A Good Knife's Work

Sheila York

FIVE STAR
A part of Gale, Cengage Learning

Detroit • New York • San Francisco • New Haven, Conn • Waterville, Maine • London

GALE
CENGAGE Learning

Copyright © 2010 by Sheila Mayhew.
Radio City® is a registered trademark of Radio City Music Hall and its use herein shall not be deemed to imply Radio City's endorsement or sponsorship of this Work.
Five Star Publishing, a part of Gale, Cengage Learning.

Set in 11 pt. Plantin.
Printed on permanent paper.

LIBRARY OF CONGRESS CATALOGING-IN-PUBLICATION DATA

York, Sheila.
    A good knife's work / Sheila York. — 1st ed.
        p. cm.
    ISBN-13: 978-1-59414-841-5 (alk. paper)
    ISBN-10: 1-59414-841-4 (alk. paper)
    1. Women screenwriters—Fiction. 2. Private investigators—Fiction. 3. Radio producers and directors—Fiction. 4. Murder—Investigation—Fiction. [1. New York (N.Y.)—Fiction.] I. Title.
    PS3625.O755G66 2010
    813'.6—dc22   2009037797

First Edition. First Printing: January 2010.
Published in 2010 in conjunction with Tekno Books and Ed Gorman.

Printed in the United States of America
1 2 3 4 5 6 7 14 13 12 11 10

For Bonnie Claeson and Joe Guglielmelli

ACKNOWLEDGMENTS

Particular thanks go to Alan Dolderer and Steve Viola, who guided me to the world of 1940s radio and inspired me to write *Adam Drake;* to Mark Lentz, my guide to 1940s New York; to Valerie Yaros and David Salper, who remain my guides to 1940s LA and Hollywood; to my editor Denise Dietz, for her gentle direction; to John Billheimer, for his wise counsel; and to my husband, David, for being himself.

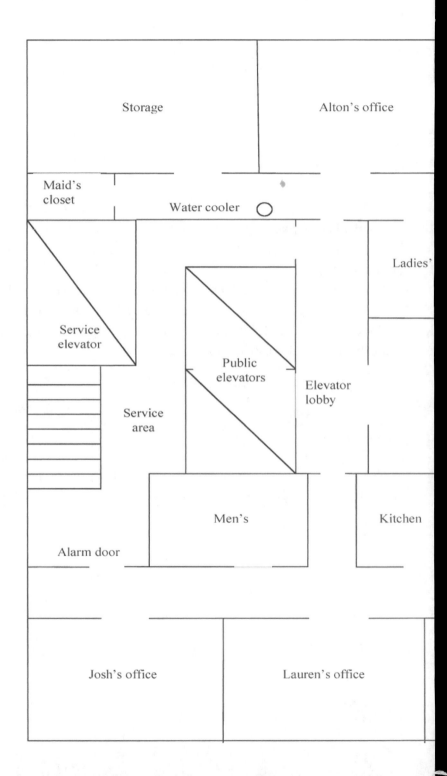

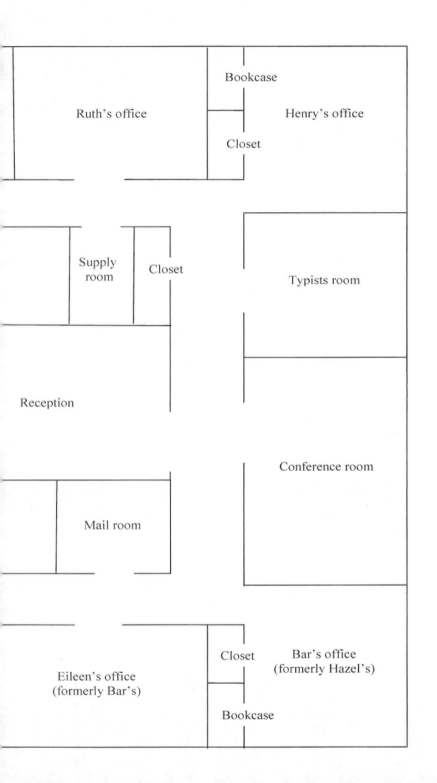

CAST OF CHARACTERS

Lauren Atwill, the screenwriter
Peter Winslow, the private detective
Hazel Keane, the producer of *Adam Drake, For Hire*
Bar Benjamin, her estranged husband
Henry Keane, her brother, who produces *Love Always*
George Keane, her other brother, head of the advertising agency
Ruth Linden, who writes *Love Always*
Eileen Walters, who writes *Adam Drake*
Josh Connally, her cohort at *Adam Drake*
Sophie Millsinberger, the receptionist
Alton Peake, the bookkeeper
Winnie Embert, the secretary
Jeannie Devine & Marty Lubrano, the typists
Al Alletter, the night watchman
Willa Mitchell, the office maid
Nathan Mitchell, her husband
Adora Watson, the Keanes' housekeeper
Sky Donovan, who plays Adam Drake
Karen Dunn, who plays Maisie Lane
Hal Lombardi, the production manager of *Adam Drake*
Lola Staton, the new ingénue
Mash Burton, the sound effects specialist
Lawrence Clayton, the doctor
Edward Crandall Lewis, the lawyer

Zack Eisler, the painter
Elizabeth Devine, Jeannie's mother
Sam Ross, a producer at Marathon Studios

New York City
October 1946

The elevator doors opened and I stepped out. Ahead of me was a wall of glass and, beyond that, the point of no return.

I stood there for a moment, fake eyeglasses perching on my nose and a smart little blue hat nesting in my brunette-dyed hair. I swallowed and thought about the possibility that I was putting my life in danger again, this time for a woman I had known for all of two hours and twenty minutes.

Then I pushed open one of the glass doors and went in.

It wasn't the sort of place where you'd expect a murder to have been committed: gleaming cherrywood paneling and thick, burnt-umber carpeting; a sofa upholstered in syrupy gold; chairs, in muted copper. The floor lamps had saucer shades of frosted glass that breathed soft light onto the ceiling.

The woman behind the desk was past the age of most receptionists—by maybe half a century—with hair so densely black that it could not possibly have been natural. A roll of bangs stopped mid-forehead; the rest was parted down the center and folded back onto her neck, framing a leathery, square-jawed prune of a face. There wasn't a quarter-inch of her skin that didn't have a crease, seam, sag, bag, pouch, line or furrow.

"Can I help you, dear?" she croaked at me with a smoke-scarred, gravelly frog-groan of a voice. Not the voice of most receptionists.

"I'm here to see Mr. Benjamin. I have an appointment. Mrs.

Tanner," I said, using my new fake name.

"I'll tell him you're here. Have a seat. Take the sofa. The chairs are bricks." She turned to the PBX cabinet, picked up a headset and pressed the earpiece to her ear. She plucked a cord from the base and stuck it into the switchboard panel. She spoke into the headset's horn.

As I slipped out of my coat, I tried to look like I was only mildly curious about my surroundings. Lithographs of the programs that were produced here lined the walls. For the "soap opera" *Love Always,* men and women in chaste romantic embraces. For the detective series *Adam Drake, For Hire,* one of the detective disarming a gunman and another of him holding the wrist of a beautiful woman, bringing the match in her hand up to his cigarette. Drake's face was turned away, revealing a terrific profile.

Against the rear wall stood a Keane console radio of burled mahogany, one of the first, from back when radios were still the amusement of the rich and when some, like this one, cost as much as a working man made in a year. In its base was the speaker, covered in gold shirred silk and surrounded by elaborate Chinese flowers of inlaid ivory. Above was a cabinet, open to reveal the same design on the inside of the door panels and the glass-covered frequency window and three dials that had been necessary fifteen years ago to tune in a station. The source of the Keane family wealth.

I sat down and pulled out my compact, to pretend to powder my nose while I examined my disguise. Then I noticed the L.A. engraved on its lid, for Lauren Atwill, my real name. I had forgotten about that. Some detective I was. I dropped the compact back into my bag.

Through the room's long glass front wall, I could see both elevators and the service door beside them. These were the only means of escape the killer could have used. Somehow, he had figured out how to conceal himself inside the offices at the end of the workday so that no one had noticed. He had waited until his victim was alone, then committed a violent murder with four people not forty feet away, without raising any alarm.

But his plan of escape had depended on those four people deserting the reception area when the body was discovered, allowing him to bolt unseen.

It was a madman's plan. And yet, it had worked.

Chapter 1

PASADENA, CALIFORNIA
SEVEN WEEKS EARLIER

I never thought that I'd end up in another murder case.

Until the first day of that summer, I'd never been closer to a crime than my typewriter. Then for the next six weeks, I was closer than I ever wanted to be again. But that was before I met Hazel Keane and before I knew I would have to leave California. As it turned out, both events occurred on the same day. Friday, September 13.

At eight o'clock in the morning, I was already sitting at my desk in my home in Pasadena, having been awakened an hour before by the first phone calls from reporters.

The study door opened. A man with a gun walked in.

He was dark and fit, in his late thirties, about six foot two of the kind of trouble most women like to get into. He closed the door and walked over to me slowly, giving me a glimpse of the Colt M-1911 under his left arm. It was a big gun for a man to carry concealed. It was the sort of gun a man wore when he wanted people to know he was carrying it.

I swiveled my chair to face him, crossed my legs, and regarded him steadily. "Who the hell are you?"

He took a good look at what he could see of my bare legs beneath my summer skirt before he said, "I heard you might need a little help."

"And you think you're the man for the job?"

He pulled me to my feet and spent some time proving that, in fact, he was. Then I said, "Some bodyguard you are. I haven't

seen you for a week."

"I've been working a case."

"Hmm."

He slid his hands down my back, over my hips and pressed me to him. He kissed me again, taking his time, which was just fine with me. Then he said, "It's getting worse."

"I'm out of practice and whose fault is that?"

"I meant outside."

"Ah." Reluctantly, I eased out of Peter Winslow's arms and went over to the windows, pulled the draperies back a couple of inches and took a look at my front lawn.

He was right. He usually was.

At the end of the drive, dozens of reporters, some with cameras and all with determined faces, were teeming on the sidewalk, held back by some of Peter's men. Radio, newspapers, newsreels, news services, news magazines, fan magazines, and probably foreign press as well. The last time I'd looked out, there had been six.

He closed the drapes. "Don't let them get a shot of you. It makes you look furtive."

"Furtive?"

"I like to use a dictionary once a month." He took off his hat and tossed it onto the sofa.

"We had to take the phones off the hook," I said.

"Yeah, Johnny told me." Johnny was Peter's younger brother, who had spent much of the last two months recovering from bullet wounds suffered in an attack that had nearly cost me my life as well. He had just returned to duty, acting now as one of my bodyguards, protecting me from the possibility that the killer I had caught that summer might arrange some revenge.

"We'll get someone over here to answer the phones," Peter said. "I brought some more men. They'll keep them off the yard and out of your trees."

"My trees?" There was a knock on the door. I wiped a bit of lipstick off Peter's face before I said, "Come in."

My housekeeper, Juanita, brought in a coffee tray and set it down on the table in front of the sofa.

"Have you had breakfast?" she asked Peter.

"I'll get something later."

"Why don't you fix some eggs?" I said to her.

"I'm fine," Peter said.

"I'll need to go to the market to feed all these new men," she said to me.

"Don't worry about the men," Peter said.

"Don't go alone," I said.

She nodded and went out, closing the door after her.

Peter said, "I like the way the women in this house pay attention when I say something."

"We're good at it." I walked over to him and we made up a little more for lost time.

While I straightened my clothes, Peter poured himself a cup of coffee and went back to work. He called Sam Ross, a producer at Marathon Studios, which our investigation had tossed into a scandal and then saved from the worst of it. So grateful was the studio that they'd hired me to write a couple of screenplays for them.

Peter convinced Sam to send over a secretary, at the studio's expense, to be the villain who wouldn't let reporters talk to me. Then he handed me the phone. "He wants to talk to you."

As usual, Sam shot me a series of questions before he paused for an answer. "Hey, how are you? How's my favorite blonde I've never been married to? You doing all right? You holding up? Hey, got a question for you, okay? You know that radio show *Adam Drake,* that detective show? You know it? We're thinking about doing a picture, you ever listen to it? Think you might be interested in writing it?"

18

He took a breath, and I stepped in. Yes, I said, I knew it, and yes, I might be interested.

"Good. We brought the producer out here. Hazel Keane. She wants to meet you."

"You want me to audition for a radio producer?"

"No, no. It's a meeting. That's it. That's all. A meeting."

"I'm having a little trouble getting out of the house."

"We'll work it out. Call her. She's at the Beverly." He rat-tatted a phone number and hung up. I disconnected, then laid the receiver down on the desktop.

There was another tap on the door, and Juanita rolled a chrome bar cart into the room: a crystal pitcher of orange juice, a china serving dish piled with ham and bacon, a silver rack of toast, and a small chafing dish full of a fluffy, lightly browned French omelet stuffed with cheese and onions. Peter's favorite.

When she had gone, I said, "She likes you."

"That's why she scowls at me."

"She's naturally suspicious of men, but she appreciates one who saved my life. Twice."

I loaded plates for us, and we sat there and ate like a couple of ordinary people, not a private detective and his client who had fallen in love while solving a case that, given the identities of the participants—guilty and innocent—was proving to be one of the biggest in California history. For the last six weeks—through the delays contrived by the defense attorney—the DA had tried to keep my identity a secret, which meant that Peter and I hadn't been able to see each other often. The reporters knew he was involved, and he didn't want to lead them to me. But too many other people knew that I was the woman who had hired him. It was inevitable the press would find out.

Apparently, they didn't yet know the extent of my involvement—that I was the one who had, in fact, identified the killer—but I was married (although separated for well over a year) to

Franklin Atwill, one of Marathon's stars, and he had managed to get himself into some trouble in connection with the case, through a little but not much of his own fault, and that was plenty for the press.

But I couldn't talk to them. How would I answer their questions? Why did you hire Winslow? Because, for no reason that made any sense, I was being blackmailed. And, oh yes, my husband might have been involved.

When the secretary arrived, we set her up in the telephone alcove in the foyer and put the phone back on the hook. It rang immediately.

"Let me get you a drink," Peter said, "then go on up and get some rest."

"A light one." The usual strength of Peter's cocktails would render me incapable for the entire day. He brought me back a mild gin and tonic, full of ice. I thought it would make a perfect afternoon if I could spend it in bed with him and some iced cocktails, but it wasn't possible, so I went up to my bedroom alone and took off my clothes. Alone.

I unplugged my extension, put on my dressing gown and started running a bath. I poured some salts under the tap and, while they foamed, went back to the bedroom, re-plugged the phone and eased the receiver out of the cradle. When I heard the dial tone, I pulled out the number Sam had given me and called the Beverly Hills Hotel. During the Depression, that grand old lady had fallen on hard times, but she was now refurbished and fashionable again. Marathon placed its special guests there—the ones who didn't require private bungalows to pass their spare time with orgies.

I asked for Hazel Keane. She answered the phone herself, a little breathless.

"I hope this isn't a bad time," I said when I had introduced myself.

"I was halfway down the hall when I heard the phone ring. I was headed to the beach. Is it like this out here all the time?"

"Sunshine, blue skies, clean water. It toughens you up."

She laughed. She had a good laugh, a good voice, warm and low-pitched; if she was a native New Yorker, she'd made a determined effort to get rid of her accent. Every once in a while, as we talked, a vowel that should have been "ah" veered toward "aw," but that was it.

"Why don't we get together?" she said. "I've heard a lot about Chasen's, but I won't be back before lunch."

"Chasen's isn't open for lunch."

"Then we better make it dinner."

I explained about my constant companions.

"I saw the stories. Hell with them," she said. "Come have some dinner. I'll get Marathon to make the reservations."

"Do you have an escort?" I asked.

"I'm sure the studio can take care of that."

"If you don't mind, I'd rather not get a stranger involved. I'll bring the man. I'll have the studio leave the reservation under your name."

"Fine. Don't worry about people staring at you. I'm so gorgeous, they won't give you a second look."

"I'll be the tall blonde with the reporter wrapped around her ankle."

"I'll be the redhead in the scarlet suit."

Peter put on his best suit and a smaller gun. Johnny drove and quickly lost the posse of press that tried to tail us. He parked the car deep in Chasen's parking lot, and since any car that I rode in these days was never left unattended, he stayed with it.

When David Chasen saw me, he took charge himself. A small man with thick horn-rimmed glasses—at five-three, he barely came up to my shoulder—he was dressed as always in perfect formal clothes, with his trademark red-silk-lined jacket. David's first career was playing the stooge in a comic Vaudeville act, the second banana who never spoke and took all the punishment, but he had found his true calling cooking up pots of chili for the casts backstage. Chasen's had begun as a chili-and-ribs joint, became a hangout for Hollywood, and was now a lavish, phenomenally successful restaurant, constantly expanding.

Our party didn't rate a table in the front "red room," named after its ten deep-red semicircular leather booths, but a call from Marathon could get us a booth in the "green room" next door. The people we passed, used to others looking at them, hardly glanced at us.

Hazel Keane did indeed have red hair. Judging from the brows, it had originally been a rather ordinary shade of earthy brown but had been mined enthusiastically to gleaming copper. She wore an evening suit that had obviously been made for her. It fit in the way only personally tailored clothes do, with perfect smoothness through the shoulders and without a pucker or roll at the waist. It had small, scalloped cutouts just below the collar bones, the latest fashion. Her evening hat fit close to her head and its soft spray of feathers brushed her temple.

Her face had good, strong bones, but not in an arrangement that usually led to the word handsome. She'd been tough on her naturally fair skin, too. Beneath the flawless makeup, there were heavy splashes of freckling and deep lines at the corners of her eyes. She looked as if she'd be more at home steering a sailboat or training horses than sipping champagne in a six-hundred-dollar suit.

"So," she said, "I'm not gorgeous."

I laughed, then introduced Peter. "I'm Mrs. Atwill's body-guard," he explained.

"Does that mean I can't talk to you?"

"I don't need to be entertained."

"You'd be the first man. Sit down." She slid to the center of the booth. Peter motioned me into the seat on her right, and he took the other one, the one with the better view of the entrance.

"What are you having?" Hazel asked me.

"Champagne sounds good," I said.

"Nothing for me," said Peter.

David Chasen raised his hand for the waiter, who materialized a second glass and filled it from the bottle in the freestanding silver bucket. David handed us menus and left us alone. I took a sip and told Hazel how much I liked *Adam Drake*. She stripped off her gauntlet gloves and tossed them down on the table.

"All right, what's the name of Adam's secretary?"

I blinked at her. "Maisie Lane."

"What was last week's show about?"

"Adam rescued a kidnapped actress in time for the curtain."

"What's Adam's favorite bar?"

"O'Malley's. The owner's called Tack. He's an ex-cop. I take it a lot of people out here are telling you how much they love the show."

"They apparently listen to it all the time, even when they don't know what night it's on." She reached for the menu. "So, what do you recommend?"

"The chili's great. Or the chicken curry or sole."

"I don't see chili."

"It's not on the menu, but you can get it if you know to ask." She didn't examine the menu further. We ordered the chili. We agreed that it would go well with champagne. Peter ordered the butterflied steak.

She said, "I don't want my show turned into some knock-it-out B movie. I need a star, but a star won't do it unless he knows there'll be a first-rate script."

I conceded that was true. Any star would be reluctant to play a character another actor had already made famous, even if that actor was only a voice.

"Of course, the money's tempting," she said. "I had no idea how much of it you people have out here."

"Which agency do you work for?" Almost all of the shows on the networks were created by advertising agencies for sponsors. The networks did little but sell time on the air.

"I don't. The D.W. Davis agency represents Miles and Foster Tobacco. They make Traveler cigarettes, our sponsor, but my family owns the agency, so I don't have to answer to any twenty-eight-year-old vice president."

"Uh," I said. "You wouldn't be Keane as in Keane Radio, would you?"

"My father was. It gave me a leg up."

"I'll bet."

"I started out acting, even the *Lux Theater*, when it was still in New York. Between us, I stunk."

The *Lux Radio Theater* had started in New York, but moved to Los Angeles ten years ago and since then had mostly presented Hollywood stars re-creating their roles in one-hour versions of their films. It had a huge audience and a hefty budget from Lux soap. My husband once made three thousand dollars for re-creating his role in a movie I wrote for him called *The Brantley Case*. As the hired pen on the picture, I got nothing.

Hazel continued, "I was always a better writer. My brothers did some acting, too, but what we really wanted to do was produce our own shows. We started with a soap opera. But *Adam Drake* was always my dream. How about you?"

"My uncle was Bennett Lauren, the oil man. I was named for him. Mabel Lauren Tanner's my maiden name. He helped me get a job. The studio told me I could be a secretary. I wanted to be a writer. We compromised. They let me write, but they didn't

24

use anything. Then I got a break with *The Brantley Case*. After that—"

"I know your work. Why'd you stop writing?"

"I didn't."

"I haven't seen your name on anything in three or four years, except that *Scarlet Spy* a few years ago."

I flinched. "I hope you don't count that."

"You owe me a quarter. I only went to see it because your name was on it."

"It went through two other writers. I've had a hand in several scripts in the last few years, off the record."

"A script doctor?"

"I was married," I said, a bit defensively, determinedly not looking at Peter. Instead my gaze dropped to her left hand. There was a simple gold band and a diamond not quite as big as Cleopatra's Needle.

"My husband directs *Adam Drake*."

That was all she said about him, and all we said about the show. There wasn't much to be done at this stage. She wasn't looking for ideas. She was seeing if she trusted me, so we talked about inconsequential, vital things. It turned out that we had quite a bit in common. We were both writers who loved to work on mysteries. We had both gone to Vassar. We knew the same professors and the same ways of getting around them, which had mostly required that we admire their opinions with wide-eyed enthusiasm, the more unoriginal the idea, the greater the enthusiasm. It had been great training for the entertainment business.

We had both been left wealthy by men we adored. We spent most of that evening talking about my uncle and her father.

When we finished, David Chasen brought the tab himself, which Hazel signed to the studio. "I'm afraid someone told the press you were here," he whispered to Peter.

Peter suggested Hazel wait and take a cab back to the hotel. We said good-bye and Peter walked me to the front door, where I stayed with David, out of sight of the crowd on the curb while he went to get the car. When he returned, he said, "Don't cover your face, but don't look at them. And don't frown." He took me by the arm and propelled me out the door, across the sidewalk beneath the green-and-white awning, and into the backseat. He jumped in after me and slammed the door.

Faces pressed against the car windows.

"Lauren! Lauren, is it true there was blackmail? What do you know about the killings? Why did you and Frank separate?"

And then, just as we pulled away from the curb:

"Did you hire Winslow because you thought Frank was a killer?"

CHAPTER 2

I had known that inevitably someone would ask it, but it didn't make it any easier to take. The rest of the reporters had heard it, and now would ask it too. The mere repetition would give it authenticity. If people hear anything enough, they start to believe it. Advertising and the Nazis had taught us that.

For the next two weeks, everywhere I went, I was followed. Johnny usually managed to shake them, but they had lists of my friends and could try to guess where I was going. When I visited Helen—Sam Ross's wife and my best friend—we went out to sit by her pool, and Johnny dragged a couple of cameras with men attached to them out of the rhododendrons. The next morning, I came up from the wash sink at my hairdresser to find a cheerful young woman in rollers standing beside me. "Lauren, hi. Mimsy Dodd, *Photoplay.* Did you witness any of the killings? How about Frank? Is your hair naturally blonde?"

Although Peter fired the bodyguard who had been with me that day, I decided to stay home. Hazel returned to New York and continued to negotiate with Marathon, holding out for a star. I signed a contract to write the script if Marathon made the deal, then went back to the one I'd been working on.

Hazel dropped me a note saying that she hoped the press scrutiny would become less intense. It didn't. Even the Nazi trials in Nuremberg couldn't shove the story below the fold.

I didn't see Franklin at all after the story broke and spoke to him only a few times. He was still shooting *The Final Line,* the picture I was doctoring when the case began. Because the schedule had been interrupted, he now spent long hours on the set to wrap by the middle of October. In addition, the studio didn't want him out much. They wanted to control all contact with the press and were busy delivering publicity through their staff and friendly columnists. Still, relentlessly, the speculation continued about the reasons I was involved, which meant that Franklin's name appeared as well, constantly connected to several murders. I knew that I had to leave town, and soon.

At the end of the second week, Peter and I were having coffee in the study after dinner. He sat across from me in his shirtsleeves, reading the evening editions, his shoulder holster on the table beside him. I stirred my coffee long after the sugar cubes had melted and watched his hands folding back the pages, the sudden intense rush of longing too sharply mingled with the hopeless dread of losing him.

It would take a miracle for him to go away with me. Even if his boss would allow his best investigator to leave town, Peter would have almost nothing to do except sleep with me. He would never submit to feeling like a kept man.

I'd go away, and he'd go back to his life, the one that included girls who wore tangerine lipstick and only stayed one night, if that long. I'd send letters, not too many, not too often. Careful letters that would not betray me as miserably lonely and near-desperate for the touch of those hands. But I had to go. I couldn't stay here.

He laid down the papers. "You can't stay here."

"What?" My hand jerked and coffee sloshed into the saucer.

"The best thing you can do for your husband is leave town."

I took my time pouring the spilt coffee into the china bowl on the tray. "I know."

"Do you have anyone you could stay with?"

I took a napkin, wiped the saucer carefully, then the bottom of the cup. "Sally Wallace has a house up near Santa Barbara," I said, striving to sound casual. "There's a studio on the property. She'd let me use it."

"Can she keep her mouth shut?"

"Yes. And she and her husband will be in Paris until at least Christmas. Would you like more coffee?"

"I'm not the one who spilled mine. What's wrong?"

"Nothing," I said. "It's been a long couple of weeks. And I hate packing."

"And here I thought it had something to do with me."

Forget the brave face. In the next second, I was weeping into my napkin. He stood up and drew me into his arms. I replaced the napkin with his shirtfront.

"It's not that far," he said into my hair. He slipped his hand up my back and rested his fingers on my neck, cool and then warm. "It would only be until the trial starts."

"That shouldn't be longer than a year. Jeez, Winslow, look what you've done to me."

"Look what you've done to my tie."

"I'm sorry."

"It's an old tie."

"That's not what I meant."

"I know," he said softly. "I know."

At midnight Saturday, October 5, Juanita, Johnny and I slipped out my back door and into the garage where Lou Brandesi, a squat, rock-hard man in a bruised fedora, waited beside a borrowed Cadillac with phony plates. He was one of Peter's men, and I'd worked with him, briefly, that summer. He held the door, and Juanita and I climbed into the backseat and ducked down. As Johnny slid behind the wheel, Lou raised the garage door, waited for Johnny to back out the car, then closed the garage door and climbed into his Oldsmobile. Johnny eased down the drive, past the knot of suddenly alert reporters and photographers camped at the end of it, and we sped off. Lou took off in the other direction.

Inevitably, some of them tailed us, and inevitably, Johnny lost them. When the Cadillac reached the 101, it roared north into the night. When it arrived at the house Sally had loaned me, Juanita and Johnny got out and went inside.

Meanwhile, I was on my way to New York.

As Johnny had sped down Wilshire, he had made a quick detour into a side street, just long enough for me to jump out and into a nondescript Chevy with Peter at the wheel.

We drove around until Peter was satisfied that, if anyone had been on Johnny's tail, he hadn't picked up the switch. Then we pulled into an alley, where we changed again—this time to a car that had been loaded with my luggage the day before—and another of Peter's men drove us through the night to San Francisco where we caught the City of San Francisco to Chicago, then the Broadway Limited to New York.

In the end, it was Sam Ross who helped me decide to go to New York. He made a deal with Hazel Keane.

Three days before I was set to leave for Sally's, the secretary who was answering my calls came into the study to tell me that Mr. Bluepoint Vance was on the phone. It was Sam's alias, a character in Dashiell Hammett's *The Big Knockover*. He'd insisted on it, so that I'd be able to tell it was really him calling.

I picked up the phone. "Hello, Bluepoint."

"Pretty good, huh? It works, doesn't it? Hey, called for a couple of things, okay? One, we're getting ready to put out the story about how Frank's headed down to Cuba when the movie wraps, you'll probably join him, you're still good friends, you trust him, what a great guy he is, you know, what we all agreed on. In case anybody calls."

"I'm not taking calls from anyone not named Bluepoint Vance."

Sam barked a laugh. "Right. Second, I can give you something to do while you're not in Cuba. We're going to sign the deal for *Adam Drake.*"

"That's good news. I'd love to do it."

"You don't have much choice, do you?"

"You got me cheap, Sam."

"Be the first time."

So I went to New York. Peter went with me, paid as my bodyguard, for a month. I'd absorb a little atmosphere and do the necessary research. It would also give us another month to test whether Sally's house was safe. If Juanita and Johnny hadn't been discovered, I'd join them in Santa Barbara.

Paxton, the agency Peter worked for, had a reciprocal arrangement with an agency in New York called Vanguard. One of their men met us at Penn Station, and by paying no attention to lanes, lights or pedestrians, he made sure that, if anyone had somehow discovered where I'd gone and arranged for a reporter to meet the trains, he'd never be able to follow us.

The Marquette was a small, private hotel on East 53rd between Park and Madison, seven stories of maroon brick with its name appearing only on the discreet brass plaque beside the beveled glass door. Its silent lobby had oak wainscoting, darkened to coffee over the years, a parquet floor covered with thinning Persian carpets, fringed Victorian velvet chairs, and a burnished gold-leaf chandelier that gave off soft sherry-colored light. The sober-faced desk clerks wore black suits and remembered only what they were supposed to. We registered under assumed names. Only the manager knew who I really was.

Our suite's living room wore the same shabby elegance as the lobby: an overstuffed sofa and chairs slipcovered in faded roses and a carpet rippling rhythmically with age. The first bedroom had taken some notice of the last decades. Intended as the lady's boudoir, its furniture was made of lighter woods and the bed had a pleated-taffeta headboard in soft rose and a satin counterpane to match.

The other was the man's room and only slightly more updated than the living room, with a brown-and-gold carpet that was not too frayed and a leather winged chair not too scuffed. Sporting prints featured lots of pointing dogs set to warn their masters if a flock of birds attacked.

For several reasons, I thought Peter would find my bedroom a more pleasant place to be. He appeared to agree, so it was a while before we got around to the unpacking. Then he put his pants back on, gathered up the rest of his clothes, which in spite of his eagerness had been carefully draped over the furniture, and went off to his room.

"Stop by next time you're in town," I called after him.

After I slipped on my dressing gown, I gently folded my stockings into their linen case. I needed to protect them. I couldn't use contacts in New York to get more. I wasn't supposed to be here. And a woman needed contacts these days. Although the hosiery mills were no longer making parachutes and soldiers' socks, they couldn't keep up with the demand for stockings. Block-long lines were still not uncommon, and stores often imposed limits on the number of pairs a woman could buy. My own hosiery shop had instituted a lottery system. Winners sometimes brought men with them to claim their prizes, just to make sure no losers tried to snatch a little justice.

When Peter returned, fully dressed, I was sitting at the dressing table. He leaned on the wall and watched me arrange my modest collection of feminine necessities: sapphire-glass jars of face cream and cleansing cream, white enamel bottles of body lotion and bath salts, a gold-veined box of dusting powder and tall frosted crystal vials of perfume and toilet water.

"I'd like to call Hazel," I said.

"And you're asking me first?"

"Jeez, Winslow, what does a girl have to do to put you in a good mood?"

He laughed. "When do you want to do this?"

"It's almost one. She might be at lunch. Two-thirty?"

"Okay. You hungry?"

"Not yet."

"Then I'm going out for a while."

"I'll go with you. I could use some air."

"Not till I've had a look around. Don't answer the door while I'm gone, don't answer the phone, don't make any calls."

"Yes, sir."

"I mean it. And think about what you're going to say to her, so you don't accidentally tip her to where you are." I made a face. "How are you going to handle the operator?"

"What operator?"

"Exactly. There won't be a long-distance operator."

"Hazel won't answer the phone. I only have to fool the switchboard girl."

"Think it out. I told the manager we'd need a new lock. I'll take care of it." He pulled himself off the wall. "Then you can practice picking it."

In the early part of my career, when I wrote my first Phil Marsh mystery, I'd been diligent in my research—and naive enough to think that Hollywood cared. The retired locksmith I'd interviewed, amused by my enthusiasm, had given me a set of picks.

The movie's producer had been shocked, as if showing an actual lock-picking would undermine the morals of our youth. So Phil Marsh usually got a "skeleton" key, which miraculously seemed to open any lock. If Phil was with a woman, the producers liked him to ask for a hairpin, which seemed to do just as well, though I'd never found them to be much good at holding up my hair.

I dressed, hauled out my typewriter and set it up on the dining table. I'd have to get the hotel to send up a card table, as the dainty little thing they called a desk was far too small. But not until Peter came back. He said no calls. I didn't want to begin our time together by going off and doing things my own way. Juanita says that I'm stubborn. Given some of the trouble I got into over the summer, I was trying to give her point of view a chance.

Peter returned with two bags of groceries and a locksmith. He sent me into the bedroom before he let the man in to install the new cylinder. In a half hour, he called out, "You can come out now."

He was in the tiny kitchen, putting things away: a can of Maxwell House, a quart bottle of milk, a box of sugar, some apples to go with the oranges we brought from California, a small loaf of bread, margarine (even though the war had ended a year ago, there was still no butter to be had), and a little ham and cheese to make late-night sandwiches. He had been to a liquor store, too. There were bottles of bourbon, gin, tonic and a good brandy.

"Do I ever get to leave the suite?" I asked.

"If you're a good girl. You want to call Miss Keane now?"

When the hotel operator gave me a local line, I dialed Hazel's office number, draped my handkerchief over the mouthpiece and made a stab at a Southern accent.

"This is operator forty-seven. I have a long-distance call for Miss Hazel Keane from Mrs. Lauren Atwill."

"One moment please," the switchboard operator said.

Hazel was on the line almost immediately. "Yes, operator, put her through. Hello?"

"Hazel, it's Lauren."

"This is a great connection. Where are you calling from?"

"I'm not supposed to say."

"I heard you were on your way to Cuba. Hold on a second." She turned away from the phone. "Here's the money," she said to someone else. "Go pick up the cakes, and whatever goes in that punch Willa makes. Sorry," she said to me. "We're having a little going-away party for one of our girls today."

"Sam Ross told me you'd agreed to a deal."

"We'll sign next week. He gave me a list of actors and said he'd put it in writing that one of them would do the movie."

"When would you have time to talk about the script?"

"I have to dash over to rehearsal, then after the party, I have a writers meeting. If you were here, I'd invite you over. Why don't you call me about ten tomorrow. Ten, my time. You're not by yourself, are you?"

"I have a bodyguard."

"Mr. Winslow?"

"Yes."

"Well, then you don't need New York. Say hello for me."

That evening, Peter and I ate a quiet dinner in the hotel's restaurant. No reporters found us. Before climbing into my bed, Peter rumpled the sheets and blankets of his own. He was even more discreet than the Marquette.

The next morning, having not quite adjusted to New York time, I didn't get up until after nine. Peter's side of the bed was empty. I wondered how he planned to conceal from the maids that he'd been sleeping there. I slipped into my dressing gown and a pair of mules. Still only half awake, I managed to rinse my face, brush my teeth and pay more attention to my hair than I usually did first thing in the morning. It was, after all, our first full night together.

Peter sat at the table, fully dressed except for his jacket, reading a newspaper from what seemed to be a stack of them. He looked up as I padded into the kitchen, but said nothing. He'd already made coffee. I fumbled for a cup, filled it, aimed a spoonful of sugar at it and took a few sips. A little of the netting in front of my eyes lifted.

I went back into the living room, stifling a yawn. He was standing up now. There was an odd expression on his face.

I said, "I'm never going to look any better in the morning, so you might as well get used to it."

He took the hot coffee out of my hand.

"What? What is it?" I asked.

"Lauren," he said, "Hazel Keane's dead. She was murdered last night."

CHAPTER 3

ADAM DRAKE CREATOR MURDERED

Below the headline in the *Tribune* was a picture of Hazel, smiling—a publicity shot of a woman whose dream of doing her own detective show had finally come true.

"She had a meeting last night," Peter said. "She stayed on after. The maid found her."

Immediately, I thought that, if I'd told her the truth about being in New York, she might have been out having dinner with me. She might still be alive.

I read the story. The writers meeting had broken up about seven-thirty, it said, and everyone had gone home, except the office maid, the night watchman, and Hazel, who had gone into her office to finish some work. About ten, a Doctor Lawrence Clayton, described as "a family friend," had arrived to take her to a late supper. The maid had gone to tell Hazel he was there and had found her behind her desk, beaten to death.

"The office has a night watchman?" I said. "How could anyone attack her with a night watchman there?"

"We don't know where he was, how far away."

"But why? Why would anyone even try to break in?"

"In the *Post*, it says there's jewelry missing, some money."

"That's not enough to break into an office with a guard."

"It'll probably turn out there's a jeweler in the building, and some hophead broke into the wrong place."

"Why didn't the watchman hear anything? Why didn't the

maid hear anything?"

"You know the papers get a lot of it wrong, especially right after something happens. Nothing's going to make sense to you right now."

Nevertheless, I sat down and read the other papers. There wasn't much more, except the *Post* said she had been stabbed and the *World-Telegram* hinted that the police had some strong leads. But the police were likely to say that. Hazel was rich, her show famous.

"Come on," Peter said when I finished. "Let's get you out of here for a while."

I dressed, covered my hair with a scarf and my eyes with sunglasses. Peter wore his hat low on his forehead, but there were no reporters lurking outside the hotel. No one gave us a second look.

When we reached Madison, we turned north, toward Central Park. Then I noticed that 520 Madison was just across the street. The papers had said Hazel's office was at 390. I took Peter's arm and turned south. He knew what I was doing, but he let me do it.

The Emory Building was twelve stories tall and sat on the northwest corner of East 47th Street, taking up about a third of the block. There was no sign that a violent crime had been committed, no police cars on the curb, no officers stationed at the information desk in the black granite lobby.

There were two banks of elevators, one that went to the second through sixth floors; the other, seven through twelve. The directory showed Keane Productions was the only business on the eighth floor. There was no jeweler in the building, nor any other company that sounded like it would keep valuables lying around.

"Lauren," Peter said, "there's nothing to see. You won't be able to get up there."

He drew me back out but let me go around the corner into 47th and take a look at the metal service door near the rear of the building. It was locked; a sign next to it, bolted into the brick, said all deliveries had to check in with the front desk. It didn't look like the sort of place that your wandering hophead would decide was an easy mark.

Just a few feet away, an alley not much wider than a good stretch ran between the rear of the Emory and the side of a narrow three-story building. A fire escape was tucked up behind the Emory, but it only extended to the fifth floor. Peter took a couple of steps toward it to get a better look.

The service door swung open, and a man came out dressed in dark blue coveralls with EMORY BUILDING stitched in red above the left pocket on his chest. He didn't even glance at me and turned toward Madison. The door started to close. I jumped through it. It slammed behind me, the noise echoing in the long, dim hallway. Immediately there was the staccato rapping of Peter's knuckles on the metal. "Lauren? Lauren, I know you can hear me. Open the door." I didn't.

I hurried to the end of the hall. On one side was a door marked LOBBY ENTRANCE; on the other, the service elevator and stairs. I hurried up the stairs. By the time I reached the eighth-floor landing, I was no longer hurrying. What I was doing would be better described as grasping the rail and gasping for breath. I hauled myself up the last step and looked around while I dragged in some air. On the right was a grimy window. I looked out: the fire escape was directly beneath, but three floors down. A door, which appeared to be practically new, stood in the wall directly opposite the top of the stairs. A red-lettered sign on it said FIRE DOOR WITH ALARM. DO NOT OPEN.

I went back, past the stairs. On the left was the alcove for the service elevator; on the right, another door. I opened it slowly and peered out through a six-inch crack into the waiting area for the public elevators. At either end were doors, but without knobs or keyholes.

Across from me stretched a wall of glass and beyond that, the reception area of Keane Productions. A man in a dark-blue uniform sat on a gold-colored sofa, reading a Tom and Jerry comic book. He had a bit of thin sandy hair running down the center of his head, some more above his ears and a crisp sand-and-pepper moustache. I didn't see any sign of the police. I dipped back into the service area, whipped off the sunglasses and scarf, and dropped them into my coat pocket. I wrote a name and address in a small notebook I carried in my handbag, then went out and knocked lightly on the glass door.

The man got up, giving me a nearsighted squint. When he was within five feet, the squint cleared. "Sorry. No reporters, miss."

"I'm not a reporter." I tried to look confused about why he would say that. "I think I'm lost," I said, helplessly, plaintively. "I was supposed to meet a friend at her office. Sally Wallace?"

"No, miss."

I pulled out the notebook and read the address, then showed it to him. "Maybe I wrote it down wrong. Is there a Bluepoint Design in the building, do you know?"

"Don't think so," he said through the glass. "You could check in the lobby."

"I didn't see it on the directory, but I thought I'd check up here anyway. Could I use your phone?"

"I'm sorry, miss. We're closed."

"Please," I said, drawing it out girlishly. "She's going to wonder what happened to me. Just two minutes. One call. Scout's honor." I gave him what I hoped was the scout's salute, three fingers raised together.

He looked me up and down, then said, "Well, all right, but we have to stay in here." He unlocked the door.

"Oh, thank you so much, Mr. . . . ?"

"Alletter."

He led me to the PBX in the center of the room and plugged one of the cords into the switchboard. I gave him the number of the Marquette Hotel. It was the only number in New York I knew. If he waited till they answered, my story would break down in a hurry. I got lucky. He didn't. He dialed the number on the rotary dial sitting on the PBX's shelf and handed me the headset.

"Hi, is Sally there?" I said into its horn. I waited a second, ignoring the desk clerk's confused response. "Sally? Hi, it's me. I have the wrong address. Where are you? Oh, okay, thanks. I'll be there as soon as I can. Bye."

I nodded to Alletter and he pulled the cord out. I handed back the headset. "Thanks a lot. It's Three-Ninety Lexington. I don't know why I wrote down Madison."

He started toward the door, ready to let me out, but I stayed where I was, examining the lithographs on the walls. "What do you do here that you thought I was a reporter?"

"This is where they write the *Adam Drake* show," he said, a touch proudly, a touch ominously.

"Really? That's swell."

He frowned at me. "Didn't you see the papers?"

"No, I'm at a hotel. Why?"

"We had a murder here last night."

I waved a hand at him. "Sure you did. Did Adam solve it?"

"I'm serious, miss. The lady who produced *Adam Drake* was killed down in her office, not thirty feet from where you're standing." He gestured at the double doors behind me. I wheeled around and stared at them.

"How can you stay here by yourself? Aren't you scared?"

He drew himself up. "We all have to do our duty, miss."

"Do they know who did it?"

"The doctor saw him right out there in the hallway coming out of her office."

"The doctor?"

"There was a doctor here last night, a friend of Miss Keane, waiting for her."

"He saw the killer?"

"He must have thought he was just working late. He should have told me, of course, but I wouldn't say that to anyone."

"You were here?"

"Yes, ma'am. And when I heard the doctor tell the police he'd seen a man in coveralls, I told them about that handyman, works right here in the building. Miss Keane threatened to get him fired. I told them all about it."

Behind him, the elevator doors opened. A uniformed officer got out, followed by a man who could only have been a police detective. He had a natural scowl, so his expression didn't change when he saw me.

"The police," I whispered to Alletter, whose squint turned quickly to a sheepish sort of alarm. He rushed over and unlocked the door.

"She was lost," he explained. "I just let her use the phone. That's all she did."

"Let's see some ID," the detective snapped at me.

"Of course, sir," I said, reaching into my handbag. "I'm visiting New York."

He glanced at the license, just long enough to see it was out of state. "And you wanted to see where a killing happened."

"I was meeting a friend. I wrote the address down wrong."

"Sure you did. Time to move along, missus."

I dropped my chin and looked at him from under my lashes with an embarrassed smile. His scowl softened a little. I took a chance. "You're right. I read about it in the papers. I didn't mean to get anyone into trouble. I'm sorry," I said. I fumbled into my bag for my gloves and dropped one of them. I crouched to pick it up and let my skirt slip up my thighs. "You see, back in Pasadena, where I come from, nothing much ever happens."

"Let me see that bag."

I gave it to him, and he went through it, probably looking for press credentials, because when he handed it back, he said, "What the hell, give you a little souvenir from New York." He strode to the double doors and opened one of them. "Two minutes, missus. Let's go."

The hallway on the other side appeared to form a U-shape around the reception area. The part I could see was about sixty feet long and eight feet wide, carpeted in serviceable gray-and-black tweed.

"How much you read in the papers?" he asked.

"Everything. I'm a big fan of the show."

"I figured, you take the trouble to come up here."

"How much are you allowed to tell me about what happened?"

He grunted and started down the hall. "This place was practically empty, a couple of people out in the waiting room. One of them, a doctor, comes out here to get himself a drink from the watercooler down that other hall." He jerked his head toward the other end. "And he sees a man come out of this door." He stopped outside Hazel's office. It was at the end of the main hall, its door facing down the side hallway.

"Didn't he ask him what he was doing?"

"He's wearing coveralls, a cap. He figures the guy's working. That late at night. I wouldn't take my *tonsils* to a guy that dumb. You didn't hear that."

"No, sir."

He opened the door. "Here it is, missus. But you don't go inside."

The walls were the same color as the hallway, but the carpeting was a smooth, soft, expensive pearl gray. I saw Hazel's desk, a well-carved mahogany with a built-in green leather blotter. I saw the pale aqua curtains. I saw the splattering of blood on them, and on the carpet, the back of her chair, and the wall behind it.

But it was the smell that rooted me to the spot, pushing down violently on sickness and the sudden urge to weep. The body had been removed long ago, the windows were open, and still the smell of death hung there, of blood and of the last discharges from the body of a dying woman.

"Maybe you don't think this was such a good idea now," he said.

It took a while to find my voice. "You must think I'm a ghoul."

"What I've seen, you're an amateur."

"Will you find out who did this?"

"Don't worry. We got him. Guy works in the building, turns out. Had a beef with the lady. Doctor picked him out of a lineup. Looks like he hid out here till she was alone. You seen enough, I think. Let's go."

When I reached the building's lobby, Peter didn't say anything, but took me firmly by the arm and steered me north through the crowds. I didn't protest, breathing gratefully of the chilled scent of car exhaust.

As we reached the next block, a bus pulled to its stop. We climbed on, and Peter dropped the nickels into the box. We rode silently to 59th, where we got off. He took my arm again and we headed west toward Central Park.

"I just wanted to see the layout," I explained, clipping along to keep up with his stride.

"Then the cops showed up. I saw them go in. What if they'd hauled you down to the precinct, where there'd be a dozen reporters asking questions about the killing? Any one of them might have recognized you. Do you trust me?"

"Of course."

"Why do you think I want to keep an eye on you?"

I stopped and yanked my arm away. "Don't patronize me, Winslow."

"Then don't make my job harder."

I glared at him, but he could out-glare a German battalion, so I gave up and snipped off toward the park. At Fifth Avenue, traffic was stalled; even the intersection was jammed with cars. Drivers were laying on their horns as if that would miraculously cure the problem. The light changed and pedestrians flowed off the curb and around the bumpers. I went with them. Halfway across, a space suddenly opened and a gray Dodge tried to get through us to claim it. He pushed his hood into the flow, jack-hammered his horn and kept coming. Peter stepped up beside me and laid his hand hard on the hood. He looked at the driver. The car bumped to a stop and the horn died.

I slipped my arm through Peter's then and we proceeded uninterrupted through the crowd and cacophony into the park, down a set of cracked concrete steps tucked into the southeastern wall, and along a curved finger of lake. The water was deep green and murky, impervious to the sunlight. Overgrown shrubs lined the rutted path along with splintered benches, some missing slats. During the Depression, the park had been home and refuge to legions of homeless families, New York having been particularly hard-hit by the downward spiral of lives. The war had followed, and recovering resources were obviously being funneled to places other than the park.

I said, "The detective said they'd arrested someone." I told him about the handyman. "The doctor, the man waiting for Hazel, saw him leave her office."

"And didn't stop him?"

"He was wearing coveralls. The doctor thought he was working."

"That late at night?"

"The detective said the same thing, that the doctor must be stupid, but it wouldn't have made any difference," I said hollowly. "She was already dead. They caught him. At least there's that. The doctor picked him out of a lineup."

Soot-edged clouds rolled over, the temperature dropped and the wind picked up, chasing the dead leaves before us. I wasn't dressed for it, so we turned back to the hotel. Peter called down to the restaurant and ordered me breakfast. It came with the midday edition of the *Tribune*.

ADAM DRAKE KILLER CAPTURED

His name was Nestor Cupp, and, according to police, he had been repairing the plumbing in the *Drake* offices a few hours before Hazel was killed and had argued recently with her about his drinking on the job. His bloodstained coveralls had been found in a trash can two blocks from the scene. The commissioner praised the detectives for their quick work.

The *Tribune* had Cupp's mug shot. He was a gaunt, sullen-looking man (although I had never seen anyone who looked particularly cheerful in a mug shot), with pale hair cut long on the top and close to his head at the sides. He had the flinty eyes and prominent facial bones I'd seen often in pictures of Appalachian families. The paper said that he had come to New York from the coal mines of West Virginia and found a better life, implying that he had betrayed the city by brutally murdering a helpless woman.

"Finish your egg," Peter said. He poured me another cup of coffee and waited while I managed the egg and half a slice of toast. "Now," he said, "start at the beginning. Tell me everything they told you up there."

CHAPTER 4

I told him what I had learned from the night watchman and the detective. We went over the layout of the offices, as much as I had seen.

"So," Peter said, "this doctor was headed to the opposite end of the hall, to get a drink?"

"I didn't see a watercooler, so it must have been around the corner, but yes, in the opposite direction from Hazel's office."

"How far is it between the doors to reception and her office?" he asked.

"Maybe thirty feet."

"How wide's the hall?"

"Maybe eight."

"And her office door faced down a side hall?"

"Yes."

"Did the door open into her office or out into the hall?"

"Into her office."

He got up and disappeared into my bedroom.

"What are you doing?" I asked.

He called back, "The kitchen door's how far from this one?"

"Maybe twelve feet."

"Let's say I'm the killer. I'm in Miss Keane's office. I leave." He came out and strode quickly into the kitchen. From there, he called, "What did you see?"

"I got a pretty good look at your profile, your clothes."

"The killer had to be headed down that side hall. If he was

headed toward the doctor, he would have known he was spotted and run, but he didn't. The question is how good a look did the doctor get at his face?"

"Especially with the cap."

"The what?"

"I forgot. The detective said he was wearing a cap."

We stared at each other.

Then Peter said, "Let's not make too much of this. We don't know exactly what happened yet."

"We only have the doctor's word there was anyone there at all."

"If it turns out that those coveralls do have Miss Keane's blood type on them, I don't see how the doctor could have done it. How'd he manage to get the coveralls into that trash can? He was a material witness. The police wouldn't have let him out of their sight. The cops probably have the right guy. I know what you're thinking. If I'd let you tell her you were in New York—"

"I'm not blaming you. Please don't think that."

"She had a meeting, she had a date with this doctor. You've got no guarantee she would've changed her plans in between just because you told her you were in New York."

"I can't stop thinking about it."

"Okay, look, if it'll make you feel any better, I'll go over to Vanguard, see what their contacts are like. Maybe we can find out what else the cops have."

I slipped my hand into his. "Thank you."

"I'm not promising anything. They'll want to see some money. A hundred should cover the retainer."

Out of my makeup case, I took the thick envelope of cash I'd brought along because we didn't want to have to use checks with my name on them. I gave Peter the hundred, and he went off to Vanguard, able to do something. I stayed there, with nothing to do except order more newspapers. There was nothing new, nothing to push back the nagging sense that something was wrong with this whole setup.

I sat back and listened to the fresh autumn wind shudder against the windows.

The handyman worked in the building, worked in Hazel's offices. Maybe the doctor had seen him there before and would have been able to recognize him easily in the scant seconds it took for the killer to cross that hallway.

Then again, maybe he hadn't got that good a look. Hazel had been a friend. He would naturally have been in shock. Could he have picked this Cupp out of the lineup because he looked familiar, not realizing that he hadn't seen him that night, but days, maybe weeks ago?

But what could we do about it? We were supposed to be in Cuba.

Peter returned about seven, just as I was ready to give up and order dinner.

"Have you eaten?" I asked.

"Not yet."

He hung up his coat and, while he poured himself a bourbon and me a short gin and tonic, I ordered steaks. Then we sat down on the sofa and he flipped open his notebook.

"This might be tough to hear," he said.

"I'm fine. Go on."

"All right. Here's what we managed to pull out of Vanguard's contacts. She died from two blows to the head, either one would have been fatal. There was one stab wound in the neck that bled very little for that kind of wound, meaning that she was stabbed after she was dead or almost dead."

"Why would the killer suddenly change weapons when she was dead?"

"A good question. The cops found a wrench and a knife in

her office, large pocket knife, four-inch blade. The wrench belonged to Cupp. He engraved his initials on the handle. Cupp's prints were on the wrench and the knife."

"He sneaks in and kills her without making any noise, then drops both weapons where the police will trip over them?"

Peter went on, consulting his notebook. "The killer emptied her purse and he took a gold bracelet and diamond ring, both worth plenty. They haven't been recovered yet. The cops searched the Emory Building as soon as they got there, but they didn't find anyone except the elevator operator and the building's doorman. They're the only ones on duty after eight, when they lock the front doors. I had a twenty-dollar talk with the building's superintendent about how someone might be able to get into the building at night. Before eight, the elevator operator would see them. After eight, when the front door's locked, anyone who wants in has to ring a bell. The service door is locked from the outside and checked every hour by the door-man."

"What about the fire escape?"

"The police found all the windows on it locked, and even if someone did manage to get in the building that way or through the service door, how would he get into the *Drake* offices? The guy said they're locked up tighter than a drum. Cupp was fixing the plumbing up there earlier, but clocked out at five-forty-five. That doesn't mean he left, but he had to figure out how to get back into the offices without anybody seeing him. The cops showed the superintendent the coveralls they found. They were old ones. The staff got new ones about a month ago, but there were a few old ones down in the basement, in a cardboard box."

"The police told the papers they were Cupp's."

"I don't see how they could know that. Still, it doesn't mean he didn't do it. He could have grabbed an old set rather than use his own. The super gave me the names and phone numbers of the other men who work in the building. I called some of them already."

"Pretending to be the police?"

He shrugged and grinned. "Miss Keane's meeting ended somewhere around seven-forty-five. The elevator operator on duty can't swear to whether all the people from *Adam Drake* left. He's new, and doesn't know people in the building too well yet. There was nothing special about last night, no reason for him to pay attention to who got on, and other people in the building were leaving too. After seven o'clock, there's only one elevator operating from the seventh through twelfth floors and it's pretty busy. The doorman couldn't swear to anything. The building's front door wasn't locked yet." Peter flipped to another page in the notebook. "There were seven people at Miss Keane's meeting. The show's writers, Eileen Walters and Josh Connally; the director, Barnard Benjamin—"

"Hazel's husband. She said he was the director."

"Her *estranged* husband. They hadn't lived together in six months."

"Interesting."

"Since they separated, she's been living in her late father's house, a mansion up in the east eighties. Her brother owns it now, George. He runs the ad agency, D.W. Davis, and Henry, her other brother, produces *Love Always,* the soap opera. They were both at the meeting, too. The actor who plays Drake was there, Sky Donovan. And Karen Dunn, who plays his secretary, Maisie. After the meeting broke up, there were supposedly only two people left in the offices beside Miss Keane: the maid, Willa Mitchell, and the night watchman, Albert Alletter, you already met."

Peter looked up from the notebook. "The elevator operator and the doorman were listening to the radio together in the lobby. They're both sure about one thing. Only two people went *up* last night after eight. And they both went to the eighth floor. A tall, blond man about forty, who arrived just before nine-thirty. The elevator operator is sure of the time, because the guy insisted on being taken up right away, so the operator missed the end of *Duffy's Tavern*. Must be this Doctor Clayton. The other was a guy who came every night to pick up his wife. A Negro police officer named Mitchell, who arrived about nine-forty-five."

"Funny, none of the papers said anything about a policeman being there when the body was found."

The steaks came. After we ate, Peter sat down at the telephone and made the rest of his calls to the men who worked in the Emory Building.

In a perfect cop voice, he told them he was "Garrity, from Mid-Manhattan," and he was double-checking the preliminary reports, asking if they remembered anything they hadn't told the detectives earlier. His bosses didn't want any screwups.

None of them had anything to add. They had all gone home after work. There were only a few tight alibis, but they all claimed they didn't know Miss Keane. Cupp did all the work on that floor. Yeah, they'd heard that he didn't get along with her, but they were surprised he'd kill her. Of course, he was from the hills. They settled things different down there.

I finished the evening editions, then took a long bath. When I came to bed, Peter folded me in his arms.

"We'll just have to see how this plays out," he said.

"I know."

Eventually, he fell asleep. I lay there for a long time, staring at the city night pressing in around the drawn curtains. Finally, I folded back the sheet.

"Huh?" Peter asked groggily.

"I think I'll make some hot milk. Go back to sleep."

He muttered something unintelligible and rolled over.

I pushed my feet into my slippers, pulled on my dressing gown and went into the living room, closing the bedroom door softly after me. Outside, even through the thick curtains, I could hear the muted rumble of traffic. One o'clock in the morning and New York was still moving.

One o'clock. Ten o'clock in Los Angeles.

I lifted the phone quietly, rang the front desk, and whispered for a long-distance operator. I placed a call to Sam Ross at his home in Beverly Hills. Being so late, the call went right through. The operator didn't have to call me back. Sam answered. I told him what was on my mind.

"I was going to call her brothers," he said, "tell them how sorry I am and that we're going to honor the deal, even though we hadn't signed yet. But I can't ask them what you want me to, not now. That'd be crude, even for me."

"Of course. I just wanted to know if you'd be willing."

"Does your bodyguard know about this?"

"Not yet."

"Tell me you're not going to do anything stupid."

"Of course not."

"Yeah," he said and hung up.

Nestor Cupp was charged with murder, and the story disappeared from the papers. Peter kept digging, but there was nothing else to find. The police slammed the door, probably because they'd found out someone had been calling witnesses, impersonating a cop.

From Hollywood, there were carefully controlled stories about the wrapping of Franklin's movie, and how all the cast would be getting away for a while, recovering from the strain of the constant publicity. Everyone still thought that I was in Cuba and that Franklin was joining me there.

We saw some of New York while I did a little research for the *Adam Drake* script. Peter still carried a gun, but he grew more comfortable with my being outside, more confident that no one had found us. We stayed away from fancy restaurants and supper clubs. We didn't want to risk my being recognized by Hollywood visitors, and I was afraid he'd pick up the tab and not put it on his expense account.

On Thursday night, two weeks and a day after Hazel was killed, we went to see *Oklahoma!*, a show that had been so successful—running now well over three years—that it had discouraged other musicals from opening, producers being afraid they couldn't draw a house against it. I thought ballet on the prairie was silly, but maybe I lack sophistication.

When we returned to the hotel, we ordered sandwiches from the desk clerk, and he handed Peter the stack of late editions he had collected for us. When we reached the suite, I tossed my fur across the sofa and went into the kitchen to get ice and a bottle of tonic. When I came out, Peter was picking up a folded sheet of vellum paper that had apparently fallen out of the stack of newspapers.

He opened it. His face hardened.

"What's this?" he demanded and handed me the hotel's note, which said: *Mr. Bluepoint Vance called. He said he did what you asked, and the answer is yes. What's next?*

"What the hell is this? When did you call Ross?"

"A couple of weeks ago."

"I told you not to make calls." He hadn't, at least on that particular day, but I thought he wouldn't appreciate the quibbling. "What the hell were you thinking? The long-distance operator probably gave his secretary her operator number. Do you have any idea how much some people would pay for that number? They get it, they can find out where the call came from."

"I called Sam at home," I said simply.

"What did you ask him to do?" Peter snapped.

"I thought he was going to wait until he heard from me."

"What did you ask him to do?"

"Find out if *Adam Drake* was going to hire a new writer, since Hazel was gone."

"What the hell were you thinking?"

"Do you think this case is airtight?"

"It doesn't matter, damn it. You're not going in."

"The police are sure Cupp's guilty. They won't do one more thing and you know it."

"They have an eyewitness!"

"What if he's mistaken? What if he's lying? Does it make any sense that the killer would use a knife after she was already dead and then leave the weapons behind? If the doctor's wrong, it's an inside job."

"You're not going in!"

"If you had a case like this in LA—"

"I don't have a case! You don't have a case! You're not going in there! Just because you got lucky in LA, you think you can do any damn thing you want! You almost got yourself killed out there! You almost got my brother killed!"

I didn't trust myself to say anything, and I was smart enough to know that if I did, whatever he would say would only be worse, worse even than blaming me for Johnny. I snatched up my coat and stalked off to the bedroom.

He didn't follow me. Soon I heard him growling around the suite, then ice cubes being flung into a glass. Ten minutes later, I heard more ice. The bell rang, the bellboy with the sandwiches. I stayed where I was, sitting at the dressing table, creaming my face.

Finally, Peter came to the bedroom door. "The food's here," he said shortly.

"I've lost my appetite."

He turned and stalked back out.

He slept in his own bed that night.

For most of the eight hours that I didn't sleep, I thought about what he'd said. He was wrong about Johnny, and I was furious that he'd use it in an argument, but he was right about the rest. I was stubborn. I was fully prepared to believe I was right, no matter what. In addition, I was gifted with and plagued by the artist's inability to censor ideas. If I had one, I went with it. It was a blessing in my career. A problem in my personal life.

At seven o'clock, I smelled coffee. I slipped out of my nightgown and into my dressing gown. You never know when an unpleasant truth might need a little silk and skin.

Peter was staring out the living-room window, a coffee cup in his hand. The bourbon bottle was almost empty.

I said, "I'm about as hardheaded as a woman can be, and I'm not likely to change. But I'm not stupid. I was careful when I called Sam, and I still think it's an idea worth considering. And as for my being in danger from a certain party in LA, I've been thinking about that. And as much as I appreciate having you around all the time, Winslow, I can't imagine that you didn't tell a certain party that, if anything ever happened to me, the certain party would be dead within twenty-four hours. Is that about right?"

After a moment, he said, "Forty-eight. I'm not that good."

I went over to him, close enough to feel the heat from his body. "I hate fighting with you."

"Then stop doing things behind my back. Just because you have an idea doesn't mean you have to jump on it."

"I know."

He set down his cup and headed for the coat closet.

"Will you be gone long?" I asked.

"As long as it takes to see a lawyer."

"About what?"

"We can't get a new one for Cupp. Neither one of us wants to go that far, but I've been thinking about that knife. About why the killer would use it too. One thing about the autopsy I didn't tell you. Miss Keane was hit hard a couple of times, but the blows didn't break the skin. If the killer wanted to frame Cupp, he had to get blood on the coveralls. And blunt instruments don't always give that to you."

"Oh, Peter."

"I figure Miss Keane must have had insurance. Let's see who the beneficiary is. If I can convince the insurance company lawyers that they could be paying off the killer, they might put somebody on it."

"You?"

"They've got plenty of their own men."

"What time will you be back?"

He shrugged into his coat. "It could take all day."

"I'd like to go out for a while."

"To do what?"

"Anything. The walls are closing in."

"Take cabs, stay where there are plenty of people. And make sure you're back before dark."

"I promise."

He took his hat off the shelf, then came over to me slowly. "I'm sorry, what I said about Johnny. You weren't to blame for that. I never thought you were." I nodded. He put on the hat. "You are hardheaded as hell, that's for sure. But you weren't just lucky. You were good."

There was a little hop in my step as I went back to the bedroom. Quickly, I changed, and pulled out an *Adam Drake* radio script that Sam had sent me when I was still in LA. I read it over again, reminding myself of the show's conventions, then I rolled paper into my typewriter. In case Peter changed his mind, I intended to be prepared.

The sounds of a circus. Calliope and laughing children. Distantly, a ringmaster.

Drake: I hadn't been to a circus in a long time. The clowns I usually end up with don't get paid for it. I never much liked the circus, even as a kid, except for the high-wire acts. Those were the only guys I wanted to see, balancing on a line as thin as an alibi, where one wrong breath can tip you. And you're never sure how many of those people, smiling up at you, are just waiting to see you die.

CHAPTER 5

At one o'clock, I stacked my pages together and finished off the last of a sandwich, then took a cab—as I promised Peter I would do—the eleven blocks and one avenue to the main branch of the New York Public Library.

In the publications room, I ordered the city edition of each of the New York papers for a couple of weeks following the final arrest in the Los Angeles case, then another stack of the papers published since September 13, when my identity was revealed. I scoured them for pictures of Peter and me.

In the first set, there were none of me, and since he had avoided the press, few of Peter. Most were shots of him on the move—coming out of the hospital or the DA's office. I didn't think they did him justice. And he was wearing his hat low on his forehead.

In the second set, there were plenty of me. A few were years-old studio-staged publicity shots of Franklin and other stars at openings and parties, with me standing awkwardly beside my husband. However, most were the portrait I had given him to keep in his dressing room when we were first married, the same picture that had been in all the Los Angeles papers, sold to the Associated Press by the portrait artist. I had been furious then; now I was grateful. I looked even younger than I had been at the time, my eyes full of dewy-eyed devotion and my hair laying softly on my shoulders. If I dyed my hair, wore it up and wore glasses, would anyone who didn't know me recognize me from that shot?

Then I searched the magazines that featured news. *Look, Life, Saturday Evening Post, Newsweek,* and—bless the Public Library—the most popular movie confidential magazines. There, in *Movie Star,* was a shot of me ducking into the car at Chasen's with Peter behind me. It was the only picture I found of the two of us together, and the only one in which I thought I looked like myself.

Would any of the *Adam Drake* staff be keen readers of *Movie Star?*

I looked at my watch. Cripes! It was almost five. I'd promised Peter I'd be back before dark. I rushed my magazines back to the desk, then scurried out, my heels clacking on the marble floors.

The temperature had dropped a full twenty degrees. I gathered my coat collar around my neck, yanked on my heavy-enough-for-California gloves and scrambled down the long flight of steps to the sidewalk. Fifth was clogged with rush-hour traffic. All the cabs were taken.

Just as the light changed, I scampered across Fifth and began to walk fast—even faster than the natives—but it was dark by the time I reached the hotel. My legs were ice. I darted into the elevator and tried not to tap my frozen foot while the ancient operator stood up slowly from his stool, slowly closed the doors, then the gate, then dropped the lever to raise the car slowly, slowly. We stopped within six inches of my floor and I jumped out.

Peter hadn't come back yet. I dashed into my bedroom, stuffing my gloves into my pocket. I tore off the coat, threw it onto a hanger and into my closet. I unpinned my hat and dropped it on the dressing table. The dress, of course, had a dozen buttons. While my thawing fingers worked on them, I stood in front of the fiery radiator, stamping blood back into my legs. Finally, I freed myself, threw the dress onto the chair and pinched out my hairpins. I ran my fingers roughly over my chilled scalp until I was no longer cold to the touch. Then I tackled the girdle and stockings.

I had just enough time to get into slacks and a sweater, tie back my hair, pull out a magazine, and throw myself into an armchair in the living room before I heard the key in the door.

Peter's collar was turned up against the bitter weather, his scarf wrapped high across his throat. He pulled off his gloves and rubbed his hands together briskly.

I said, "They just don't know how to make a winter out in LA, do they?"

His ears and cheeks were pink and chilled. I took his hat off and kissed them. I kept kissing them till they got warmer. It was one of the few times Peter Winslow didn't stop to hang up his coat.

"How would you like to go out tonight?" Peter asked, raking my hair with his fingers and spreading it onto his bare chest.

"Hmm," I said, moving my cheek over the smooth skin of his shoulder. "It's too cold. Maybe we could just stay in."

He chuckled and got up, naked, to retrieve his notebook from the living room. He climbed back in bed, shoved the pillow behind him, and flipped the notebook open.

"The insurance company wants me to look into it," he announced.

I sat up. "How did you manage that?"

"Sometimes you forget who the shamus is around here. The chief investigator at Mutual was very interested in what I had to say. It turns out they have two policies on Hazel Keane's life, each for a hundred grand. The first one she bought when she got married. The second was purchased by Keane Productions when the company was formed."

"And the beneficiaries are . . . ?"

"For the first one, her husband, Barnard Benjamin. For the second, everything goes to the production company, which will be run by her brothers now. Since all three men were in the offices the night she died, the investigator thought it would be a good idea to ask a few questions before they paid off. He decided to let me do it. He liked my references."

"I'll bet he did."

"Then I got a look at her will."

"You're good at this, aren't you?"

"A will's a matter of public record once it's been submitted for probate. I hope you're not disappointed."

I ran my hand up his thigh. "Not so far. Did she have much to leave?"

"Enough. Most of it probably came from her father, Morris Keane. He died in March. He had a stroke last year and never recovered. He was a widower. The brothers, George and Henry, are the only other children. Henry was married once, but it was annulled. George has never married. There are no grandchildren.

"Hazel Keane's will was dated last March, two weeks after her father died. She left half of everything to her husband—which looks like it could be worth at least a half million—and the rest to her college, a theater company and a Catholic orphanage. She left her rights to the shows to her brothers, but no money. Thirty thousand went to Adora Watson. I don't know who that is yet. A hundred thousand went to. . . ." He paused for effect.

"Our witness, the good Doctor Clayton," I said. "I knew it! I knew it!"

"It gets more complicated. She also left ten thousand to Willa Mitchell, the maid who found the body."

"And her husband's a policeman, who was there every night, able to look around. Wouldn't you love to have a talk with those two?"

"You're going to get your chance."

"What?"

"The power of a gold-plated lawyer. Mutual's got one and he used to be a prosecutor. Very good connections. He called the cops' top brass. They're not too eager for it to get into the papers that the insurance company has doubts about their case, so we agreed to keep it quiet, and they agreed to let us take a look at what a good job they did. One call to Mitchell's captain, and Officer Mitchell and his wife have decided that they can find time to have a talk."

He turned the notebook to me. At the bottom of the page was written: "Club 131. 131 W.131. 10:00."

"We're meeting at a nightclub?"

"I think Officer Mitchell would like to be among friends."

In spite of the turn in the weather, I was going to wear my wool-lined cape, not my fur, but Peter pointed out that, no matter what I wore, I would be conspicuous, a blonde in a Harlem nightclub, so I wore the fur and stayed warm.

One Thirty-One and 133 were fawn-colored townhouses whose facades had been painted black from the first floors down; all the windows in the painted part had been replaced by opaque glass bricks. At the top of the stoop to 131, on the front door, there was a hand-lettered sign that said: CLUB IS DOWN-STAIRS. DON'T RING OUR BELLS.

The club's front door was tucked beneath the stoop, and had a small, black, scuffed awning above it with 131 and a pair of eighth notes painted in silver. Music pulsed out onto the side-walk.

As Peter put his hand on the door, it swung open. On the

other side stood a Negro man who couldn't have been more than six-eight. He was extremely skinny and stooped and probably a great deal older than he looked in the dim light of the small lobby: his close-cropped hair was full of tiny corkscrews of white. His shiny evening clothes hung from him, the jacket sleeves not quite long enough, so that an inch of white shirt cuff shot out from under them. Beyond him, on the other side of a silver beaded curtain, the audience whooped for an encore.

"Nathan Mitchell, please," Peter said. The man looked over into a dark alcove on the other side of the room, where another man sat on a stool. At least I thought it was a stool. His bulk covered it entirely and took up most of the alcove as well. He wore all black: suit, shirt, tie. In the pale spill of light, I could see his hands working in front of his belly, cleaning long fingernails with the curved end of a narrow silver file. "Twelve," he rumbled. That was all. He went back to his file.

We checked our coats with a girl in a red Chinese dress, then Peter paid two dollars each for the cover and the skinny man took us in through the beaded curtain. Beneath the heavy layer of smoke, we snaked our way through the tightly packed patrons to an empty table about the size of a serving plate. Peter handed the man some coins, and we wedged ourselves in. The couples around us continued applauding, but they eyed us as we sat down. On the opposite side of the room were the only other white people, six of them, all in one group, gathered around two tables smothered with glasses. Our waiter came over and we ordered drinks.

Finally, the singer returned through a beaded curtain beside the band. She was small and thin to the point of fragility, her yellow gown cut with deep folds draping across her bosom and hips, making her figure appear more generous than it was. Her head was large for her frame and her hair had been arranged on top in big, looping curls.

She stepped to the mike. "Thank you," she said in a growling whisper. "Thank you so much."

She made no attempt to end the cheering but stood acknowledging it with small inclinations of her head, until it died away. "Next week," she said then. "Next week, as you may know, I will be going on tour with Mr. Dizzy Gillespie." The audience applauded heartily. "Then, then in December, we'll return to New York to the Aquarium Club for the holidays."

"We be there, baby!" a voice called out from the other side of the room. The rest of the room laughed and joined in, shouting, "Yeah, we be there! Look for us, honey!"

"And since," she went on, "many of you might not be able to attend. . . ."

The woman at the table beside me called out, "We 'tend, honey! We tend the ladies' room!" There was more laughter and shouts of, "You tell it! Tell it, sister!"

"I won't be with you for the holidays, but you know where my heart is." She lifted the hand at her side almost imperceptibly. The band began to play and she sparkled her way through "Christmas Night in Harlem."

When she finished, she bowed, again only her head, and went off through the beaded curtain. The crowd continued to roar. She took one more series of bows, then went out. The band struck up "Diga Diga Doo."

"Mr. Winslow?" a man's voice said, practically in my ear.

I turned. Less than two feet away were a pair of intense, deep-set eyes with a shallow furrow between them and a chin almost as good as Peter's. The man's hair was slicked back tightly so that the dense waves were very nearly smooth against his scalp.

"Officer Mitchell," Peter said.

Nathan Mitchell's head was turned toward us, but he kept his body facing the stage. "Your company's got a lawyer gets straight through to the captain."

"He knows some people," Peter allowed.

"My lieutenant said you wanted to talk to Willa. I told him I wasn't going to let her talk to anyone alone. I told him that was the only reason I was going along."

Peter said, "Thanks for not making it the precinct."

"I could have. I still might."

"I understand."

"This is my wife."

Willa Mitchell had an attractive—if somewhat girlish—face, with round cheeks and a slight overbite. She wore a powder-blue gown with a square neck and cathedral sleeves. Her hair was gathered back into a discreet chignon.

Peter introduced me as Mrs. Tanner. Tanner was my maiden name. Mabel Lauren Tanner.

"Why's the insurance company asking questions?" Nathan Mitchell asked.

"It's standard when there's this much money."

Mitchell didn't look entirely convinced.

Peter said, "For what it's worth, I don't think you or your wife killed Miss Keane. You'd be crazy to do it there, where your wife would be the chief suspect."

"There's my mother-in-law," Mitchell said. "She weighs all of ninety pounds."

Peter didn't betray that we hadn't known who Adora Watson was until now. "When did she find out she was a beneficiary?"

"Last week, when we found out about our money."

"Ninety pounds," Peter said.

"Ninety-two, maybe. Can't keep her away from the cake."

Our drinks came. We sipped silently for a while before Peter said, "I'd like Mrs. Mitchell to tell me what happened that night, in her own words."

"The detectives are the ones to talk to," Mitchell said.

"I'll talk to them."

I took another sip and watched them watching each other.

Peter said, "I understand there was a meeting that night."

Nathan Mitchell glanced at his wife and, after a moment, nodded. She shifted in her chair and spoke then, using a voice very different from the one she'd used to call out to the singer— soft, measured. "A writers meeting. They get together once a month or so and decide what to write."

"Is it always at the same time?"

"It usually starts at five, but they had a party that night for one of the typists who was leaving to get married, so the meeting didn't start till almost six-thirty."

Peter took his notebook out of his jacket. "Can you start with when you came to work that night?"

She stared at the notebook. Mitchell slipped his hand over hers. "Go on," he said.

"Well," she said, "I got there about four, just like I always do, and changed into my uniform in the ladies'. Now, that's on the *Love* side, so I—"

"Did you say 'love side'?" Peter leaned toward her.

A smile pulled on her lips. "They write two shows up there. *Love Always*, that's one of those soap operas, and *Adam Drake*, the detective show." She opened her evening bag and looked inside, then said to her husband. "Do you have a pen?"

"Here, use this one," Peter said. She eyed him for a moment before taking it.

On a cocktail napkin, she drew a large U, squared at the bottom, and filled it in with a rough draft of the office floor plan, which turned out to be very accurate when, a few days later, we were able to draw a more detailed one. "The office looks sort of like this," she said. Peter got up and wedged himself into a chair at their table so he could see better. She gave the pen back and traced left to right along the bottom of the U with her finger.

"Here, in this corner, they have Miss Keane's office, then the conference room, then the typists room, and then Mr. Keane's office at the other corner. That's Miss Keane's brother, Henry Keane. He produces *Love Always*."

She pointed to the right side of the U. "On this side is where they write that show. On the other side, they write *Adam Drake*. So, they call those hallways the *Love* side and the *Drake* side. After I finished changing, I went around picking up everybody's coffee cups and things that need to be washed. Is that what you want?"

"Yes, exactly."

"I made up some punch in a bowl that Miss Keane keeps and rinsed out the glasses. I set it all out in reception and the cakes and helped everybody get served." She placed her finger in the middle of the U. "The reception room is here, where we had the party."

"Did you see Nestor Cupp?" Peter asked.

"I saw him in the ladies' room when I first got there. He was working on the plumbing. I asked him to step out for a bit so I could change. Then I saw him later at the party. I think Miss Walters invited him. She's one of the writers. I didn't hear her ask him, but he told me she'd said it was all right for him to come have some cake."

"Did you notice if he had his toolbox with him?" Peter asked.

"He wasn't carrying it. I don't know where it was."

"Did you see him leave?"

"No."

"Did you see him there after five-forty-five?" Peter asked. I remembered that the building's super said Cupp had clocked out at five-forty-five.

"I don't remember. I wasn't in the reception room for the whole party. I was emptying ashtrays and taking the cups and dishes to the kitchen some of the time."

"Do you know who called him to come make repairs that day?"

"He wasn't making repairs, as such. He replaced the drainpipes to the sinks and re-tiled around them. He'd done the men's room the day before."

"Did everyone know he was going to be there?"

"There were signs up for a few days, telling everybody the sinks were going to be worked on."

Peter made a note, then asked, "When did the party end?"

"I know it was after six, and everybody went home except the people at the meeting and Mr. Alletter, he's the night watchman. I know that the meeting had started by six-thirty because there's a clock in the kitchen here," she said and pointed to its location in the *Drake* hallway. "That's where I was when the alarm went off."

Chapter 6

"The alarm?" Peter asked.

"It's so loud, it scared me so. I dropped a glass and broke it. The alarm's up there at the top of the *Drake* side, and the kitchen's not that far away. Miss Keane had some sandwiches sent up for the meeting, and the delivery boy decided to take the stairs down. He was a new boy and didn't know about the alarm. He was so scared, he just froze up, and Mr. Alletter had to move him out of the door so he could close it."

Peter frowned at the drawing.

Mitchell said, "Thinking the boy let someone in?"

"It would have to be somebody with access to the coveralls and Cupp's tools. And what would he think he was going to find up there? Would an outsider think there was anything up there worth stealing?"

Willa said, "I never thought there was, maybe some petty cash that the bookkeeper has."

"I'll have a talk with the boy anyway," Peter said. "Does the alarm have to be reset?"

"No," Willa said. "It goes on when the door's opened and stops when it's closed."

"Who made it this hard to get in and out of there?"

"Miss Keane. A year or so ago, they caught the maid going through the desks, stealing story ideas for another show. That's when she asked me to work for her there. And she got a new door for that back staircase and put an alarm on it."

"Who was at the writers meeting?"

"Mr. Connally and Miss Walters—the *Adam Drake* writers—Miss Keane and both Mr. Keanes, Henry and George. George Keane comes to the meetings, too, though he only stays a little while. Mr. Benjamin was there. He directs the show. And Mr. Donovan and Miss Dunn. They play Adam Drake and Maisie Lane. And Miss Keane, of course."

"I understand that Miss Keane and her husband were separated," Peter said.

"Since just after Christmas. That's all I have to say about that."

"Then we'll stick to what you did that night. What happened after the boy left?"

"Everybody went back to work. I finished washing up. I put the punch bowl and glasses away in the closet in Miss Keane's office, so I know there was no one hiding there, not then anyway. Then I vacuumed her office and emptied the trash. I took my cart down to the end of the *Drake* side and started cleaning and emptying the trash there too. I vacuumed under those desks, so I can tell you no one was hiding under them either. Then I cleaned the reception room and took my cart around to the *Love* side. I was in Mr. Keane's office when I heard them coming out of that meeting. Then there was a lot of commotion because the rod in the hall closet had fallen down. They went to get their coats and found them all on the closet floor. Miss Keane got Mr. Alletter to come fix it, and when he came out of reception, I heard her tell him that she was going to do some work. She'd get ideas during the meetings and want to work on them right away. She said she should be finished before ten but he should call her then in case she lost track of time."

"When was this?" Peter asked.

"I'm not sure. But the meetings didn't usually last much more than an hour, so maybe a bit after seven-thirty. I got a screwdriver for Mr. Alletter from the toolbox in the storage room, then I finished Mr. Keane's office, took the dishes out of the conference room and washed them, then I cleaned the conference room, the typists room and the hallway, and went back to the *Love* side and started cleaning there."

"Once you were on the *Love* side, were you ever in a position to see Miss Keane's door again?"

"No."

"What time did you start cleaning that side?"

"It couldn't have been later than eight-thirty. I'm always on the *Love* side before eight-thirty."

Mitchell said, "Nobody would have seen Miss Keane's door after eight-thirty. But from nine till nine-thirty, Mr. Alletter always takes his dinner in the kitchen. He couldn't see her door from there, but he would have seen anyone in the *Drake* hall."

Peter made some more notes. "Go on," he said to Willa.

"When I finished up, it was just before ten. I put my cart away in the storage room—that's on the *Love* side—and changed in the ladies' room, which is on that side, too. I got my coat and went into reception. Nathan was there and Mr. Alletter and Doctor Clayton. He'd come to pick up Miss Keane.

"I wouldn't have gone into her office at all, except I wanted to tell her about the broken glass. She wouldn't be angry, but I wanted her to know. And she'd told Mr. Alletter to let her know when it was ten o'clock. I knocked on her door, but she didn't answer. I knocked again and opened the door. All I saw were her shoes. Her feet on the other side of the desk. I thought she had a heart attack, so I ran back out and got the doctor. I didn't go in. I didn't see her."

Peter nodded. "I have just a few more questions," he said gently. "Do you have any idea how someone could get in or out of the offices at night without setting off the alarm or being seen by Mr. Alletter?"

She looked at her husband, then said, "I don't think they could, not when he's out in reception. There's glass all along the front, so Mr. Alletter could see anyone getting off the elevators or coming out of the service stairs. Those side doors near the elevators are always locked from the outside. The fire door has that alarm. And the front door's locked at seven. They'd have to have a key."

"Who has one?"

"I don't. Mr. Alletter does. I guess Miss Keane did, but I don't know."

"Once somebody was inside—sneaked inside somehow or stayed after the party or the meeting—where could he hide?"

Mitchell said, "If somebody knew the layout of the offices, there are plenty of places. There's a supply room and a mail room. My wife didn't clean them that night."

"When does she usually clean them?"

Willa said, "On Tuesdays and Thursdays, I mop those floors and wash down the cabinets."

Mitchell said, "The doors to those rooms weren't locked. I searched the offices after we found the body, and they weren't locked."

"Are they supposed to be?" Peter asked Willa.

"No," she replied, "we don't lock those doors."

"The police think Cupp hid in the coat closet."

"Maybe because the rod fell down."

"Doesn't seem like a smart choice, with people having to get their coats."

"There are plenty of other places he could have hidden," Mitchell said.

"Where's the watercooler?" Peter asked Willa.

"On the *Love* side, near the ladies' room."

"Did you see Doctor Clayton in the hall?"

"I know he said he went for a drink, that's when he saw Mr.

73

Cupp, but I must have been vacuuming in one of the offices."

"Did the detectives ask whether you'd seen Clayton?"

Mitchell said, "I think you've had your 'few more questions.' "

"I take it they didn't ask."

Willa watched her husband and said nothing. After a moment, Peter picked up his drink. He sipped and stared out at the dance floor.

I said, "Mrs. Mitchell, may I ask something? It has nothing to do with the detectives. Do you clean the offices the same way every night?"

"I have my routine. It makes it easier."

"Did having that party and the meeting change anything?"

"I did a few more dishes, but, no, not much."

"So anyone who'd been up there in the evenings could have figured out that you'd be on the *Love* side after eight-thirty and stay there."

"I guess so."

"Do the writers often stay late?"

"Not often. But from time to time, yes, I'd see them there. Sometimes Mr. Keane—Henry Keane—or Mr. Benjamin, too."

Peter said, "If the killer knew the routine, he'd know people worked late. He'd know he might be seen."

Willa said, "Not on meeting nights. No one ever stayed late after meetings, except Miss Keane."

"Never?"

"Not as long as I've been there."

I said, "Did you ever see Cupp up there late?"

"No, never."

"Then how could he know the office routine well enough to—?"

"Lauren Atwill?" a voice called from the edge of the dance floor where a lithe blond man bent forward, squinting into the gloom. "My God, it is you!" He came over, hips swaying as he wove his way through the tables. "I heard you were in Cuba."

It was Geoffrey Jonas, one of the top hair stylists in Hollywood. Just my luck, he'd done my hair for a few parties when Franklin and I were still together. Just my luck, he never forgot a face.

"Geoffrey," I said. "How are you?" I introduced the Mitchells, then Peter, who stood up, topping Geoffrey by almost a foot. "I'm her bodyguard," he said.

"Lucky for her."

"Sit down," I offered, and Geoffrey squeezed in beside me. "I'd appreciate it if you wouldn't tell anybody you saw me. Tell your friends I'm someone else."

"Hiding out, are we?"

"The reporters were hounding me to death."

"Oh," he said, suddenly serious, "I guess they were."

"Please don't tell anyone I'm in New York."

"My dear, you know all secrets are safe with me. All those I hear first, anyway."

"I'd appreciate it. What are you doing here?"

He glanced at Peter. "Nothing as exciting as you. I'm on my way to Madrid, but I'll be here for another week. I'm staying at the Plaza, in case you need somebody to tell you all the secrets I didn't hear first." He stood up, took my hand and kissed it. "I have some friends who are sleeping better these days because of you." He said good-bye to all of us, then waved playfully to his companions across the room and went to join them. Peter sat back down.

"Atwill?" Mitchell said to him.

"Mrs. Franklin Atwill," I said and explained who I really was. "You know the case?"

"I know some innocent people got shot."

Peter said, "I didn't shoot any of them."

"None of the innocent ones."

The band started up a rumba. There were whoops of delight from the crowd, and the dance floor filled up. Geoffrey grabbed one of the tightly coiffed and corseted matrons in his group and led her out onto the floor. Neither one of them glanced our way.

Mitchell said, "We don't talk about what the detectives did or didn't do that night."

"All right," said Peter. "Can we talk about what you did?"

"My shift starts at midnight, so I pick Willa up and take her home, then go on to the precinct. I got there about nine-forty-five. The doctor was already there, reading a magazine. He didn't say anything. Alletter and I talked a little baseball."

"Did the doctor leave the room?"

"Whenever he went for that drink, it was before I got there. When Willa came running in, we all ran into Miss Keane's office. She was dead. I didn't need the doctor to tell me that, but I told Alletter to call the ambulance anyway, and the police, and to call the man downstairs on the front door, to warn him, in case the killer was on the way downstairs. I sent Willa out with Alletter. I didn't want her to see that. I told the doctor not to touch anything, and I went out and searched. I started up by the alarm door and worked my way around. I kept one eye on the hallways when I went into the offices, but I didn't find anybody."

"And the alarm was working?"

"Yes. After I finished searching the offices, I went out that door, and closed it after me. I went up to the roof and down to the lobby by the service stairs, but no one was there. I checked the windows along the way. They were all locked. By the time I reached the first floor, the first patrol cars arrived, the detectives right after that. They let me call George Keane, to tell him what had happened, since I knew him, then I called Henry Keane at his apartment."

Peter said, "Did you notice anything to indicate someone had been hiding in any of those offices?"

"I wasn't looking for anything smaller than the killer, but I did notice that the cabinet in the mail room was open."

"Did Doctor Clayton tell you he'd seen someone outside Miss Keane's office?"

"He talked to the detectives. I didn't hear anything he told them."

Peter took another sip of his bourbon, which was now mostly water. "Did you work for Miss Keane before you came to *Adam Drake?*" he asked Willa.

"I started cleaning for her at her home about ten years ago. Then when they caught that maid stealing, Miss Keane asked me if I wanted the job. She wanted somebody she could trust."

"Do you still take care of her apartment?"

"I clean for Mr. Benjamin now. Miss Keane went to live with her father when she and Mr. Benjamin separated and stayed on after he died. My mother takes care of that house, that's the house where George Keane lives now. She worked for Morris Keane for thirty years."

"Do you know of anyone besides Cupp who'd had trouble with Miss Keane? Did anyone ever threaten her? Was there anyone she was afraid of?"

"I can tell you," Willa said, "Miss Keane wasn't afraid of anybody."

"When her marriage broke up, did she and Mr. Benjamin fight?"

"Mr. Benjamin wouldn't do something like this."

"Mr. Winslow," Mitchell said, "do you have any more questions about what happened the night of the killing?"

They looked at each other across the tiny table, then Peter said, "I guess that'll be all. Thank you." He handed Mitchell a card with Vanguard's phone number on it. "I'd like to talk to your mother-in-law."

"Why?"

"Because she knew Hazel Keane for thirty years." He got up and took his wallet out of his jacket. He put three dollars on our table to cover the drinks and tip.

Mitchell said, "Were you ever a cop?"

"No. When I was a kid, I used to run hooch for a guy out in LA. When they repealed Prohibition, he sent me to a friend of his who owned an agency. He didn't think I was cut out to be a gangster."

"Too soft."

"Yeah."

We were in the cab, careening down Columbus, before I said anything. "All right, what's bothering you?"

Peter said, "Nathan Mitchell knows that if Clayton didn't see a man in the hall, his wife could be in jail. She was alone in those hallways. The family got forty thousand. When I ask too many questions about what the cops did, he shuts me off, but he never once mentions the lineup. The one thing that prevents his wife from being a suspect, and he doesn't even mention it."

He took a long breath and stared out the window. It was a full twenty blocks before he spoke again. "When we get to the hotel, call Sam Ross."

CHAPTER 7

It didn't take Henry Keane long to decide that, as long as
Marathon was honoring the movie deal, he could do Sam Ross
a favor and give a friend of his an interview, as long as they
were thinking about adding another writer for *Adam Drake,*
temporarily anyway.

"You know, this story you've got?" Sam said to me, after he
made the call to Henry.

"Yes, I do," I said dryly. "I made it up." I was a recent di-
vorcée, my family was friends with the Rosses. Before I married, I'd done some writing in Hollywood, and was trying to get
back into the business now, in another town.

"Well, you know, it sounds like you might be my, uh. . . ."

"I'm flattered, Sam."

"Well, if it doesn't bother your bodyguard that those people'll
think this fat old Jew's got himself a little package on the East
Coast, it doesn't bother me. Take care of yourself, whatever
you're up to."

"I will. Tell Helen I'll write her."

"I'm not telling her anything. She'll make herself crazy wor-
rying about you."

And so by Tuesday morning, I was sitting on the syrupy gold
sofa in the reception room at Keane Productions, wearing phony
glasses and freshly dyed—and completely unflattering—brunette
hair (Geoffrey had made me promise never to tell anyone who
had done it). While the seam-faced, smoky-throated receptionist

called Henry Keane, I looked around the room, at the lithographs, the Keane cabinet radio, and the near impossibility of anyone's having got into the offices after the front door was locked at seven.

Cupp had clocked out at five-forty-five, so he had plenty of time to return and slip through the people at the party to hide. No one would pay attention to him. He had been working on the plumbing.

If he was guilty.

If he was not, it was the perfect night to frame him. A party, a meeting, people going in and out, and he was a man with a grudge and a set of heavy tools.

Whoever the killer was, he had managed to conceal himself where no one saw him, then slip out and creep into Hazel's office, surprising her so completely that she had not even been able to cry out for help.

I wasn't sure exactly when Clayton claimed to have seen the man in the hall, but it had to have been between the time the elevator operator took Clayton up—just before nine-thirty—and when Nathan Mitchell arrived at nine-forty-five because Nathan said the doctor never left reception. Why didn't the killer just go straight from Hazel's office, out the alarm door, and scramble down the service stairs? He could have made the street before anyone figured out what was going on. But instead, his plan of escape had been to gamble that when the body was found, no one would stay in reception to call an ambulance and see him dash out across the elevator waiting area.

It was a madman's plan.

"Mrs. Tanner?" said a voice right above me.

I jumped. "I'm sorry. I didn't hear you. Yes, Mabel Tanner."

"Bar Benjamin," he said. I stood up and we shook hands. He was tall and thin, with longish, lank light brown hair that wouldn't stay combed back despite hair oil. It fell in pieces over his ears. Beneath a wide forehead, he had forlorn dark-brown eyes, shadowed in their sockets. Hazel had been thirty-five. He looked maybe thirty. His long fingers brushed his hair back, and it fell again almost immediately.

"Let's go on back to my office," he said.

The door into the hallway opened silently. The killer, coming out of Hazel's office, would not have heard Clayton—presuming Clayton actually saw someone.

We went into her office. "Sit down," he said, and I did, across from his desk. It was new, as was the carpeting, the chair and the drapes and paint behind it.

He asked me how I was finding New York, had I been here before? Finally, he said, "I read the script you sent, Mrs. Tanner. It was impressive for a beginner."

"Thank you, but I'm not really a beginner. I did some writing in Hollywood, before my marriage."

"Um, yes, Mr. Ross mentioned that. But, you see, we have much tighter deadlines than the movies. You know that we lost our producer recently."

"Yes, I heard. I'm so sorry."

"She wrote as well. So, you see, we really need someone who can hit the ground running." He waited. I thought he was waiting for me to throw in the towel.

I said, "Why don't you let me show you what I can do?"

"We have your script."

"I meant today. This morning. Let me show you what I can do with a deadline." I gave him a cheery little smile.

He hesitated, but he couldn't be rude to Sam Ross's protégée. "Very well. Let me give you a script idea and see what you can give me by lunch. Say, one o'clock. I'll need the first ten minutes and an outline for the rest. He took a page out of his desk drawer and handed it to me. "This is something we were thinking about using." He turned to his typing table and

81

grabbed a fresh stack of paper and a couple of pencils. "I'll show you an office where you can work."

As we crossed the hallway into the *Drake* side, I calculated how much time Clayton had to see the killer. One-thousand-one, one-thousand two. Two seconds to invisibility.

The *Drake* side had three doors along the left-hand wall, all of them closed. Bar opened the second and showed me into a room with the same gray walls and tweed carpet as the hallway. It had two blind-covered windows close together and a radiator between them. There was a varnished maple kneehole desk with nothing but a typewriter and a telephone on it. Behind it, a rolling wooden chair. A simple hard chair in front. An empty bookcase. On each wall were pale rectangles where pictures used to be.

"This was Eileen's office. Eileen Walters," he said. "She's moved next door. I'll be leaving soon, to go to the *Love Always* broadcast. I direct that show as well. If you have any questions, I'll be back about eleven." He left me there.

I sat down and looked over the story idea. Maisie (Drake's secretary) brings a friend to see her boss. The friend's husband has disappeared. His company says he embezzled, but she knows he wouldn't, and so on and so on.

Nothing very exciting. The first thing I had to do was put some juice into that dull setup. At least there could be a storm raging. What if Maisie's not there yet? Drake, after an insomniac night, is there early when a beautiful stranger appears, claiming that she's a friend of Maisie's. Isn't Maisie here yet? It must be this terrible weather. My husband. . . . Oh, Mr. Drake, I need your help very badly.

But Maisie has been kidnapped to insure that Drake finds the missing man, who has stolen money from dangerous people. And his "wife" appears to give Drake the details before he can find out what's happened and strong-arm the messenger into telling him where Maisie is. That had possibilities.

Drake's office door opens, and there she is.

My own office door opened.

A tall, plump woman stood in it, her short, dyed-blond hair brushed backed carelessly. She wore a good black wool skirt and purple silk blouse. Both strained a little at the waistline darts. Anger flashed across her face, then disappeared in the next instant. "Sorry, wrong room," she said and started back out.

"Are you Eileen Walters?" I asked.

"This used to be my office. My mind was somewhere else. You the one getting the tryout? What's he got you doing?" I handed her the setup. She read it and rolled her eyes. "Good luck," she said and left.

By twelve-thirty, I'd finished the first ten minutes and the outline. I created a few pages of false starts to add to what was already in the wastebasket, then went to see Bar Benjamin. "I'm done."

He glanced at his desk clock. "Well, good, let's see what we have." I handed him the pages and sat down. He ran over the opening and his brows went up a touch. He read on. I sat there, imagining a smug little smile, even if I couldn't make one. When he looked up, I had my hopeful-supplicant expression in place.

"Well, you obviously have talent. I encourage you to continue pursuing your career." He cleared his throat and folded his hands on top of my script. "However, as I said, we really need someone who can step in, hit the ground running. We've been talking to Barton Loomis. You won't know him, but he's an old hand in radio, and I think we'll be inviting him to join us. But I don't want you to be discouraged."

I stared at him while he went on with his little speech about the promise I showed and how I could have a future, with work and perseverance. My enormous ego. It had never occurred to me that he wouldn't be bowled over and grinning like a fool at his good fortune to have found me.

I said, "Thank you, Mr. Benjamin. For your time and your advice. If anything should turn up, or if you decide to use my idea, I hope you'll give me a shot at it."

I went back to the hotel and threw a few things around the suite.

"Hmm," Peter said when I'd calmed down enough to tell him about Bar Benjamin's incredible lack of artistic judgment.

"That's all you can say?"

"It was always a long shot."

"It was?"

"Don't get hot. It was a long shot he'd take a flier on an unknown. A plan doesn't work, you try something else."

"Such as?"

"We could try the original one, the one where I do the detective work. Get your coat. We have an appointment with Adora Watson."

"You've changed your hair," Willa Mitchell said when she opened the apartment door. She didn't say it looked better.

"I thought I might be able to get a job at *Adam Drake*, to find out what was going on there, but it didn't work out."

"That's too bad." I wasn't sure if she meant the job or the hair. Or both.

She led us into the living room, where Nathan Mitchell stood beside a chair slipcovered in lilacs. In it sat his mother-in-law. Adora Watson could not have been much more than five feet, with the same round, girlish face as her daughter, but there was heavy indigo shadowing beneath her eyes. She wore a navy-blue silk dress with tiny white flowers and a white collar and cuffs.

"Sit down, please," she said. She indicated the sofa. Her small hands had large knuckles and prominent veins.

Willa sat in the other armchair. Nathan took his place beside Adora in a hard chair that had been brought over from the dining table. "Nathan told me that you knew Miss Hazel."

I said, "We met in LA. She wanted me to write her movie."

"You liked her?"

"I did. Very much. We want her killer caught."

She turned to Peter. "You know the doctor saw that man."

"I know he believes he did," Peter said, "but the truth is that eyewitness testimony is frequently wrong. And we have to consider the possibility that the doctor is lying."

"Did he get money, then?"

"Yes. A hundred thousand in her will."

"I see."

I said, "You weren't fond of him."

"That man broke Miss Hazel's heart once," she said. "This would have been in nineteen twenty-eight, and Mr. Keane's radios were just starting to make him rich. I always thought it was her money he was after, but she was head over heels for that man. He was handsome, oh my, he was that, and a smooth talker, so her parents tried to keep an eye on her. Then they found out he had some other women, was still keeping a little dancer, even though he was engaged, and he wasn't likely to give all that up. She cried herself sick over that man, then she went away with her mother for about a year, to Europe, and when she came back, she went off to college, then started her career, acting, then writing, with her brothers."

Peter asked, "How long have you worked for the family?"

"Goodness, most of my life. I came up here in nineteen fifteen from a little town you never heard of called Senatobia, Mississippi, to live with my brother Isaiah. He's passed on now. He worked at the Edison plant downtown where Mr. Morris Keane was an engineer back then. Mr. Keane and his wife were looking for someone to take care of their home and the children, and he asked Isaiah if he knew anybody. Mr. Keane was going off to France. He volunteered for one of those ambulance corps that went off to help the soldiers. I have a picture of him here." She picked up the silver-framed portrait on the table beside her. "He and his wife gave this to me. I asked for one, on their thirtieth anniversary, in nineteen thirty-five. I thought you might like to see what he looked like."

It was a solemn picture. Most people of Morris Keane's generation still looked somber in pictures, no matter how pleasant the occasion. Despite the serious expression, he had friendly eyes. Mrs. Keane wore a satin gown that showed perhaps a bit too much upper arm for a woman of her years, but she had strong bones that kept her handsome, and there was a curve of contentment on her lips.

"Miss Hazel was born in nineteen eleven, Mr. George in nineteen fourteen and Mr. Henry in nineteen fifteen. Mrs. Keane never quite got her health back after Mr. Henry was born. She died not a year after that picture was taken. Mr. Keane took her passing very hard. Then just when I thought he had found someone else to share his last years, he had that terrible stroke. This would have been a year ago last summer. It affected his mind. He didn't know his own children. That hurt Miss Hazel particularly. She was very close to her father."

"Was there any difficulty between Miss Keane and her brothers?" Peter asked.

"Mr. Henry and Mr. George can account for where they were that night," she said staunchly.

"I'm sorry that I have to ask these questions, but they're beneficiaries."

"I know they didn't kill her, because I was with them."

"Would you tell me about it?"

"Of course. Mr. George had invited some friends to come over that night after the theater for drinks and a late supper. I'm not sure when he got home—I know he had a meeting that evening—but he came down to the kitchen to see how things were going just as I was putting the ham in, so I know it was about eight-fifteen. Mr. Henry arrived a few minutes after, came straight down, still in his coat and hat. He went around sampling all the other food, just like when he was a little boy. But I could tell there was something wrong. They were talking to me, but not to each other. They went on upstairs, then. I finished the cooking and went up to the dining room to ice the cake. I always leave it up there to cool, and ice it there. It's too warm in the kitchen, with all that cooking. Once I've finished the cooking, I always stay up in the dining room and set the buffet table—the linen and flowers and all—until the kitchen's cooled down a bit.

"When the icing was done, I took a slice up to Mr. George, like I always do when I bake for parties. Two slices, of course, one for Mr. Henry too that night. Just before he opened the door, I heard Mr. George say something sharp to Mr. Henry about how Mr. Henry was going to have to grow up. Mr. Henry was in the other room, playing billiards, and told Mr. George to stop acting like his big brother all the time.

"I went back down to the dining room and then, in just a few minutes, I heard them arguing. Then Mr. Henry came downstairs, putting on his coat and hat. Mr. George yelled for him to come back, but he didn't. He just called out good night to me and slammed out of the house. Then Mr. George slammed his own door and all I could hear was his radio up there. Not too long after, he turned it off and came on down and apologized for the way they acted. I gave him another slice of cake and he ate it, while we listened to my radio for a while. I have a little one that I always bring up with me."

"Do you know what George and Henry fought about?" I asked.

"A program they're starting, a new soap opera. Just before

Mr. Henry came downstairs, I heard him say it was his show. And Mr. George said not without sponsors, and then Mr. Henry said that he was tired of having to ask permission for everything he wanted to do."

"Was there anyone else in the house, who might have heard more? Does George Keane have a manservant? Were there maids?"

"It was Mr. Hawthorne's night off. The maids come by day."

"Do you know what time this was, that Henry Keane left?" asked Peter.

"I do. I was listening to WEAF and at nine, they had Judy Stevens on, and Frank Sinatra. Mr. Henry left after the program started, during the first song. Mr. George and I listened till the show was over, then he went up to his study till the guests started arriving. Not long after that, Nathan called to tell him what had happened. I showed the guests out and made some tea. Mr. Henry came back then. Such an awful night."

I said, "We understand that Miss Keane was living in the house at that time, too."

"Since January, when she and her husband separated."

"Did she have trouble with him?" I asked.

"Not like you mean."

"Do you think Clayton was the reason they separated?"

"There were problems before she met that man again," she said, reluctantly. "Miss Hazel wanted children for a long time, but Mr. Benjamin was still a young man when they married. She thought he'd change his mind, but he didn't."

I said, "You said that Morris Keane might have found someone. Was he planning to marry again?"

"He told me he was. I never knew her last name, only that she was called Rachel. He never brought her to the house. He'd go off to pick her up for dinner, all dressed in his evening clothes. It was good to see him happy again."

"How did the children feel about her?" Peter asked.

"I don't think this could have anything to do with Miss Hazel's death."

"It might," he said, "if this woman thought Miss Keane was the reason Mr. Keane didn't marry her."

"I hadn't thought of that. The children were against it. They thought she was after his money, but I think it was mostly because she was Jewish. I was surprised they'd feel that way, but they thought it would be hard for him, with his own friends, with business. He told me he was too old to care about that sort of thing anymore. Then he had that terrible stroke. I saw the young lady a few more times, when she came to visit him. A pretty lady, dark hair, about your age, Mrs. Atwill. But he didn't know who she was. After a while, she stopped coming." She shook her head, tears in her eyes, and looked down at her hands. She kept staring at them.

"Is there something else?" I asked.

Nathan said quietly, "Go on. Tell them about that day, mom."

"I don't know if it means anything," Adora said, "but I guess I should tell you everything. This would have been back in early April. I don't remember exactly when, but not long after Mr. Morris died. I knew the children had planned to go through his papers, but when I got to work, at first, I thought there'd been a robbery. The drawers in the study were open, everything pulled out. Books all over the floor. Then I heard Mr. Henry's voice down at the other end of the hall. He was going through all the books in that room, Miss Hazel searching through picture albums. Mr. George had the pictures down off the wall, looking behind them."

"What did they say?" I asked.

"That there were some things unaccounted for and they thought Mr. Keane must have hidden them. After his stroke," she explained, "he was, well, as I said, he wasn't himself. He'd

89

wander all over the house in his wheelchair. He could do that because there's an elevator. He'd hide things, mostly foolish things, like his socks, but one time, Miss Hazel found some money and jewelry was missing. The nurse told her that it was probably me, but Miss Hazel set her straight right away, and then she found her father one night hiding money in a book. She found all the missing money and jewelry in the bookcase in the study. After that, they never left anything valuable where he could find it, so I didn't understand how there could be things unaccounted for."

Or, I thought, why they would be searching so desperately.

"What did you think they were looking for?" Peter asked.

"I don't know."

"Did they say or do anything that gave you an idea?"

"I don't know."

"A new will?"

Nathan said, "She doesn't know."

"It was something that scared them bad enough that they tore the house apart looking for it," Peter said to him. "I don't think they left any bearer bonds laying around where their father could get his hands on them. So let's say, for the sake of argument, that while they were going through his papers, they found some indication that he'd made a new will before his stroke and that he'd left this woman, his new fiancée, more money than they were willing to part with."

I said, "They'd be searching for it in every place that he might have hidden it *after* his stroke."

"For the sake of argument," Nathan said, "why wouldn't his lawyer know about it?"

Peter said, "Morris Keane wouldn't be the first man to keep things from his lawyer, especially if he thought the lawyer would try to talk him out of it. Did they find anything, do you know?" he asked Adora.

"I don't think so. They tore up the whole house."

I said, "If his fiancée knew he intended to make a new will, when the old one was presented for probate, she'd be pretty angry."

Peter said to Adora, "Do you know anything else at all about this woman? Where she lived, what she did?"

"No, only her first name."

"Did you ever hear Mr. Keane mention a new will?" I asked.

"No, and, of course, after his stroke, what he said didn't make much sense. Memories all jumbled up with the present. He mistook his children for other people. Me for his wife even, called me his darling, kissed my hand. The children would apologize, but I knew he couldn't help himself. All the years I worked for him, he was never anything but a gentleman."

Peter said, "We've taken up enough of your time. There may be a few other things I'll need later. May I call you?"

"Yes, young man, you may."

Nathan showed us to the door. "When did you decide to try to get Mrs. Atwill into *Adam Drake*?"

"After I found out how hard it was to get in and out of that place, and that the killer probably knew your wife's routine."

"Have you seen the detectives' reports?"

"Not yet. Even the insurance company's going to have trouble getting files while the case is still active."

"The Keanes have been good to my family," Nathan said. "We want Miss Keane's killer caught. So I won't tell anyone who you are and what you're really doing. But that's as far as I go."

"I understand," Peter said.

Nathan opened the door and we left. Once again, he never said a word about the lineup.

At the hotel, the manager handed me a message for Mabel Tanner. Would I please call Mr. Bar Benjamin?

The next day I started working as a junior writer on *Adam Drake, For Hire.*

Chapter 8

"I'm Mabel Tanner, the new writer."

The receptionist gave me a smile and redistributed the seams in her face. "Sophie Millsinberger, glad to meet you," she said, in her smoky-throated growl. She offered a thin, age-spotted hand, and I took it. She had a grip. "I'll tell Mrs. Embert you're here. Don't let her scare you."

As she turned to the PBX, two men in coveralls came out of the service stairs and in the front door. One pushed a dolly with furniture padding folded on it; the other carried a coil of rope and a sheet of paper, which he handed to Sophie.

"Over there," she said, nodding at the console radio.

"Where's it going?" I asked.

"Bar's loaned it to Radio City for an exhibition they're having." She turned to the men. "And if you so much as scratch it. . . ."

"Yeah, I know," the first guy said, "I'll be sorry."

"It's a classic," Sophie pointed out.

"Hey, Morty," he observed to his colleague, "hear that? A classic."

"Huh," Morty returned. "Guess we better not drop it out the window, then."

A board-straight woman in a black suit marched into reception. She had thick, lustrous dark hair, but she wasn't letting that get in the way. She had it pulled back tightly and skewered with hairpins the size of rivets.

"I'm Mrs. Embert," she said crisply. "Come with me."

I followed the impeccably straight seams of her stockings, which stopped long enough for me to hang up my coat, then headed straight into the corner office on the *Love* side. The seams turned, went out and left me there.

Henry Keane stood up from his desk and re-buttoned his suit coat slowly, looking me up and down. Bar Benjamin stood sullenly by the window. Henry was a strapping, handsome man, with carefully oiled wavy auburn hair and a fresh shave. Like his sister, his fair skin had seen a bit too much sun and there was a light freckling on his forehead.

I offered my hand. We shook, and he held on.

"Bar tells me you've got a lot of promise. Always glad to give a leg up to a newcomer, especially such a pretty one. How's Sam Ross?"

"Quite well, the last time I spoke to him."

"I've been reading some good things about that movie he just finished. What's it called?"

"*The Final Line.*"

"Right, right." He kept staring at me. I was sure he was on to me. Finally, he released my hand. "Sit down."

I said, "If you don't mind, I'd rather you didn't tell anyone else that I know Sam. They might think I'm not really qualified to do the job."

"Sure, we can do that, can't we, Bar?" He went on without giving Bar a chance to answer. "You understand that this is a tryout period."

"Yes. Thank you for the opportunity, Mr. Keane."

"Henry, please, Henry."

We discussed the terms of my sixty-day trial. It wasn't really a discussion. He talked and I nodded at appropriate moments, then we shook hands again. He held on for a while, but not as long as before.

When Bar and I were outside, past the typists room, he finally said, "While you're here, you answer to me."

"Of course."

"*Adam Drake*'s my show."

"Of course."

We turned into the *Drake* hallway, and he stopped at the first office. It looked the same as the one in which I'd written my audition script, except that it was personalized with framed photographs on the walls and tan curtains with interlocking squares of olive and aqua scattered over them.

Eileen Walters sat on a hard chair, smoking, her feet up on the radiator, a copy of *Vogue* under them to protect her shoes. Another woman sat behind the desk, staring at the paper rolled into the typewriter. Without looking up, she slid an ashtray across the desk toward Eileen, who dutifully dropped her ash in it.

Bar said, "This is Mabel Tanner, our new writer."

"Oh, hi. We met before," said Eileen. "Welcome aboard. Meet Ruth Linden."

Ruth had exotic looks: Southern Italian coloring and black eyes, with a beauty mark high on her right cheekbone. The soft waves around her face set it off like an expensive frame to a classic painting.

"How do you do?" she said, without much warmth. Her eyes appraised me, and I didn't feel real good about the look in them.

Eileen said to Bar, "I think we've fixed the opening. Somebody runs Adam off the road while he's on the way to see the client."

"How much time will it add?" Bar asked. "That second scene has a lot of exposition."

Ruth said, "Maybe our problem is that the second scene has a lot of exposition." They looked at each other. I had the distinct feeling that Bar had written the second scene.

Quickly, Eileen said, "The drive out could take care of some of that, a little narration over the engine whine. Why don't we bring you what we've got in an hour or so?"

"Do that," Bar said to her. He turned and continued down the hall. I followed. When we came to the last office, something white flew out the door, bounced off my skirt, and landed on the carpet. It was a thick triangle about three inches on its longest side, made from several sheets of paper, folded and tucked into themselves. There were others just like it scattered in the doorway and inside the metal wastebasket beside it.

"Sorry," said the man behind the desk. "I play with these footballs when I'm trying not to work." He grinned at Bar, then said to me, "You must be the new one." He stood up, but he didn't offer to shake hands. In fact, he put his hands in his pockets.

Josh Connally was no taller than I, but with a broad chest and shoulders that suggested he might have been an athlete at school. His tightly curling black hair receded so evenly that it looked like a sort of curly black headband. He wore brown flannels, a rust-colored Argyle pullover sweater-vest, and a white shirt with the sleeves rolled up. His forearms looked strong.

Bar said to him, "How's it coming?"

"Still trying to get Adam out of the trunk."

"We'll let you get back to work," Bar said.

As we stepped back into the hall, a triangle twanged into the wastebasket.

Bar escorted me into my new office, which someone had supplied with a battered dictionary, a stack of typing paper, a stapler, and a cup of freshly sharpened pencils.

"Finish that script you started last week. If you need anything, ask Mrs. Embert. There's coffee in the kitchen."

"Thanks." He went out, and I took off my hat and settled in.

I rolled paper into the typewriter and made a list of things I needed to fix up the place. Plants, books, some curtains. Then I got up to start my investigation. First off, I stuck my head out and looked down the hall at the alarm, which sat above the fire-escape door opposite Josh's office: a red metal dome six inches across. One of Peter's theories about the killer's escape was that he'd stuffed a rag up into the alarm, attached to a string, then after the door closed, pulled it out after him under the door, concealing his route. I couldn't examine it more closely, not with Josh in there, but the door's fit looked awfully tight to have allowed that.

So instead, I went off in search of places the killer might have hidden. In the kitchen across the hall, there was nothing in the cabinet below the sink except the elbow pipe, a dish rack and drain board, a box of dishwashing powder and one of ant powder. There was enough room for someone to hide, barely, but it would have been an insane choice, with Willa cleaning up after the party.

I went along next door to the mail room, where I found the usual things. A rack of mail slots with employees' names, typed on strips of paper and glued to the wood. A pine table for sorting the stuff that came in, and a hand-printed sign on the wall above it that said personal mail had to have correct postage attached. A postage scale on a metal cabinet, whose drawer held sealing tape and balls of twine, and whose doors concealed a couple of rolls of brown wrapping paper and plenty of space to hide if your joints were good. The night Hazel died, Nathan Mitchell had found this cabinet's door open.

Out in the hallway, Mrs. Embert said, "I'm sorry, Mr. Keane, but I thought you knew."

There was angry knocking on Bar's door and Henry didn't wait for an answer before going in. I didn't wait for an invitation to eavesdrop. I sneaked my head into the hall.

Mrs. Embert stood stiffly in Bar's doorway. I couldn't see Henry or Bar, but I could hear them. "You do not loan my family's property out without asking me first!" Henry shouted. "Get on the phone and tell them to bring that radio back now!"

"You never gave a damn about that thing before," Bar said.

"I do now. Get it back."

"That radio was Hazel's. So it belongs to me now," Bar pointed out. "I'll do what I want with it. If you'll excuse us, Mrs. Embert?"

"Of course." Before she closed the door, I heard Bar say, "It was Hazel's. Now it's mine. If I want to give the damn thing away, I can do it."

I nipped back across to my office, leaving the door open in case there was something else to overhear. There wasn't. So I spent the morning fleshing out my villain and creating a sidekick for him to add a little comic relief. The sooner I finished the script, the more free time I'd have to sleuth.

About twelve-thirty, Eileen appeared in the doorway. "You want to go to lunch?"

"Uh. Sure." Suddenly I couldn't remember a single one of the strategies Peter and I had discussed to get people to talk about the murder. I leaned over to get my handbag and hat out of the bottom drawer, and took a few breaths while I was down there.

Eileen said, "We need to go a little early, so we can get over there by two."

"Over where?"

"Bar didn't tell you anything, did he? Rehearsal. We do the show on Thursday nights, did he mention that? We're doing one of my scripts this week, so I need to be there. You should come along, see how things work. On Mondays, we pull out the script for the show, rewrite if we need to. Cast on Tuesday. Rehearse on Wednesday, then do the show on Thursday at nine and again at midnight for the West Coast. We transcribe the first one—record it—but we've always done both shows live. Come on. I need to go to the ladies' first. Did Bar introduce you to anyone besides Josh?"

"I met Mrs. Embert."

"Oh, God, we can't stop there."

A counter separated the typists room from the hallway. Mrs. Embert sat at her desk just on the other side, slicing letters with a long opener. Across from her was a smaller desk, empty. At desks near the windows, two girls, neither one of whom could have been much out of high school, were busily typing.

Eileen gestured at them. "These are our princesses." One of them giggled, a giggle cut short by Mrs. Embert's reprimanding scowl. Eileen went on. "This is Jeannie Devine and Martha Lubrano, called Marty, if you want her to answer."

Jeannie was a ripe peach of a girl, with a woman's figure, glowing rosy skin and soft dark-gold hair brushing her shoulders. She wore a pink sweater set that might have been borrowed from her mother, as it was a bit too big for her. Marty was thin and square-jawed, with rather heavy, straight brows above serious dark eyes. Her hair was cut in a short sports cut and tucked behind her ears. She wore no jewelry and beneath her russet jacket, a man's-style shirt.

Eileen said, "They type our scripts, decipher our handwriting and our intentions. They respond to bribes of chocolate."

Mrs. Embert said, "We have work to do, Miss Walters."

"And I wouldn't interrupt it for the world."

"Nice to meet you," I said to the girls. They smiled. Mrs. Embert sliced another letter.

Eileen gave me an eye roll as we stepped away from the counter and continued past Henry's closed door into the other hallway. "This is what we call the *Love* side. We're the *Drake* side. We do the *Love Always* show from here. It airs every day from ten until ten-fifteen, in case you're one of the sixteen women in America who doesn't listen. Henry produces. Bar directs. So they're both in and out all the time."

The first door past Henry's was closed as well. "That's Ruth's office. Don't disturb her if the door's shut."

"Why do you need me if you have three writers already?" Most half-hour programs had two at the most.

"Ruth doesn't write for us. She writes for *Love.* She was just giving me a hand this morning. She can write anything." Eileen stopped at the next office. "And this is accounting. Alton, this is our new girl, Mabel Tanner. Alton Peake, our bookkeeper. He makes out your check, so be nice to him too."

The man rose stiffly, then took my hand with ceremony and bowed over it. "A pleasure, my dear lady. I hope that you will find us pleasant working companions."

Alton was well past sixty and had a six-foot frame that had lost a couple of inches to the slight bend in his back. Behind his old-fashioned, silver-rimmed glasses, the eyelids folded onto his lashes. His hair had gone mostly to salt, although there was still a sprinkling of pepper in it. It was thin enough to show a rosy scalp and a long, narrow scar on the side of his head above his left ear.

"We're on our way to lunch," Eileen said. "Want us to get you anything? Maybe a bit of dessert?"

"Do not tempt me with your offers of cake, young woman."

"One day, I'll seduce you."

"She is sure to be a bad influence on you," he informed me.

"I hope so."

He wheezed a little chuckle.

"It was good to meet you, sir," I said.

"And you, kind lady."

When we reached the ladies' room, I said, "He's a character."

"He's our pet. The word is he was fired from the place he'd

worked his whole life when his wife was dying and he had to take care of her. He knew the Keanes somehow and they gave him a job."

The ladies' room had pale-pink paint and cream tiles. The pipes beneath the sink and the tiles around them were brand new. The work Nestor Cupp had done the day Hazel died.

Eileen disappeared into the only stall. I set my things on the shelf below the mirror and pinned on my hat. Above the stall, there was a small vent in the ceiling, not nearly big enough for anyone to get through. The killer certainly had not hidden nor come and gone through there.

Back at the hall closet, I told her which coat was mine and she pulled it out and tossed it to me. She had just reached in for her own when the doors to reception opened and Mrs. Embert came through, accompanied by a tall, dark-haired man in a brown overcoat, carrying his hat. He nodded perfunctorily to us and followed her into Henry's office. Eileen watched him all the way, her left arm still in the closet.

"Va va voom," she said when Henry's door closed. She snatched out her coat and scurried into reception.

"Who was *that?*" she asked Sophie.

"The private detective, dear."

"*Love's* got a private detective? Since when?"

"He's a real one."

"Oh, come on!" Eileen laughed. "No real detective looks like that."

"He *is*. Mrs. Embert made him show her his badge."

I said, "I think you mean license." Somebody was bound to ask, which was why Peter was forced to use his real name.

"Well, whatever he had. He's working for the insurance company that had Hazel's policies."

Suddenly, Eileen's face was stone serious. "Are you sure?"

"I do not dispense incorrect information."

"Sorry I questioned your grapevine, dear. What does he want to see Henry for?"

"Not that I would eavesdrop on calls, but if I did, I probably would have overheard the insurance lawyer tell Henry this morning that he was holding up the payment until their man asked some questions."

"What kind of questions?" Eileen asked.

Sophie shrugged.

"Well, the next time you're not eavesdropping, see what you can find out. We're going to lunch, then over to rehearsal. Can we get you something on the way back?"

"You could get yourself some manners. You didn't even offer to introduce me."

"Sorry," said Eileen.

"However, Mabel has manners and introduced herself this morning."

I said, "So you're the person who knows everything that goes on here."

"Have any secrets you want to tell me now?"

I laughed and hoped it sounded genuine.

Chapter 9

"Don't tell her a thing. Give her something to pass the time," Eileen said, then turned back to Sophie. "But work on the detective first, okay? Come on," she said to me, "I'm starving." She charged out to the elevators.

"What's going on?" I asked.

The elevator arrived. "Tell you in a minute," she said and waited till we reached the lobby, away from prying ears. "Our boss was murdered three weeks ago, right in her office. You didn't know?"

"I read something about it, out in LA, but I didn't realize it happened inside the building."

"This is our first live show since it happened. We've been using transcriptions of shows she wrote."

She told me the story as we walked up Madison, and I was glad she was doing all the talking. This was a part of New York I couldn't get used to—talking while negotiating through the thick crowds. How did these people concentrate on what they were saying? How did they look at the person beside them and not plow into someone else?

Eileen's version was simple, the police version. Cupp hid out in the offices after the party, killed Hazel, was seen by the doctor leaving Hazel's office, hid again, and then when everybody ran into her office, slipped out one of the exits.

"Probably out that door across from Josh's office," I said and slammed into somebody's briefcase. "It goes to the fire escape, doesn't it?"

"Oh, God, don't ever use it. It's got an alarm on it."

We went to a coffee shop on 48th Street, and since there was a wait for tables, hitched ourselves onto stools at the counter. I ordered the BLT. Eileen had a hot roast beef with mashed potatoes and gravy.

"Do you think the private detective will want to talk to everybody?" I asked.

"I hope he wants to talk to me," she said and wiggled her eyebrows. "I've never met a real private detective before."

"You didn't talk to one before you started writing the show?"

"Are you kidding? We don't want Adam Drake to be a real detective, crawling around under bedroom windows. What's Bar got you working on?"

"He wants me to finish that script I started the other day."

"I thought he would. He asked me to do it. I said, 'Are you crazy? You sent her packing?' Bar's a good director, but he's not a writer, even though he thinks he is. That script Ruth and I were working on this morning, Hazel had started it. Bar took a crack at finishing it. What a mess. Maybe we can fix it and use it next month. I'm not sure he's got the script judgment to take over for Hazel."

"What was she like?"

"She'd tell you what she thought and ambitious as hell, but she respected writers. We have more than most, but she wanted to make sure the scripts were first rate. We're not rushed to crank them out."

The waitress set the coffee cups down in front of us, sloshing the requisite amount into the saucers.

Eileen said, "I can just see Henry now, calculating how much he'd save if you turned out to be as good as the script. Bart Loomis may be an old sot, but Henry'd still have to pay him at least three hundred a week. They're probably not paying you more than, what, two?"

"One fifty."

"Christ!"

"I thought that was pretty good to start. I didn't have any idea what radio people are paid."

"Bar comes from old money, then married plenty. He's got no idea some people have to live on their salaries. Henry's new money. Keane Radio. He's just tight. He pays a typist thirty bucks a week and can't understand why she'd quit when the first nice boy with a good job comes along. By the way, Henry is Hazel's brother. There's another brother, George. He runs the sponsors' advertising agency."

"What's he like?"

"Nice. A nice man. Who'd believe it, comes from advertising? You should also know that Bar was married to Hazel. They were separated, but still husband and wife."

"He must have taken her death very hard."

She took a long sip of coffee rather than answer. "Are you married?" she asked then.

"Divorced, almost."

"I got mine three years ago, just before I came to work here. He was an actor. Word of warning. Stay away from them."

"I promise. About the offices. Since you moved closer to Bar's, is there some sort of hierarchy?"

"Don't worry. Josh turned yours down. He likes it where he is, tucked back there in the corner. Makes him feel like a bad boy."

"Is he?"

"Josh likes to pretend he's slumming. Makes a big show of not working too hard."

"What about Ruth? Does she want to write for *Drake*?"

"Wouldn't do any good. Henry's not about to let her go. She

has a contract, and *Love*'s a gold mine."

The sandwiches came and she stirred the gravy well into the potatoes and salted them before she tasted them. I took a bite of my sandwich, pausing before I launched into my next attempt at information-gathering.

"The actor who plays Drake—what's he like? Will he want a lot of changes?"

"Sky Donovan. A bit full of himself, plenty full of himself, actually, but okay."

"How about Maisie, the actress who plays her?"

"Karen Dunn. She can be a pill, but what a voice. You'd think she was a tall, slinky brunette, which is exactly what she's supposed to be, but she's really a stout little bleached blonde, still claiming she's thirty-five. You can bet she won't be in the movie. They're making a movie, did you know? Marathon made a deal with Hazel just before she died. They might give Sky an audition, just to be polite, but there's no chance, although I don't think he knows that yet. He's got Hollywood dreams. You know who'd be great? Frank Atwill. But I guess he won't be doing any murder mysteries for a while. So has Henry given you the treatment yet?"

"What?"

"My first day here, he gave me a friendly little pat on the ass. Secretaries kept quitting, and the secretary's the assistant on both shows, so you can imagine how tough it was to keep finding new ones. Finally, Hazel got fed up and hired Mrs. Embert. She won't put up with that nonsense. If he tries anything with you, come talk to Aunt Eileen."

CBS was at 485 Madison, near 51st, so we didn't have much of a walk to the studio from lunch. The door from the hall opened into a sort of air lock, with another well-sealed door on the other side leading to the studio, so that people could come in during a broadcast if they absolutely had to, without dragging in sounds from the hallway. Inside the air lock was a short flight of stairs to the control room, which was about six feet above the studio floor and looked down on it through a large plate-glass window. Bar and Mrs. Embert were already in the control room, sitting with another man at an L-shaped console containing a set of turntables, and the dials, meters and switches that helped broadcast illusion. There were copies of the script in front of them, full of notes in pencil.

Down in the studio, a soundman positioned a couple of freestanding doors on rolling pallets beside a two-turntable console near a short, standing mike. One door was stained dark and well polished; the other had weathered gray paint and a pebbled glass window. Behind the two-turntable console stood another freestanding unit, a sturdy frame with what appeared to be household screening inside it. Next to that was a set of drapes for a midget—curtains hung from rings on a rack about three feet high. Next to them, perpendicular to the console, was a long table with nothing on it yet, but beneath it were a half dozen black boxes, each two feet square, full of secrets.

Eileen took off her coat and tossed it on the frayed sofa at the far end of the control room while Bar introduced me to the other man. "This is Hal Lombardi, our engineer and production man. Mabel Tanner, our new writer."

Hal was a New Yorker—short, dark, with features that weren't the least bit shy. "Good to meet you," he said. He got up briefly and crushed my hand, then went back to work.

Bar ran down his cast list. "Holland Rogers for the ex-wife and the cook. Jim Lillard'll do the victim and the detective. Vic Wager, the partner and the cousin. Karen covers the daffy aunt and the maid."

Eileen said, "Karen's doing three roles?"

"She wanted to," Bar said. "Give her a stretch. Maisie doesn't have much to do this week."

"Who's playing the new wife?" Eileen asked.

"New girl," Bar said. "Bill Paley recommended her."

Another man, in a heavy herringbone overcoat, came into the control room. Everyone stood up.

"Hello, George," Hal said. "Nice surprise."

"Thank you. I thought I should be here today."

The rest of them, even Mrs. Embert, said hello with that sort of over-cheerfulness with which one greets the bereaved.

He shrugged out of his coat and draped it over his arm. "Is this our new writer?"

George Keane had hair like his brother's, wavy and auburn, just not nearly as much of it. A fringe ran a few inches above his ears, but above that, nothing. He also carried another twenty pounds. His green eyes had the same friendly lines around them that I had seen in his father's portrait. I introduced myself and offered my hand. Unlike his brother, he didn't keep it any longer than he was supposed to.

"Ever seen a show produced?" he asked.

"No," I said before I realized that it made me sound like the complete amateur I was. Everybody else in the room stared at me. "My writing was for the movies."

"Then you must be a natural, to have impressed Bar and Henry so. How's everyone treating you?"

"We're sucking her in," Josh Connally remarked casually from the doorway, "then we'll turn on her like piranha."

He peeled himself off the frame and strolled over to the sofa, his hands in the pockets of his overcoat, and flopped down on it. "I came over to see that new girl, the one we're looking at for Maisie."

"Josh," Bar said.

"Sorry, thought everybody knew. Henry told me."

Bar said, "Henry talks too much," and went back to his script.

George said, "Can we have a script for Mrs. Tanner?" Hal handed me one, then went down to the studio floor to arrange chairs around the table beneath the studio window. George took my coat and hung it up along with his own and his hat on the rack in the corner.

The script was about thirty pages long, stapled at the left corner. Each line of each character's speech was numbered in the left-hand margin, which would make it easier for the actors and crew to find their places for changes and pickups in rehearsals. The plot seemed to be about art forgery and a dead society art dealer, with a greedy partner, a jealous ex-wife, some avaricious relatives and a sexy young widow.

George said, "We're just waiting for the cast now. Let me introduce you to our soundman." As we went down into the studio, he said, "I'm sorry I mentioned your lack of experience in front of everyone."

"That's all right. They'd have figured it out pretty soon."

Behind us, the studio door swung open and three people came in, two men and a woman. The supporting actors, I assumed. The woman had a cloud of curly dark hair that would not be restrained. Hairpins stood out all over her head like croquet hoops. One of the men was older, with white hair and pouchy eyes. The other looked like a tall jockey, slightly built but tightly muscled. Immediately, they came over to George and greeted him warmly. He introduced us. "Holland Rogers, Jim Lillard and Vic Wager, regulars with us. This is Mabel Tanner."

The woman offered her hand. "Are you the new wife?"

"I'm sorry?"

"Are you playing the new wife?"

"I'm a new writer on the show, sort of learning the ropes."

"You looked familiar there for a moment. I thought you were an actress."

The door opened again and saved me. Adam Drake's secretary, Maisie Lane, walked in. I recognized Karen Dunn from Eileen's description. Under her coat, she wore a suit the color of a green pepper, with bold arabesques of piping on the lapels, which did nothing to disguise her shape. The jacket was cut for someone with a longer body, and maybe smaller hips, so that it folded at the waist. A black velvet hat shaped like a gravy boat sat in her platinum waves.

Right behind her appeared a tall, well-built, dark-haired young man, sporting a fedora, a long white scarf, and a walking stick. Sky Donovan was certainly attractive, by radio or any other standards, with a fine, straight nose, strong mouth and deep-set brown eyes. He had thick, immaculately groomed dark hair and a small, well-kept moustache. But there was maybe a touch too much flesh below the jaw for movie leading-man looks.

"He's carrying a cane," I observed.

"Our Adam," George whispered. "Not your average private eye. Let me introduce you."

Sky laid his things on the grand piano in the corner, then helped Karen off with her coat and draped it beside his.

"Sky, Karen, meet our new writer, Mabel Tanner. Sky Donovan and Karen Dunn."

"I've admired your work," I told them.

"Very good to meet you," said Sky, with an intense gaze that most women probably found exciting.

Karen said, "Thank you," then inspected my outfit.

From the center of the room, Hal announced, "We've got a few changes, when you get settled." Which meant, let's go, you're on the clock.

The actors followed Hal to the table, where Bar, Mrs. Embert and Eileen took seats as well.

Eileen asked, "Where's the new wife?"

Bar said, "She'll be a little late. She's doing a spot at NBC."

"Let's go meet Mash before they start," George said to me.

"Who?"

"Mash Burton."

Over in the sound area a few props had now been arranged on the tabletop: A highball glass with three dice in it, an envelope and a folded sheet of good vellum notepaper, wrinkled sheets of cellophane, and two wooden boxes with buzzers on top.

"Mash?" George called.

A man appeared from the other side of the polished freestanding door and straightened to his full five-two. He had a shock of dense wiry hair that appeared to have been combed with static electricity. He strode over, snatched my hand and gave it a crisp, jerking shake.

"How do you do, Mabel," he said.

"You hear pretty well through solid oak."

"I've got the best ears in the business," he said, no bragging, just fact.

I gestured to the table. "Do you lay out the effects in the order in which they're used?"

He turned to George. "She's pretty green."

"Pretty green."

"Well, Daisy Mae," said Mash, "we assemble our props in the most convenient locations given what we have to do with them and how often. Now, where do I start with such a bumpkin? Doors. You recognize doors?"

"I do, sir."

He gave the polished one a hearty slap. "Solid oak, as you said. You have to build a door that's a real door. On the other side, we've got baffling, to give it a good thunk when it closes, like a real door to a real room. And stage keys to lock it down to the floor, so you can slam it if you have to. Over here is the door to Adam's office, with a little rattling hardware, so it sounds like an office where you don't pay too much rent. Here we have our storm for this week, the thunder for our storm."

Set inside a four-by-two wooden frame was a sheet of copper screening. A wooden bar with an electrical socket at one end crossed the frame about a quarter of the way down. Hanging from the center of the bar, facing the screen was—

"A phonograph pickup," Mash said. "A 'needle' to the hoi polloi. It takes the sound directly to the control-room console through the wire from that plug."

"And you make thunder by hitting the screen with a tympani hammer," I said proudly.

"Stick. Tympani stick. You do not hit drums with hammers."

The door to the studio flew open and a young man came in, bare-headed, his cashmere coat open over a well-cut gray suit. He tossed his coat onto the piano and strolled over to us.

"You're late," Mash said.

"Sorry, old thing," the young man said and gave Mash a pat on the shoulder. "Got held up at lunch. Some old college friends, you know. Couldn't get away." He glanced at me, and Mash introduced me to Chaunce Hubley.

"Call me Chance," he said. "Everybody does. Come to visit our little playpen? What can we show you?"

Mash said, "I'll take care of Mabel. You finish the props."

"They're here."

"Where's the canvas?"

"In the box."

"That's a *roll* of canvas. Did you read the script? Adam slashes the forged painting. We need framed canvases, tight ones. And what are those crates doing here?"

"But we need them," Chance protested. He reached into one of the black boxes on the floor and pulled out a stack of fruit crates—thin wooden baskets each about a foot and a half long.

He set them at the end of the table. "There's a fight in the second act. I did read the script, old thing. What do you say, let's break a few chairs when Adam fights with the cousin."

"We are not breaking furniture. Go get the canvases and the doorbells. These aren't the right ones. We need the ones that chime, the mansion doorbells. Bring two. We'll need backup."

"Yes, sir," Chance said, and snapped a small salute. He picked up the doorbell boxes and went off, whistling.

George said to Mash, "I'll speak to his uncle again." He turned to me. "His uncle's, well, important at the network. We took him on to train, as a favor."

"He's got no soul for this work," Mash said.

"Is there a story behind your name?" I asked him.

He cheered back up immediately. "I can create any effect of the macabre, grotesque and gruesome with flair and finesse. A body landing on the pavement from the roof? I'm your man. You take a good just-ripe spaghetti squash, eight pounds, only from Italian markets. Need to cut off a head with a guillotine? I've got the watermelon and the cleaver. Want someone hit on the head? I can give you a light tap, a temporary stun, a knockout blow. I can give you the sound of a human skull being pulverized by a. . . ."

"Mash," I cautioned, shaking my head.

"What? What did—? Oh." He glanced at George, his face suddenly flaming. "Sorry. Sorry, George. Wasn't thinking."

"It's all right," George said, but his own face was pale.

The actors scraped back their chairs. The script meeting was over. While they took their places around the standing mikes in the center of the studio, Eileen joined us.

"Mash show you his secrets?"

He said, "She now reveres me above all others."

Briskly, Hal assigned the actors to their mikes. "We're going to start without our ingenue. We're running late, so—"

His mouth stopped moving, but it stayed open. The last member of the cast had arrived. She paused in the doorway and let everyone notice her. She could have been riding a roller coaster at midnight and they would have noticed.

She was a tall, willowy brunette with generous curves pushing the limits of a flame-colored jersey dress. Immediately, I began to think of very bad similes.

She had big brown eyes, as soft and dangerous as a forbidden bed.

She had a build like a racetrack, with the kind of curves only a pro could handle.

She had legs like a life of crime, they started out small and neat and ended up in big trouble.

Fortunately, Eileen interrupted. "Close you mouth, Hal. You look like a gargoyle."

CHAPTER 10

"Look who I found lost in the hallway," Henry Keane said as he came in behind her. "Let me introduce everyone. This is Lola Staton."

Bar said, "That will have to wait. There are no changes to your role, Miss Staton, so let's get started."

"Of course," she said. Hal handed her a script and showed her which mike to use, then went back up to the control room. George steered me over beneath its window, out of the way. Chance, the sound assistant, returned with several small framed canvases and two filigree-covered wooden doorbell boxes, which he set down on the table. I opened my script.

First the actors did a sound rehearsal, which concentrated on the effects and the actors' positions at the mikes. Apparently by standing at a certain angle from the mike's center, an actor could make it seem as if he were on the other side of a room from the actor standing only a foot away.

Mash and Chance worked through timing and choreography, Mash spending a good deal of time jerking his head at Chance, showing him where to go next. Chance was late on the first door cue, then whipped the curtains closed so awkwardly that they sounded more like flapping wings than draperies. Bar kept glancing that way, frowning. Nothing Chance did seemed integrated with the story, ruining the illusion that the characters were actually performing the actions.

The second read-through, which Mrs. Embert dutifully

tracked on her stopwatch, was for timing. Chance did not improve, and the actors' performances suffered, as they had to feel their way to the next sound cue. Bar's mouth got tighter and tighter.

"Okay, let's go. Once more, please," he said.

But Mash and Chance were standing in front of Adam Drake's door, arguing. "I knocked," Chance protested.

"Not like Maisie. Two raps, light, fast, then you open the door right away. She doesn't wait for an answer."

Chance knocked twice on the pebbled glass. "There."

"Light, fast. You're a girl."

"Oh, really, old thing. No one can tell the difference between a boy and a girl by a knock."

Bar snatched my script from my hand as he stormed past me, bearing down on them. Mash had the presence of mind to jump out of the way. My script sailed at Chance, who didn't get his hands up in time. It struck him on the forehead.

"Get out!" Bar shouted. "Now!" His own script followed mine, smacking Chance on his forearm as he raised it over his face. "Out! Now!" Bar grabbed both Mash and Chance's scripts, and they sailed one after the other across the room, chasing Chance as he scuttled around the far end of the effects table. Bar went after him, snatching up fruit crates and throwing them one after the other. They splintered on Chance's back, sounding as if someone were breaking chairs on him.

"And don't ever set foot in my studio again!" The final crate splintered on the studio door. Chance was gone.

Bar turned back to a roomful of silence. He collected the scripts from the floor and handed Mash's back to him. "Can you manage?"

"Yes."

He returned mine without comment.

"All right, ladies and gentlemen, we'll be starting at the top.

Karen, if you please."

Karen stepped to the mike, and they began, moving smoothly through the show, pausing only a few seconds where the commercial breaks would be. They finished promptly at the two-hour mark. There would be no overtime pay for the actors. The price of competence.

George said to Bar, "I'll drop in on Chance's uncle. I think he'll have to find his nephew a new line of work." Then he turned to me. "I hope you'll be able to come to our party on Saturday. We're celebrating our third anniversary."

"I'd love to."

"Just a small affair, under the circumstances, only people connected to the show. Here, let me give you my card." He pulled one from a gold case. With a small gold pencil, he scribbled the address on the back. "Cocktails at seven. Dinner starts about eight. It's buffet, so come anytime." He went off to mollify Chance's uncle.

I stayed for another hour, watching Bar working out the cues. And thinking about his volcanic temper. As long as Hazel was alive, he was dependent on her for his job and money, and his marriage was in trouble. But if she died. . . .

Finally, at five, I went back to the Emory Building. Eventually, I had to face the night watchman, the only person at Keane Productions who had ever seen me before.

The console radio Bar had loaned to Radio City had been replaced with a slightly more recent and far less expensive model, one that looked as if it had been a family's hard-used companion. I wondered if Bar had selected this one to needle Henry for shouting at him.

Al Alletter, the night watchman, whom I'd last seen the morning after Hazel died, was sitting in Sophie's chair. I pushed my glasses back up the bridge of my nose, went straight to him and introduced myself, offering my hand. I was grateful for my gloves, as my palms started sweating the second his nearsighted squint cleared and I knew he could see me. He stood up and practically clicked his heels when we shook.

"Welcome to the show. We'll take good care of you here."

"Thank you." I pitched my voice low, hoping the sound didn't trigger any memories.

"Sophie left a message for you, came this afternoon." He handed it to me.

"Thanks. I don't think I'll be long. I'm only going to pick up a few things." I walked, when I wanted to scurry, through the hall doors, examining the message. A Mr. Stone had called. There was a phone number. Stone was Peter's alias.

The offices were quiet. Everyone seemed to be gone. I didn't see Willa, but her maid's cart was parked on the *Drake* side near the men's room. I grabbed the script I was working on and left. I couldn't call Peter from my office. Alletter would have to connect me to an outside line and I couldn't count on his not listening in.

On the way out, I stopped long enough to examine the rod in the coat closet, the one that had fallen the night of the murder. At each end, the rod sat in a simple U-shaped holder, with a tab that flipped down across the top of the rod and was screwed in place. Over time, that screw could have come loose. But the combination of its having come loose and the bar, weighted down by winter coats, falling out of its holder on its own seemed unlikely. The police said Cupp had hidden there, but it would have been a ridiculous choice. Perhaps he realized that, and moved somewhere else, knocking the rod down. Or had it been pulled down by someone else, the real killer, as a diversion? But a diversion from what?

Peter had moved out of the hotel suite, leaving no sign of himself behind. I called the number on the message. A woman answered. "Mr. Stone's office."

"This is Mrs. Tanner. Is he in?"

"Not at the moment. I can give him a message."

"Tell him I'm at the hotel. He has the number."

I pulled the cover off my typewriter and pounded out notes on what I'd learned during the day, then stared into the tiny refrigerator longer than it should have taken for me to realize that there was nothing to eat in it.

The phone rang. It was Peter. "I'm over at the Roger Smith. I'll be bunking here. It's not that far away, over on Lexington. That number I left goes into Vanguard. You can tell whoever answers anything you need to. How'd the day go?"

"No one blew the whistle on me. What about you?"

"Henry Keane's not going to roll out the red carpet. He's going to make me wait to get a look at the office. He said things would be fairly quiet Friday. And he said he wouldn't have time to talk to me until next week. Our eyewitness, Doctor Clayton, has declined my invitation to meet."

"I'm shocked."

"What time do you have to be in tomorrow?"

"Looking for a late-night visitor?"

"Keep your mind on your work, gumshoe. We have a meeting with Hazel Keane's lawyer."

"His name's Edward Crandall Lewis," Peter said as our cab shot south on Park. "He was Miss Keane's lawyer and her father's, but not Henry or George's, so there's no conflict of interest. I had to tell him the truth, who I was, what I was up to. He wasn't going to tell me anything as long as he thought this was just about insurance. Turns out, he followed the LA case. He's looking forward to meeting you."

I said nothing about whether this Edward Crandall Lewis could be trusted to keep his mouth shut. Peter would never have exposed me if he thought it would endanger me.

I gave him my notes on my day.

"Anything I should look at now?" he asked.

"No."

He pulled out his notebook, folded the notes into it, then tore a page out of the front. "You have an apartment," he said as he handed it to me. "Here's the address. Good locks. You can move in over the weekend. It belongs to the office manager at Vanguard. She's willing to loan it to you for the rent and an extra hundred a month while she's gone to stay with her mother. Here's your copy of the keys."

"Why do I have to move?"

"Because Mabel Tanner is a woman trying to save money, and we won't have to worry about anybody seeing me go in and out. You won't give anyone the real address."

"Does that mean you'll come to visit?"

He slipped his hand over my knee and ran it lightly up my stockings on the inside of my thigh till he reached bare skin. I savored the distraction all the way downtown.

The Ocean King restaurant was on 8th Street, the "Main Street" of Greenwich Village, tucked between the Philosophers Bookstore and Grimbaldi Art Supply. Its two long rooms ran parallel. The first was mostly cigarette smoke, with bits of a mahogany bar and business suits visible through it. The second was low-ceilinged and dark, and made no attempt to remedy either problem: the brass fixtures hanging from the beams did little more than provide a sobriety test for tall men. Like most New York restaurants, the tables were set so close together that, with a winter coat added to your width, you had to turn sideways to get between them.

Edward Crandall Lewis, Esquire, was ensconced in the far corner, cross-examining a large Scotch. He pulled his ample rear out of his chair about six inches to greet me. "Sit down, get a drink," he said and waved for the waiter. Lewis had a round, overfed face with features set close together in the middle of it. He wore expensive evening clothes with a dress shirt that had so much starch in it that, when he leaned his forearms on the table, the placket popped out like the prow of a ship.

"So you're the lady who took on Hollywood," he said to me.

"I wouldn't say that."

"You left five bodies out there."

"Six. I didn't kill any of them."

"What about you?" he asked Peter.

"Only one. I'm a rotten shot."

He chuckled happily. "Well, it's good to meet you."

Peter and I decided on the lobster, which in spite of the decor, cost three dollars and explained why none of the customers looked like your typical Village artists. Lewis examined his menu carefully, then ordered the lobster as well, and chowder to start.

I told him how I met Hazel in Los Angeles, then he said, "I was fond of her, and her father was a good friend. If I can help make sure the right guy goes to the chair for this, I'll do it." He glanced at Peter conspiratorially, then said to me, "I hear you're on the inside."

"I'm sorry?"

"Mr. Winslow tells me you're at *Adam Drake*."

"You realize that you can't tell *anyone* about this."

He grinned. "I'm a lawyer. I know when to keep my mouth shut. As long as I get the details when it's over. Deal?"

"Deal. How long were you Hazel's lawyer?" I asked.

"About ten years, since she started making money herself. I represented her father for thirty. Morris was smart, and lucky. He pulled most of his money out of the market just before it crashed, then radio made him a fortune. He bought some stations and an advertising agency. Gave that to George, and helped Henry and Hazel get started producing."

"He didn't expect his sons to run the company?" Peter asked.

"Morris spoiled his children. He was lucky they turned out as well as they did. George took a law degree because the old man wanted him to, but he was more interested in advertising. Henry didn't finish college. It was pretty obvious neither one of them was going to run Keane Radio. Morris picked others to do it, and they do it well. Everybody's happy."

Peter said, "Do the sons squander money?"

"Maybe Henry now and then, on some chorus girl or other, and he's paying alimony to one of them, though the marriage didn't last six months. She held Henry up for it, the only way she'd agree to an annulment. The Keanes are Catholic, very devout. I hope you're not thinking the boys did this. They didn't get any money from her, but then you know that. You wouldn't be much of a detective if you hadn't already seen her will. They got rights to both shows, but why kill the creator?"

"The production company got a hundred thousand in one of her policies," Peter said.

Lewis shook his head. "Not enough. They're each worth twenty times that, easily."

The chowder arrived, a bowl big enough for a meal.

Lewis picked up his spoon and waved it at us. "No business during dinner. I like to have conversation while I eat and that usually requires a lot of conversation."

I told him as much as I could about the LA case. He lapped that up, too. The waiter arrived with the lobster, which was meaty, tender, and accompanied by drawn butter that was real butter, so it was a while before any of us spoke. Then Lewis said, "You need to get out, see the city while you're here. Let me take you over to Zack Eisler's tonight, the artist."

I said that I'd heard of him.

"He gets a crowd together every month. Artists and patrons. I was headed on over."

"Do you need evening clothes?" I asked.

"I do, if I want the girls to give me a second look. There'll be friends of Hazel's there you could talk to." He glanced at Peter. "Always a bunch of little actresses, too. Unless. . . ." He looked back and forth between us.

"I work for her, that's it," Peter said.

When the empty cheesecake plates were taken away and the coffee poured, Lewis sat back with his brandy. "So, what do you want to know?"

Peter said, "Where Hazel's money came from and more about where it's going."

Lewis pulled a small leather notebook from his jacket. "When Morris died back in March, his children each inherited two million in trust funds. As the elder son, George got another half million in cash and the house in the city. Henry got the place in Rhode Island, and Hazel the horse farm in Maryland."

I said, "Did that create animosity, George getting more?"

"Have you seen the house? It takes a lot of money to keep that up. I think there might have been, a bit, between George and Henry, but Morris was old-fashioned. The family home went to the elder son."

"What else was in Morris Keane's will?" Peter asked.

"A gift to his housekeeper, Mrs. Watson, of ten thousand. The same to his butler, Mr. Hawthorne. Smaller amounts to other servants. There were large gifts to charities and three Catholic orphanages—Saint Benedict's, Saint Gregory's, Saint Katherine's."

I asked, "Was Mr. Keane an orphan?"

"No. Morris once told me that he had seen too many abandoned children in the city when he was young. They used to wander the streets not that long ago, you know. And he drove an ambulance in Europe in the first war, for the American Field Service. The hospitals were full of orphans. He used to visit them, when he had the time. He and his wife were very fond of children, regretted that they didn't have grandchildren."

"We've heard that Mr. Keane was considering marriage before his stroke," Peter said.

"He was seeing someone, yes, a girl named Rachel, but I never met her. They were keeping it quiet. She was quite a bit younger. The children thought she might be a gold digger, but he was serious about her."

"There was no financial provision made for her?" Peter asked.

"None that I know of."

"Doesn't that seem odd?" I said.

"Maybe the kids took care of it privately. I don't know."

Peter said, "We understand that the children thought Morris might have made a will subsequent to the one you presented."

"Who told you that? That's ridiculous. I was Morris' lawyer until the day he died. I held his final will, the one he made after his wife, Ethel, died back in thirty-six. I don't know why the kids would think there was another."

"Maybe he said something after his stroke," Peter suggested, "or maybe they found something among his papers, something about a new will in this woman's favor."

"If he was going to make a new will, he'd have come to me. And he didn't. You think this woman, this Rachel, might have thought Hazel cheated her?"

"We're looking at that. If you remember anything at all that might help me find her, I'd appreciate it."

"Sure."

"Let's move on to Miss Keane's will."

Lewis flipped further into his notebook. "Her current will was made in March, after her father died, and it replaced the will she made when she married Bar Benjamin. Back then, she and Henry had just started *Love Always,* and Benjamin was the director, younger than she was, but a real up-and-comer. In that earlier will, she left everything to him, except rights to the show and a few gifts to servants and endowments to Vassar and Saint Kay's. That's what she called Saint Katherine's. Her parents raised her to be a good society wife, do good works. She took an interest in Saint Kay's when she was still in high school."

"Do you know why she and Benjamin split up?" Peter asked.

"I was her lawyer, not a friend."

Peter waited. Then Lewis said, "One evening, back just before Christmas, she came over for dinner, a little too much wine. She started crying, and my sister took her upstairs for a heart-to-heart. Maude doesn't gossip, but she said enough about how selfish Benjamin was that I figured it out. Hazel wanted children and Benjamin said he wasn't ready to be a father. But Hazel wasn't getting any younger."

"Go on."

"That's all I know about it, except that Hazel was seeking an annulment."

"She was?" I said.

"No divorce. She was devout, as I said. But the rich can usually get annulments." Lewis glanced at his notebook. "She came to me in late March, a couple of weeks after her father died. She was going to be worth a lot more money then, from him. She told me that she and Benjamin weren't going to reconcile. That's when she told me about trying to get the annulment. Still, she left him plenty. The gifts to friends and servants would be the same. The money she took from Benjamin she used to increase her bequest to Saint Kay's—she left them the farm in Maryland as well as more money—and to leave Doctor Lawrence Clayton a hundred thousand. She also gave fifty thousand to endow a theater company, the Off–West Broadway Players. Said she'd seen their work, and wanted to give them a leg up."

"Who runs that, do you know?" Peter asked.

"Karen Dunn, plays Maisie on *Adam Drake*. Hazel took me to see a show down there. Too many angry women for my taste, but then you've met Ruth."

"Ruth Linden?" I said.

"Their playwright." He closed the notebook. "That's all there is. Except that a week before she died, Hazel called and said she wanted to make a new will. She made an appointment, but she never got to keep it."

"Did you tell the cops that?" Peter asked.

"No. They got their man, or so I thought. Anyway, what could they do with it? She didn't tell me what she was going to change, and it didn't sound urgent."

"Anyone else profit from her death?" Peter asked. "Any money set to go to her that will now go to others?"

"If there was, I never heard about it. You know," he said and tossed back the last of his brandy, "it probably doesn't mean anything, but as long as we're talking about wills. . . ."

Chapter 11

"Last spring, I ran into Hazel at a cocktail party. As soon as she saw me, she said she wanted to talk about an idea for the show, took me outside on the terrace so we were alone. Hazel was always worried about people finding out what she was planning. A little eccentric, but she was an artist.

"She asked me what would happen if a man found out that his wife was already married. Would he have any rights to her property if she died? I said I'd have to know more particulars to give her a true legal opinion, but if the property was in both their names, then he probably did have some rights. For anything else, probably not. If she died—and the bigamy were discovered, of course—the man would inherit nothing that wasn't in his name, even if she left a will. She'd be declared intestate, and everything she had would probably go to her real husband. If that man had died—presuming that he died after she married this other man—then the money would go to the children of that first marriage, and if there were no children, then to other relatives of the dead woman. A real mess."

Peter said, "You weren't sure it was for the show?"

"I was, at the time. She seemed pretty upset, but I thought it ruined an idea she had."

"When was this, do you remember?" Peter asked.

"I'd have to check my diary if you need the exact date, but I think it had to be late April. You think she was already married?"

"She was engaged to Lawrence Clayton once. If they married secretly, and she realized she'd made a bad choice, her father could have arranged a quiet annulment. Or thought he had, and she discovered years later that it wasn't valid."

According to Adora Watson, the housekeeper, the Keane children had searched Morris Keane's papers in April. Had they discovered that their sister might be a bigamist?

I said, "If Bar found out, he might want Hazel out of the way while everyone else still thought they had a legitimate marriage."

Lewis shrugged. "Or maybe she was asking for the show."

He was right. We had nothing but speculation.

Peter paid the bill and we headed over to Zack Eisler's. Peter decided that I could tag along and he'd see whether there was any sense in my staying, whether the risk of my being recognized was greater than the chance that I could learn something circulating on my own among Hazel's friends.

The party was four flights up in a five-story building that had just enough crumbling stonework to make it appropriate for an artist's lair. We could hear the party the moment we opened the building's front door. By the third flight, people carpeted the narrow staircase. Women in satin and velvet talking to women in ankle socks and ancient sweaters. Men in corduroy jackets and horn rims talking to men with tuxedos and cigarette holders.

On the fourth floor, we squeezed between the bodies draped in the doorway and into a room hung with paintings on its Chinese red walls. Through the crowd stuffed inside, I had glimpses of a few pieces of furniture: a sofa covered in puckered velvet with tattered gold fringe, a couple of chairs that looked like fallen soufflés, and, at the far end of the room, a sturdy oilcloth-covered pedestal table with a tub of ice on it, studded with beer bottles. Beside it, French doors opened into a kitchen. Another tub of beer sat on the floor; people covered the table.

Lewis took me by the elbow. "I can introduce you around."

"I wouldn't want to cramp your style with the actresses." He chuckled. I said, "Stay with Peter. I'll make my own way."

The men went off, and I made a slow circuit of the room, unbuttoning my coat, making a quick check for anyone who looked familiar. No one paid much attention to me.

All the paintings were modern, some intriguing and some, surprisingly, merely ordinary or plainly derivative. On the wall by the front door, so that I didn't see it until I had completed my tour, a five-foot canvas drew me immediately.

Executed in bold strokes of gold, amber, bronze, and their attendant shades, it was the modern world—mechanical, jangling, exhausting, exhilarating, bursting with life and possibility. Then as I approached, I noticed, pushing through the layers of paint in a half dozen places, a pentimento of a meticulously re-created Renaissance religious painting—a woman, drawn with the delicate detail of DaVinci, in the rapturous adoration of something unseen, something the modern strokes kept hidden. Or were obliterating. You wanted to peer around the edge of the paint to see the rest of her. You wanted to see what she saw.

What saved it from being an obvious comment on the trampling of traditional art or religious faith, and modern art's or modern life's right to do so, was the brilliance of its execution: You weren't sure how the artist felt. You weren't sure how you felt.

"So, what do you think?" said a man's voice beside me.

I turned. He was about my height and age, with a rogue's mouth and thick, unkempt dark curls.

I said, "Provocative, aggressive, disturbing."

"I painted it."

"I know. I saw the signature. I recognize you. Mabel Tanner." Zack Eisler's black slacks were cut tight across all the places that pants were meant to conceal. His gray shirt, open to his belt, showed off a chest that was probably pretty exciting for a painter, but I'm a tough critic, given what I was used to seeing. He had a long red kerchief tied around his neck.

"What do you think of the rest?" he asked.

"Some of it's brilliant. Some of it's. . . ."

"Crap."

". . . not up to the others' standard."

"I don't do the work for dilettantes. You come here, I'm not going to hand you an artist to support so you can impress your friends. You want to be a patron, you better know what you're doing. If you don't, you embarrass yourself. Who you come with?"

"Some friends. I'm new in town."

He pulled me to him and kissed me hard on the mouth. "Welcome to New York," he said. "Carol," he called out over his shoulder. "We need a beer over here."

A blonde in an expensive silk shirt and velvet pants slipped through the crowd and put a bottle in my hand. I peeled myself off Zack, and she replaced me. She had perfect teeth and a finishing school smile that said, Go to hell.

"So talk to me," Zack said. "How'd you get here?"

"I know Ed Lewis slightly. I met him through Hazel Keane."

"You knew Hazel?"

"A little."

"She collected Zack's paintings," Carol said. "She owned three."

"Two," Zack corrected.

"Three. If you can't sell it for more, her estate owns it."

"I'm not going to make her estate pay for it."

"Well, you'll damn well keep the deposit."

He took her hand off his shoulder. "Why don't you go mingle? Make sure everybody's having a good time."

She gave him a narrow-nosed glare and pranced off.

"Would this be the painting?" I asked.

"Yes."

"I can see why. Why she wanted it. Would you consider selling it to me?"

"It's two thousand," he said.

"Very well."

"No haggling?"

"I don't haggle over anyone's art but my own."

"Do you paint?"

"No. Look, I'd rather not talk about me."

"Why don't I take you up to the studio, show you what I have, in case you have friends who don't like to haggle either."

"I think I'm safer down here. Who's your agent? I'll call him in the morning." He gave me the name and phone number.

"At least take your coat off." He slipped me out of my coat and hung it on a rack in the corner that was already teetering under its load.

Carol came back, her arm through Peter's. "Darling," she said, and it wasn't clear if she meant Peter or Zack, "let me introduce you. Zack, Pete. Pete's new in town."

Zack said, "Mabel's buying the painting."

"Quick work," she said, "and without going to the studio."

Zack took her by the arm, tight enough that she let out a little yelp. "I think you need to sit down alone for a while and sober up. I'll see you later, Mabel. Sorry, Pete." He took her off toward the kitchen.

Lewis meandered over, taking a good, long swallow of a beer. He jerked his head toward the French doors, where Zack and Carol had disappeared. "I don't think that one knew anything anyway. I can find you some ladies, know something." The longer he stayed in our company, the more he sounded like a movie tough guy. "What's our next move?"

Peter said, "Lauren should go home. She's not going to find

anything here. You and I'll talk to Miss Keane's friends, find out if she was worried about anything, get the gossip on Clayton."

"That's one of the reasons I suggested this place."

Suddenly, Peter was very still. "Does he come here?"

"He usually shows up at these things. I thought you could—"

Peter turned to me. "Go, now."

Immediately, I moved, and, immediately, Peter yanked me to him and turned his back on the front door, shielding me. "That's him. In the door. Isn't that Clayton?" he demanded of Lewis.

Lewis said, "Yes. What's the problem?"

"He can't see us together."

"Why? Oh, Christ, he's seen me."

"Get him out of the doorway," Peter commanded. "Get his attention on you."

Obediently, Lewis raised a hand in greeting and moved quickly to the center of the room. I peeled away from Peter, dropped my head, grabbed my coat and headed for the door, keeping close to the wall, keeping people between me and Clayton. With my head down, I had no idea what he looked like. I hoped he saw as much as I did.

When I reached the front door, a group of society partygoers came in, full of the bonhomie created by a few rounds of martinis and having to be friendly to people you don't particularly like. I stepped back and let them pass. As they did, I turned and peeked over their shoulders at Lawrence Clayton, who was now standing with Lewis, his face in profile. He had the kind of looks that doctors have only in a girl's dreams, accompanied by blond hair meticulously trimmed and oiled, a perfect blond moustache, and the remains of a good North Shore tan.

Peter came over to them, and Lewis made the introductions. Before Clayton registered the name, he offered a long, elegant hand to Peter, who took it. Then there was an awkward frozen moment, and he took the hand away. Lewis kept talking, his face amiable. Clayton's tightened, but his gestures were still smooth, as he introduced the group he had come with—a middle-aged couple and a carefully arranged brunette, maybe twenty-five. Two weeks after Hazel's death, he was squiring another woman around in public.

I overslept. Useless speculation had bumped around in my head until almost two A.M.: about Hazel's last, unkept appointment with Lewis, about whether her bigamy questions had anything to do with her wanting to change her will, and about what Peter was doing in a roomful of women, pretending to be a man on his own, looking for companionship.

By the time I reached the office, it was ten-thirty.

Sophie said, "Don't worry, sweetie. Everybody comes in late on Thursday and Friday."

I hung up my coat, and rather than trying to sneak past Bar's open door, I walked right up to it. He stood beside one of his file cabinets, reading through some pages in a Manila folder. I tapped lightly on the door frame.

"Hi. I made some progress yesterday. I should have the first draft soon."

"Good," he said, distractedly. He shut the folder and added it to a stack on his desk.

"Doing a little housecleaning?"

"Just moving one of these cabinets down to storage."

Mrs. Embert appeared beside me. She had exchanged yesterday's severe black suit for a stern navy blue. She did not say good morning. "The man's here to move the cabinet."

Bar said, "I've pulled out what I need."

"Excuse us, Mrs. Tanner."

"Sorry, am I in your way?"

In my office, I took the folded script pages out of my handbag, the pages on which I had done absolutely no work last night.

Nobody came to visit me, which was a danger in places where people actually worked, so I started writing. Just before one o'clock, when nobody had asked me to hear his confession, I decided to take another look at possible hiding places.

Mrs. Embert sat at her desk, arranging letters that needed either Henry or Bar's signatures. Jeannie and Marty were typing away, neither looking up from the pages beside their typewriters.

"May I help you?" Mrs. Embert asked briskly.

"I was wondering about the routine for getting supplies. Do we ask you, or do we get things ourselves?"

"There's a supply room, around the corner, first door," she said, pointing toward the *Love* hallway.

"Is it left unlocked at night, in case I work late?"

"Yes."

"Thanks," I said and moved off. I figured two questions were about the limit with her.

The supply room smelled of mimeo ink: a machine sat on a metal cabinet against the far wall. Shelves lined the room, full of the sorts of things an office needed: envelopes, stationery, carbons, mimeos, pencils, gum erasers, bottles of ink, typewriter ribbons, staples, and steno pads. On the floor were two large cardboard boxes. One contained typewriter paper, packaged in reams; the other, rolls of toilet paper. The shelves were about eighteen inches deep, with just enough room beneath the bottom one for someone to slide in and pull the boxes in front to conceal himself. There was also enough room to crouch behind the mimeo cabinet, although not enough to crawl inside, unless the killer was a dwarf. There was no vent in the ceiling with access to the pipes, and therefore to the *Drake* side. If the killer hid here after the party or the meeting, he had gone to Hazel's office down the hallway and would have had to wait until Willa was inside one of the *Love* offices.

"Looking for something?" Henry Keane said behind me.

"Just some staples."

"Let me get them." He slid past me, closer than he had to, even given the size of the room, and lifted a box off the shelf. He smiled and presented it to me. I smiled back as if he had done something.

"Thank you." I slipped out into the hall. Mrs. Embert looked up at me, and I showed her the staples. "I found what I was looking for." She didn't comment, but her eyes slid past me to where Henry must have been standing, probably leering at my rear end.

He said to her, "Bar and I are going to lunch with some men from Pearl Soap. Be back about two-thirty or three."

I deposited my staples in a drawer, then grabbed my coat and took myself along to a nearby coffee shop to buy a sandwich. The waitress tucked the edges of the waxed paper carefully so I could slip it into my handbag. While I was out, I called Zack Eisler's agent from a phone booth to arrange to buy the painting. I didn't want to call from the office, knowing that Sophie had a habit of listening in. I couldn't give him a check with Lauren Atwill on it, so I'd have to send a check to my friend Helen in LA, then she could wire the money in my phony name. The agent asked for a phone number so he could arrange delivery once he had received the check. I gave him the one at the new apartment, but I told him I'd pick up the painting.

Back in the office kitchen, I decided to make a fresh pot of coffee. As I pulled down the canister, Alton Peake, the accountant, passed, presumably on his way back from the men's. "Let me do that," he offered. "I know the peculiarities of this machine."

"Don't trouble yourself."

"You are no inconvenience, young lady." He poured the old coffee down the drain, emptied the basket of grounds into the trash, then rinsed the basket and the percolator thoroughly.

I said, "I understand you haven't been here long, either."

"Two years, come January. I worked for quite a long time for an insurance company in Hartford." He filled the percolator with the required amount of water, then placed the rod into it. Carefully, he spooned coffee into the basket before fitting it onto the rod. He replaced the basket cover and lid and pushed the plug into the wall socket at the end of the counter.

"Someone told me you knew Morris Keane," I said.

"We were friends for fifty years. We met in the army. You wouldn't think to look at me now, but we were young and reckless once, in Cuba, which was a perfect country for the young and reckless man."

"I can imagine. What were you doing there?"

"Fighting the Spanish." He tapped the thin scar on the left side of his head. "I ran into a bullet there."

"You don't hear people talk about the Spanish War much these days."

"Too many others, too terrible. Morris and I served together with Colonel Roosevelt. Morris liked to say that we made Roosevelt president. Then we came back here and finished our educations. I went to school to learn accounting. My parents didn't want me to work with my hands. Of course, Morris made his fortune that way."

"He was an engineer, wasn't he?"

"One of the best. He left Edison and set out on his own, that would have been about twenty-seven. It takes a brave man to do that, with a wife and three children."

"And a brave wife."

"That it does. The ladies never get enough credit."

"Mr. Peake," Mrs. Embert said from the doorway. I had no idea how long she had been there. "Did Mr. Keane take those figures with him to lunch?"

"I put them in his hand so he wouldn't forget."

She glanced at me. I grinned at her, and she went away, but I thought my examination of the storage room on the *Love* side would have to wait. I didn't want people to start talking about how that Mrs. Tanner was never in her office, but always wandering around, asking people questions, poking her nose in.

When the coffee finished, I poured a cup and ate lunch at my desk. By four, having finished a very rough draft, I gathered my pages to take along to the typists and nearly slammed into Bar in my doorway.

"If you have a few minutes," he said abruptly. "In the conference room."

CHAPTER 12

"Of course. Is anything wrong?"

He didn't reply. He continued down to Josh's office and repeated the offer.

George and Henry stood at the far end of the conference table. The rest of the staff had already gathered; Alton insisted that I take his chair. Bar came in and took a seat at the near end of the table.

Henry said, "Thank you for coming. This won't take long. George has a few words." He sat down.

"As an officer of our company," George said, "and, further, as an attorney, I wanted to speak to you today. Mrs. Tanner, you won't understand all of this, but sooner or later, it will involve you as well.

"As you might have already heard, my sister's insurance company has begun an inquiry. I know that you must be concerned that this could cast doubt on the police case and cause embarrassing publicity for all of us. But I want to assure you that this sort of thing is a standard practice in a case such as this, and I have been assured by the company that they will not inform the press. You may receive a phone call from a man named Winslow. You're under no legal obligation to speak to him; nevertheless, I encourage you to answer any reasonable questions. None of us has anything to hide. However, you don't need to invite him into your home. We'll put this room at everyone's disposal. And if he makes himself in any way unpleasant, makes any implications whatsoever, let me know immediately, and I'll take care of it. And if you should be contacted by reporters, let me know at once. Does anyone have any questions?"

We glanced at each other. No one said anything.

"If you have any concerns at all, don't hesitate to call me. And please remember the party on Saturday. Thank you."

"Thank you, everyone," Henry said and stood up. George left, and the staff started to drift out.

Bar said, "If the *Drake* people could stay. I'd like to go over the script assignments. I won't keep you, Henry."

They looked at each other, then Henry sat right back down. The *Drake* writers took seats as well, and everyone else disappeared. Mrs. Embert closed the door as she went out.

Whatever Eileen might think about his script judgment, Bar was certainly organized. Quickly, he went over the script assignments from the last meeting and checked on the progress the writers had made. Then he began tossing out ideas for enough shows to carry *Adam Drake* through the New Year and asked us to think them over, decide which ones we wanted. Next week, we'd meet again and finalize the assignments. He wanted everything set before Thanksgiving.

As I didn't have anything beyond my current assignment, he suggested I think about a script in which Adam is hired as a bodyguard, and his client, who refuses to take his advice, is bumped off. That was the general outline. I was welcome to take it wherever I liked, consulting Bar along the way, of course. In exactly a half hour, he dismissed us.

It was now too late to give my script to the typists. They would be leaving soon. So I trailed Eileen back to her office. "What time should I be at the studio tonight?"

"Eight-thirty or so." She picked up her handbag. "You know, I feel like a swine for thinking that detective was cute, knowing what this could do to us, if it gets out. Can you imagine what that would be like?"

"No. No, I can't." I'd been on the receiving end of some very public, very unpleasant speculation. But no one had ever speculated that I was a killer.

Back in my office, I wrestled with my conscience for a while about what I could be doing to innocent people, then decided to go do something useful: get information.

I stuffed a few dollars into my jacket pocket, grabbed my coat and went into reception.

"I was just going out for some dinner," I said to Alletter. "I shouldn't be long. Will the door be locked?"

"We don't lock up till seven."

"Could I get you anything?"

"No, thank you, miss. I'm set."

Longing for Juanita's cooking, I bought myself another sandwich, and picked up two slices of cheesecake as well.

"Is it all right if I eat out here?" I asked Alletter, when I returned. "I need a break from my office walls."

"We're not allowed to eat out here. You'll have to use the kitchen, miss."

"All right." I took one of the slices of cake from the paper bag and showed it to him, shining against the waxed paper. "I brought an extra, just in case you changed your mind. Shall I put it in the refrigerator?"

"You know, I might just have room for that, thank you. I can lock the door early tonight. Everyone's gone except you."

In the kitchen, I found forks, plates and paper napkins and served our food at the small, round table.

I said, "Is this what you do every night, eat in here?" I took off the top slice of bread and salted my sandwich. I thought that made the question look casual.

"Just like this, but later. Nine to nine-thirty."

"Every night?"

"Every night."

"You have your routine, then?"

"I do."

I cocked my head to one side and smiled with interest and he went on. "I make my rounds, four times a night. Seven o'clock, when I lock up, then before I have my dinner and after, and again before I go, check those side doors, the ones that go out to the elevators. They lock on the outside, but I make sure they're closed all the way. Sometimes the writers work late and go out that way."

Nevertheless, from nine to nine-thirty the night Hazel died, anyone—anyone with a key—could have got in the front door.

I took a couple of bites and let a little time pass before I asked, "Do you ever get bored here by yourself?"

"I bring plenty to read, and I've got the radio."

"That radio works?"

"I have one of my own, a little compact, no bigger than a lunch pail. I don't know if that one out there works or not. The one they loaned out to Radio City, we weren't allowed to touch that one. That was worth a lot of money."

"Do you get nervous here now, I mean, after what happened?"

"He didn't get in past me."

"Oh, I didn't mean that. I heard he was already hiding here. He sneaked in during a party."

"He hid out in that coat closet after that party was over, that's what I told the police. That's why the rod was broken. He knocked it down when he sneaked out, then he must have hid in Miss Keane's closet, and waited till he thought everybody was gone, and killed her. I never liked that Cupp. He'd come in here, sour to everybody. This never would have happened if he'd been fired when he should have been."

"Fired?"

"A couple of weeks before it happened, Miss Keane caught him drinking in the ladies'. I had just come in and heard him yelling. I came out into the hall and there he was, following her to her office, yelling at her to mind her own business. I was the one who calmed him down and got him out. Mr. Keane and Mr. Benjamin were gone, and you can't expect Mr. Peake to help, not at his age. But there was Mr. Connally and Mr. Donovan, watching the whole time, and neither one of them lifting a finger to help her."

"Sky Donovan was there?"

"In her office, right in the doorway. Man his size, and didn't lift a finger."

Sky Donovan knew about Hazel's trouble with Cupp, I thought. "I wonder why he wasn't fired. Mr. Cupp, I mean."

Alletter shrugged. "He works for the building, not for us."

"But still, you'd think they would at least have moved him somewhere else."

"I wouldn't have let him back, if anybody asked me. Not to blame her, but most of those hillbillies. . . ." He tapped the side of his head with his fork hand, scattering a few crumbs of crust on his shoulder. "Not right up here."

I nodded seriously then said, "I heard George Keane left the writers meeting early. I wonder why he didn't notice the rod had fallen when he got his coat."

"I can tell you write mysteries, miss, but, you see, he uses the closet in his brother's office."

"Ah. George told us there's an insurance detective who's going to be asking some questions. He should talk to you first, it seems to me. You had to unlock the front door to let everybody out, so you can vouch that they all left."

"I wish I could, but I wouldn't lie. I saw George Keane leave, of course. That was earlier, before I'd locked up, but I was fixing that rod when the rest of them left. Mr. Benjamin said he'd unlock the door. He has a key. I saw him go into reception and the others went off with their coats and things. I finished fixing that rod and then I went and locked the front door *before* I went around to put the screwdriver away so I can tell you nobody sneaked in that way."

"That was very smart of you."

"I know my job, miss. Now, a couple of them didn't leave right away, I can tell you that. When I went to check the side doors later, before my dinner, the lights were on in both Miss Walters and Mr. Connally's offices. Willa always turns them off when she finishes a room. And I found a cigarette still burning in Miss Walters' ashtray. I put that out. And a few of those paper footballs around Mr. Connally's trash can. I put them back in his drawer, like Willa always does."

"I see you're a bit of a detective, too," I said. He nodded in satisfaction. I said, "George said the inquiry was just routine. I guess it really couldn't be anything else, since I heard there was a witness."

Alletter grunted. "The doctor. He was knocking on the front door when I came back from my dinner, asked me why wasn't I at my desk, and I told him a man is allowed to take his dinner and that Miss Keane hadn't said anything to me about him coming."

"She didn't?"

"When she came to tell me about that broken rod, Miss Keane said she was going to go do some work and if she wasn't through by ten to call her. She never said a word about him. I told him she was busy and he'd have to wait. Then he asked me for some water. I think he expected me to go get it."

The vacuum started up at the end of the hall. Alletter pressed his fork into the remaining crumbs, scraped them up and finished them off. "Well, thanks for the cake, miss. Back to work."

"You're welcome. I'll take care of the plates."

He returned to his desk. I put his plate and fork in the sink, and threw away the paper napkins, then took the remains of my sandwich and cake to my office, sat down at my desk and made notes. Now, we knew exactly when Clayton had spotted the killer, if he wasn't lying. Alletter couldn't swear to anyone's having left after the meeting except George and Bar. We knew Henry left, because he showed up at George's. Eileen and Josh had definitely stayed after, and there was no evidence that either actually left.

George and Henry had alibis, but Bar could easily have hidden in the service stairs and come back through the front door with his key while Alletter was putting away that screwdriver or was at dinner. Anyone else could have ducked into a hiding place while Alletter was fixing that rod.

Now that I thought about it, did Henry have an alibi? It would have taken timing and luck for him to leave George's just after nine, take a taxi, change into the coveralls, climb the fire escape to the fifth floor (which was as far as it went), slip up the service stairs, into the offices through the front door, and kill Hazel all before Alletter's dinner break was over, but maybe it could be done, depending on where George's house was.

And yet, if Henry was guilty, why would he sabotage the closet rod? Certainly that had been done to create confusion, allowing the killer to hide.

It wouldn't have been difficult to loosen the screw during the good-bye party, then pull the rod down after the party ended. Everybody who was going home had already retrieved their coats. Repairing it would draw Alletter out of reception, so he wouldn't notice if someone didn't leave.

I still had time to investigate the men's room as a hiding

place before I went to the broadcast, so I tucked my notes away in my handbag, and peered out into the hall. Willa was busy in Bar's office, her back to me. I scooted across into the men's. It was immaculate and smelled only of pine cleaner. There were two sinks, two urinals, and, in the corner, one stall with a painted pine door. Above the stall, a three-by-two-foot panel provided access to the pipes and, possibly, a hiding place or escape route. I went into the stall and dropped the seat, then climbed onto it. There didn't seem to be any sort of locking mechanism on the panel. I put both palms on it and pushed. Nothing happened. I pushed a little harder. Still nothing.

Then I saw, at the far end, a ring no bigger than a nickel, flush against the panel, painted the same color. Detective that I was, I decided it might mean something, so I pulled the ring down and turned it. I felt something move, a fastening tongue moving aside perhaps. I pushed hard again. The panel popped straight up and rewarded me with a brisk shower of tiny, gray, oily dust balls.

Then the bathroom doorknob rattled.

I jerked down, squatting on the toilet seat, reaching for the stall door at the same time. I pulled it toward me an eternal six inches. Whoever came in didn't seem to notice. There were footsteps, a grunt, and a zipper went down, then the sounds of urinating. Then someone else came in. They didn't acknowledge each other right away. Urinating etiquette, I assumed. Then a flush, another flush, and the water in one of the sinks came on.

"You're here late," Henry commented.

"Yeah," Josh said. He was the one at the sink. "Want to get the script in shape before the weekend."

"I had to grab a few things, then George and I are meeting some people for dinner before the broadcast. So what do you think of her, your new writer?"

"She's green." Josh turned off the tap and snapped a clean length of towel down from the roll in the dispenser. "And she's had one idea, based on someone else's. We'll see."

"Nice legs, though. Tits aren't much."

There was a knock on the door.

"Gentlemen," Willa called softly from the hall. "Gentlemen, don't use the toilet please. It's leaking. I was about to put up a sign."

"Okay," Josh called back, and the men left. Henry wasn't overly conscious of hygiene: he went out without washing his hands.

"Thank you, gentlemen," Willa said. She came in and closed the door. After a moment, she said, "You can come out now."

I scrambled down from the toilet and opened the door. "How on earth did you know I was in here?" I shook off some of the dust. There was plenty on the floor of the stall, even without my help.

"I was looking for you, to tell you they came back, in case you were up to something. You weren't anywhere else." She taped a hastily written sign that said OUT OF ORDER on the stall door.

"Next time I want to go to the men's room, I'll tell you."

She was not amused. "Go clean up. Behind your desk so no one sees that on the carpet." She stuck her head into the hall, then waved me out. I scurried across and shut my door.

As ordered, I carefully picked the remaining dust balls off my clothes and, with the help of my compact, out of my hair. I dropped as many as I could into the trash can. At least I had eliminated the panel as the killer's hiding place or escape route. No one had opened it in a very long time.

I gave myself a final dusting and went over to the *Love* side, checking to make sure that Henry was not in his office. One more place to check out: the storage room. Its floor was still damp from its regular Thursday-night mopping. There were no hiding places. Four-drawer file cabinets lined both long walls. On top of one was a green metal toolbox, probably the one from which Willa had retrieved the screwdriver. At the far end, a short stepladder leaned against the wall. There was space for the maid's cart there as well. I tiptoed on the dry spots and tried all the file drawers. Locked. I examined their labels.

When I came out, Willa was rinsing a cloth in the maid's sink. "I stepped on the dry spots." I said to her. "I see the scripts are in there. Where do they keep the transcription recordings, do you know?"

"Why do you ask that?"

"They'd take up space. I was wondering if there was storage space, some hiding place that I hadn't seen."

"They keep them at George Keane's house, with copies of all the scripts they ever did. *Love Always* and *Adam Drake*. I think you've seen everything."

"Are you sorry you agreed to let us do this?"

It took her a moment to answer. She laid the cloth on the edge of the sink and smoothed it over the porcelain. "Whoever killed her knew more about what I do every night than Mr. Cupp probably could have. It doesn't make it easier to see you sneaking around on everybody."

I nodded. I waited. Before I could think of a way to start more sneaking, she said, "What else is it you want to know?"

"Mr. Alletter was telling me about the rod in the coat closet falling down. He saw George and Bar leave. He can't swear to anyone else. Could you?"

"No, I went back to work. When I was bringing Mr. Alletter the screwdriver, I saw Miss Walters go off toward her office and Miss Dunn go into the ladies'. Miss Dunn had a package. A dress box from Lord & Taylor. But I didn't see anyone leave. Doesn't the elevator man remember?"

"Not to swear to."

"Nathan and I have been talking about that night, trying to help me remember things. This morning, I remembered that before the party, when I went to get that punch bowl from Miss Keane's closet, there were roses on her desk. I told her they were pretty, and she said, 'They think if they send a few flowers, we lose our memories.' I don't know who they were from, she didn't say. I don't know if it means anything."

"Everything helps. Thank you."

She smoothed the cloth and said nothing.

CHAPTER 13

Paper triangles littered the floor in front of Josh's doorway.

"Hello," I said. "I didn't know you were staying late."

"One second." With his left index finger holding the triangle upright, he made a circle behind it with his right thumb and middle finger. He gave it a solid thwack with the middle finger, and the triangle sailed across the room and pinged into the can, joining a half dozen brothers.

"That's six in a row," he announced.

"Bravo." I picked up the triangles from the floor and set them on his desk. "Does it help, when you're stuck, playing with those? If it does, I'd like a lesson sometime."

"Sit down."

I pulled up the spare chair and sat down next to him.

"Hang on a second. Back up a little."

I scooted the chair back and he opened the bottom drawer, which held dozens of his footballs. "Get some more ammunition."

I reached in, scooped out a dozen or so, and placed them on the desktop. He shuffled through them. "I like to make these nice and thick. Gives you more control and they last longer. But not forever." One had a badly bent corner. "That won't work." Another's folds were frayed from long use. "No good." A third was splayed at the bottom, so it looked more like a little paper hat, with nickel-sized eruptions on either side and a tear at the corner. "Somebody's put her high heel into that one."

He tossed all the rejects back into the drawer.

"I could throw them away," I offered.

"Wouldn't do any good. If Willa finds any in the trash can or on the floor, she puts them back in here. She thinks I've forgotten them. I'm not always a good boy."

"I'm shocked to hear that." He laughed, then I said, "How did you get started in this business, if you don't mind my asking?"

"I taught for a while after college, then did a little tutoring around town, trying to decide what I wanted to do. Then I got a job writing copy at D.W. Davis, the ad agency, just before the war, highbrow stuff. When I came out of the service, they let me take a crack at some scripts for their radio shows, then I came over here last year when Hazel's father got sick and she decided she didn't have time to write as much as she used to. Okay, you ready? Hold it up, the long side toward you. Hold it lightly. Point it toward the trash can. Tilt it back just a bit. Bit more. Now, use the middle finger to hit it."

I did. It flew off to the right and made it maybe halfway to the can.

"That stunk," he said.

Under his guidance, I tried a dozen more, without much improvement. He gave me a handful. "Go practice. You need it."

I went back to my office, dropped my gifts on the desk, then sat down and started making notes about coveralls. At some point, the killer had changed into them. They could be easily sneaked into the offices folded under a winter coat or in a box from Lord & Taylor, like the one Karen Dunn had been carrying that night. But what had the killer done with his coat after he changed? Maybe nothing. Maybe the killer had simply put the coveralls over the coat. It would increase the killer's bulk, which could explain Clayton's identifying the killer as a man if it were a woman.

Of course, Clayton could be lying about it all.

Josh was still typing. On my way out, I closed my office door.

When I reached the studio control room, it was eight-forty-five. Down on the floor, Mash Burton, the soundman, was making a final survey of his props. A tall, pear-shaped man I'd never seen before was standing by one of the mikes, moving his lips over a script.

"Who's that?" I asked Eileen.

"Lon Randall, our announcer."

"He doesn't rehearse with you?"

"What he has to do, he could do in his sleep."

The cast flowed in and to their places. Bar and Mrs. Embert went down to the floor; she and her stopwatch sat at the long table below us, while Bar positioned himself, script in hand, where he could be seen by everyone. George and Henry arrived.

George looked at me. "Would you like some headphones? It's more like a show that way." He handed me a spare set that was hanging on the rear wall. "See what you think." He plugged them into a jack at the end of the console. "But you have to call them cans, now that you're a pro."

"Thanks."

On the floor, Bar put on his own set of cans. Mash did the same. The actors took final sips of water from paper cups set nearby on high stools.

The second hand on the clock above the studio door ticked the final seconds toward nine. I stood close to the window, holding my cans to my ears.

Five seconds. Lon stepped to his mike.

Four. Mash switched on one of his turntables and held the record stationary on it.

Three. Bar lifted his hand.

Two. Hal, the engineer, turned on Lon's mike.

One.

The "On Air" light went on.

Bar cued Mash. He released the record. Hal rolled up a dial on his panel, and through my cans, I heard the *Adam Drake* theme begin, the lonely saxophone creating a dark gritty street in a city of restless souls.

Bar pointed to Sky.

"In the city, trouble never sleeps. It tosses and turns, gives up the fight and heads out into the street. Trouble doesn't care where it's going, who it runs into. Sometimes it finds me. Sometimes I return the favor." The sax rose and fell.

Bar pointed to Lon. "Traveler cigarettes, with the smooth taste that comes from only the finest tobacco, proudly presents *Adam Drake, For Hire*. And now, Act One of 'A Storm of Suspects.' "

Out of the music, thunder rumbled, as Mash struck his screen with the tympani stick. He rolled down the screen, and the thunder faded. As he did, he used his other hand to turn on his second turntable and rain poured out of it. Hal blended it into the fading thunder, then left the rain softly in the background. Karen and Sky stepped to opposite mikes.

Adam Drake: "It was seven o'clock on a Friday night. I was sitting at my desk, watching the rain march up Broadway and examining the bottom of a bottle of Scotch. Beside me was the statement from my bank account. I was getting close to the bottom of that, too."

Mash rapped smartly twice on the pebbled glass of the Drake door and opened it.

Maisie Lane: "Boss, you need anything before I go?"

Adam: "That's quite a dress." In his voice, you could hear how good she looked.

Maisie: "This may surprise you, but there are men in this world who like to take a girl dancing once in a while. Are you going to spend the night here?"

Adam: "I have an appointment. Marshall Prescott wants to see me up at his place on Sixty-Fifth."

Maisie: "The art dealer?"

Adam: "He sent an invitation. Take a look."

Mash slid an envelope across the effects tables in front of a low standing mike, then opened it.

Maisie: "A hundred-dollar bill. Nice calling card."

Adam: "Read the note."

Mash unfolded the sheet of heavy paper.

Maisie: "Mr. Drake, I understand that you are a man who can be discreet. I have a problem that requires your special talents. This evening. Seven-thirty. Please be prompt."

Adam: "Time to go."

Mash, who had sat down lightly on a rolling wooden chair by the mike, now smoothly rolled it back.

Adam: "Don't get that dress wet."

Maisie: "I think I'll be inside all night."

Mash struck the thunder screen again. In the control room, Hal started a turntable. Rain lashed against a window.

Lon: "Meanwhile, in the Prescott mansion on Fifth Avenue."

Mash crackled two sheets of cellophane, the fire in Prescott's study. One of the supporting actors stepped to his mike; Karen stayed where she was, to play the maid, Mary.

Mash knocked on the library door, then opened it.

Mary (with an Irish accent): "Mr. Prescott, sir, the guests have all arrived, they have."

Prescott: "Indeed."

Mash struck the screen. Karen yelped.

Prescott: "Are you frightened of storms, Mary?"

Mary: "Yes, sir, that I am. I'm closing these drapes."

Mash slid the set of drapes closed, one panel at the time, while Hal lowered the volume of the rain. The storm's intensity dropped. Karen stepped into the angle of the mike.

Prescott: "What about our guests? Are they nervous, too?"

Mary (now sounding as if she were across the room, at the windows): "Yes, sir. And I don't blame them. This awful weather."

Mash rapped on his library door again, this time delicately, tentatively, then opened it. Lola stepped to a mike, facing it straight on.

The Wife: "Sweetheart, the guests have all arrived."

Prescott: "I told you not to disturb me."

The Wife: "I brought you a whiskey."

Prescott: "Put it on the desk."

Mash rattled the dice in the glass and set the glass down.

Prescott: "You can go now. Now."

The Wife: "Very well."

Mash closed the door. As she spoke, Karen moved from the side to the front of the mike.

Karen (sounding as if she were approaching the desk): "The guests don't have much to say to each other, so I've let them wait in different rooms. They have plenty to say to me, asking all kinds of questions, about why you would be wanting them to come out on a night like this."

Prescott: "One of them knows."

Mary: "Sir?"

Prescott: "Nothing."

Mary: "Should I be telling them you'll be right down?"

Prescott: "In a minute. We're waiting for one more guest."

The show went on. Adam arrives. He and the maid go to the study and find Prescott dead.

A closed house, with a storm preventing an intruder's getting in without leaving a water trail. The suspects, who were in different rooms, have no alibis. The police arrive, and, as only private eyes in fiction can, Adam gets to stick around for the interrogations.

At ten minutes, we took our first commercial break. Lon, the announcer, stepped to his mike as the thunder faded. "We'll be right back with Act Two of 'A Storm of Suspects' on *Adam Drake, For Hire* in just a moment. But first this word from our sponsor, Traveler cigarettes."

Hal started another turntable. On the recording, Lon was interviewing a guest. "We have with us this evening Doctor Milton Granger, a specialist in internal medicine from the McKee Institute in Indianapolis, Indiana. Doctor, good evening."

"Good evening, Lon."

"Doctor, do you ever advise your patients to smoke?"

"Yes, I do, Lon. When I have a patient who suffers from digestive problems, I advise him to smoke a Traveler immediately after a meal. I recommend the same for ladies. With certain types of digestive complaints, it's exactly what the patient needs, and a very simple remedy. I'm always glad to recommend a Traveler."

"Thank you, Doctor Granger."

Then Hal signaled Lon, who continued live: "Each week, the makers of Traveler cigarettes send free Travelers to servicemen's hospitals from coast to coast. This week, Travelers go to the Veterans Home, Oakland, California; Fort Lillard Army Hospital, Columbus, Ohio; and the U.S. Naval Hospital, St. Augustine, Florida."

The *Drake* music, which Mash had re-cued during the commercial, swelled. Lon intoned, "And now, Act Two of Adam Drake and 'A Storm of Suspects.' "

By the end, Adam had discovered the killer: the ex-wife had poisoned the ice cubes to frame the new wife and get rid of her ex, who was about to cut her off because she'd been having paintings forged and selling them abroad. Promptly at 9:29:30, the closing music rose and Lon said thank-you to the audience and encouraged them to tune in next week for the next thrilling Adam Drake adventure, "A Race to Death."

"And so from *Adam Drake* and Traveler cigarettes, with the smooth taste that comes from only the finest tobacco, good night."

The "On Air" light went off.

Through my cans, I heard the network announcer moving to the next program, a musical evening live from the Tropicana. I took the cans off, and we all went down to the studio.

Bar was saying, "Good show. Good show, everyone." He sat down with Mrs. Embert and Eileen to discuss changes for the midnight broadcast. The cast came out of their characters, congratulating each other, making plans for between shows, and sharing stories while some of them picked script pages up off the floor and put them back in order. Most of the actors worked without the staple in their scripts, and just let the pages drift to the ground when they finished with them. It made less noise than flipping the pages over.

"Thanks for saving that," Lola said to Sky. "I don't know what happened. I jumped your line."

"It's fine. You were great."

She laid her hand softly on his arm. "Thank you so much. This is such a break for me."

"Okay, let me have your attention," Bar said. "We're cutting a few lines in the scene with the aunt. Sorry, Karen, but the second ten's running long. Sky had to rush the wrap-up. It only affects Sky and Karen, so the rest of you can go on. Be back at eleven-forty-five."

"Eleven-forty-five," Hal repeated. "On time, please."

Sky said to Lola, "You're joining us, aren't you? We go over to Lindy's between shows. They keep a table for us."

"That sounds like fun." Lola sat down in one of the folding chairs by the actors' mikes to wait, crossing her long legs. Sky watched while she did it. Karen gave him a hard eye, but he didn't seem to notice.

Henry strolled over to Lola, carrying her coat. "Why don't we go on over, wait for them there?"

She glanced at Sky uncertainly. "Sure. Okay. See you all over there." Henry held out her coat. She slipped into it obediently and they went off.

George appeared beside me. "Good night."

"You're not going to Lindy's?"

"Not tonight. We'll see you Saturday, I hope, for the party."

"I'm looking forward to it."

After Bar made the cuts, which appeared to be mostly Karen's lines, Eileen asked me, "Going with us?"

"I'd love to, but I promised to meet someone. I'll be back for the second show."

She, Hal, Bar and Mrs. Embert all went up to the control room to get their things. I tarried by the director's table, examining a script, trying not to look like I was eavesdropping.

Sky handed Karen's coat to her.

"Don't offer to help," she snapped. "Save your strength."

"For Christ's sake," he muttered. "Lower your voice."

"Go on. Go on over there. Henry might let you sit next to her."

"Get hold of yourself."

"To hell with you." She yanked on her coat and stormed out, paying no attention to me. Mash, at the prop table, pretended he hadn't seen a thing.

I retrieved my coat and went back to the office. Alletter was just letting Willa and Nathan Mitchell out. We nodded to each other. I told Alletter that I was going to work until the second show and he went back to his Beetle Bailey comic book.

Willa had turned off all the lights except for the small sconces beside Bar and Henry's doors. The hallway was deep in shadow and silence. Josh's door was still open, paper triangles littering the carpet. His typewriter clacked away. I didn't tell him I was there.

Quietly, I slipped into my office and shut the door again. I draped my coat on the floor, covering the space at the bottom of the door and turned on the desk lamp. I pulled out a note-pad and used it to work on my script instead of the typewriter.

I worked. I listened.

CHAPTER 14

At eleven, Josh's typing stopped. I turned off my lamp and pressed my ear to the door. After a moment, I heard him moving down the hall. I waited another minute, then opened my door and crept to the corner. I didn't hear anything. Through the shadows, I tiptoed past the conference and typists rooms, and stuck my head into the *Love* side. A thin bar of light glowed under the storage room door.

I backed up into the typists room and slipped an inch of cellophane tape from Mrs. Embert's desk dispenser, stuck it to my right index finger and started slowly down the *Love* side. I listened. Then another step, and one more. I stopped and listened again. Three more steps, and I was there. I heard a file drawer slide open, then fingers flipping through the tabbing on file folders.

It wasn't enough to know he was in there. He could have a legitimate reason, although I doubted it since he'd waited until Willa was gone, and—which was the reason I had come back—a man who likes to make a show of not working certainly doesn't tell one of the bosses, as he had told Henry in the men's room, that he was staying late. And I remembered that Bar had moved one of his file cabinets—one of Hazel's old cabinets—to the storage room that very morning.

I turned the knob slowly, silently, pushed the door open an inch and put my eye to the crack. Josh was crouched next to a cabinet toward the far end of the room, with the second drawer from the bottom pulled open. He shuffled though a sheaf of papers inside a manila folder, put that folder back, took out another, and shuffled through it. He put it back quickly and yanked out another.

I pushed open the door. "Hi."

He jumped, gasped, and sat right down on his behind. The papers slid out, fluttering toward me.

"I'm so sorry," I said. "I thought you knew I'd come back."

He scrambled onto his knees, shoving the pages back into the folder. "I was looking at some old script outlines," he said. "Don't want to repeat ourselves."

"Here, let me help." I crouched and started gathering pages.

"I'll do it, don't bother. I'll do it." He took the pages out of my hand not quite fast enough to give me a paper cut.

"Okay." I said cheerfully. "I was looking for some ink."

"The supplies are in the room down there on the right."

"Thanks." He went back to his page-gathering. Surreptitiously, I pressed the strip of cellophane against the lower corner of the unopened bottom drawer. I left him there as if I hadn't seen a thing, but Josh Connally was not looking at old script ideas. He was going though letters signed by Hazel Keane.

If Bar or Henry caught him, he could be fired. What would be worth that risk?

I hoped that, by letting him know I was around, he'd stop, and I could get a look at the files he hadn't had a chance to search. Sure enough, two minutes later he passed my open door, headed for his office. I didn't see any paper in his hand, which didn't mean a thing. I heard his door close.

I started typing furiously to give the impression I meant to stay.

At eleven-forty, he appeared in my doorway. "Going back to the show?" he asked.

"This is going too well. I'm afraid to stop."

"Well, see you tomorrow."

I typed more furious nonsense for another five minutes, then I grabbed my handbag and coat and stepped smartly into reception. First, I needed to make sure Josh was gone.

"So I guess I'm the last one out," I said to Alletter. "I think Josh left."

"Just a few minutes ago."

"Well, good night. Oops, forgot my gloves." I scooted back to the hallway.

Once the door had closed behind me, I bolted down to the storage room. The piece of cellophane tape was still there, undisturbed. He had not opened that drawer.

I scurried back to reception where Alletter was just letting someone inside, a slight, elderly man, probably the overnight watchman, but that was all I had time to notice. "I couldn't find my gloves. I might come back after the show." I jumped onto the waiting elevator and made it to the studio with two minutes to spare.

The show went smoothly into the second act, then Karen seemed to have trouble: the aunt lost some of her humorous focus. Down on the floor, Mrs. Embert showed the stopwatch to Bar. At the second commercial break, while the recorded part played, he said, "Karen, you're running long."

"Well," she snapped, "it's hard to be funny when you're racing through your lines."

Eileen stood up, staring down to the studio.

"What is it?" I asked her.

"Nothing. Second show. People get tired."

Bar said, "We need twenty seconds, ladies and gentlemen."

The "On Air" light came on, and Lon listed the hospitals to which Traveler cigarettes had been donated. Karen picked up her pace and gave them back the time they needed. Lon said good night, and the show ended.

As Bar and Mrs. Embert started toward the control room, Sky came up to Karen and tried to take her arm. She shoved him away and staggered a little with the effort.

"Christ," Eileen whispered urgently to me. "She's tight. For God's sake, get her out of here. I'll grab Bar. If he finds out, she's fired. Go."

I snatched up my coat and bag. Eileen intercepted Bar while Karen stalked out of the studio. I got her things from the piano and went out into the hall. She wasn't there.

I found her in the powder room on the far side of the elevators. The network had made it nice enough for any sponsor's wife: in the lounge, frothy green carpet, vanities with beveled mirrors and tufted velvet stools. Karen sat leaned against the wall at the far end of one of the vanities. Her eye makeup was now mostly on the handkerchief in her lap.

I said, "Eileen asked me to check on you."

"She wants you to keep me away from Barbell."

"Yes." I sat down at the other end of the vanity, draped her coat over the stool between us and set her handbag on it.

"Bastard," she said.

"Pardon?"

"The bastard. He thinks he's going to Hollywood, and he doesn't want any baggage. I was good enough when he couldn't get arrested, good enough to pay the bills. You should have heard his voice when I met him. Sounded like one of those, what do you call them, the singers with no balls?"

"Castrati."

"Yeah. I trained him, for God's sake. Introduced him around. Got him an agent."

"Wouldn't he marry you?"

"Hah, well, that's where he came off lucky. I already have a husband, down in Baltimore. We're Catholic, so no divorce, even though we haven't laid eyes on each other in ten years. You got a cigarette?"

I pulled a pack of Chelseas out of my handbag and offered it to her. Peter had told me to carry them, even though I didn't smoke. She took one. I handed her a lighter. She lit the cigarette and sank back against the wall. Through the smoke of the exhale, she tossed me back the lighter. "Eileen's a good egg. Barbell say anything?"

"No."

"He's had it easy, and he doesn't even know it. He was married to the producer, did you know that?"

"Eileen told me."

"He comes from money—or did until his father gambled it all away—but he had connections, so he slides right out of college into directing soaps, then he meets Hazel. She's pushing thirty, and he comes along, good-looking young guy, ready for the next step up, and he takes it. First, she gives him *Love Always,* then *Adam Drake*. He's never had to deal with anything but first-rate actors and scripts." She wiped her eyes again. "Christ, it'll take me an hour to clean up." She took a long drag on her cigarette and set it down on the lip of the glass ashtray. With her handkerchief, she wiped the remainder of the makeup from around her eyes.

"Why does Sky think he's going to Hollywood?" I asked. "Doesn't he have a contract with the show?"

"Just signed a new one last month. Hazel wanted two years, with no way out. He wanted to be able to get out, if he got a Hollywood deal, since his agent's been telling him he ought to be out there, but Hazel gave him a lot more money to sign. Now that Hazel's gone, Henry's going to let him go out there anyway, for a screen test. Things worked out real well for him." She took an enamel mascara compact from her bag, opened it and rubbed the tiny brush briskly across the black powder. She tilted her chin back and began stroking her false eyelashes.

"I've heard you have a theater company," I said.

"Couple of years ago, Ruth—You met Ruth?"

"Yes."

"She gave me one of her plays. It knocked me out. A few of us rented a hole and put up a sign. Now we have subscribers, a board of directors." She snapped the compact closed, took out her lipstick and applied a fresh coat of Fire and Ice. "Oh, cheer up, honey. It's not as bad as I make out." She straightened her hat, put on her coat and we went out. When we reached the street, she raised her hand. A cab floated to the curb. "Can I drop you?"

"Thanks, but I'm just around the corner."

"Well, okay, if you're sure." She opened the cab door. "The hell with today, right?"

"Right."

It was one o'clock in the morning. I went back to work.

The overnight guard sat on the sofa, a newspaper in his lap, head thrown back, fast asleep. I knocked gently on the glass and kept knocking until he woke up.

"Sorry, sorry," he said dazedly as he unlocked the door. "Must have dozed off."

"No trouble. I came back to pick up some things."

"Gloves," he said, as if I had asked him. "Your gloves."

"You have a good memory. I'm Mrs. Tanner."

"Mr. Mudder." He had patches of silver stubble along his jaw and a tuft of white hair curling out of his collar above his tie.

I said, "I may do a little work while I'm here. I had some ideas while I was watching the show tonight."

He shook his head, mystified. "Young ladies these days."

At my desk, I unlocked the bottom drawer, where, underneath a stack of new paper, I had hidden a page of script, ready to be rolled into the typewriter when I needed to look like I was working, then I took out two thin, lock-picking wires from their pouch in my handbag and slipped them inside the leg of my girdle. I scooted back to the storage room and closed the door. I took off my suit jacket, pressed it against the space at the bottom of the door and turned on the light.

I retrieved my lock picks and set to work, first on the drawer Josh had been searching. It was labeled "Adam Drake Contracts/Correspondence (January–June 46)." The lock on a standard file cabinet is fairly simple. It took me five seconds. The folders were labeled in a small square handwriting. The ones in front were the contracts, divided by months. I took out the June folder and flipped through the pages. They all seemed to be standard actor contracts for the supporting players. The actors who had worked on "Storm of Suspects" seemed to work on *Adam Drake* frequently, paid twenty-five to thirty-five dollars for the show and rehearsal, and ten dollars for the repeat broadcast. Sky's and Karen's contracts weren't there. Nor any of the writers'.

Behind the contracts, the correspondence began.

It all appeared to be listener correspondence. The letter received was on top; stapled behind it, a carbon copy of the response the secretary had typed for Hazel. Sometimes, it was answered by Hazel and sometimes, for children's letters, by Adam, whose signature looked suspiciously like Hazel's. There wasn't enough of it to be all of *Adam Drake*'s fan mail. Maybe these were letters that needed particular attention.

There were some complaints: the subject matter of a particular show had been too risqué; the portrayal of the schoolteacher had insulted the men and women who worked tirelessly with our nation's youth. Each reply had assured the listener that his complaint would be taken under serious consideration by the producers and thanked him for it.

I moved on to the bottom drawer, Contracts/Correspondence (July–December 45). The contracts were much the same, and many of the same actors' names appeared. I found nothing worth Josh's getting himself fired. What had he thought he would find in letters from listeners?

But the labels didn't say they were from listeners. Maybe he'd been looking for business correspondence.

I groaned to my feet and waited until the blood returned to my rear end. I examined the labels on the other cabinets. Scripts from *Love Always* and *Adam Drake*. And *Love*'s correspondence. Love letters. I was just punchy enough to think that was funny. The rest of the cabinets' labels indicated that they contained accounting files.

Whatever Josh was after might still be locked in Bar's office. I turned off the light, picked up my jacket and opened the door slowly, then eased down the hall, and dipped into the typists room. How had Josh unlocked the file cabinets? I pulled open the middle drawer of Mrs. Embert's desk. There were no keys, not in plain sight anyway. I lifted the pencil tray. There, hooked to the bottom of the tray was a set of small keys. Very good, Mrs. Embert. Why bother to lock the cabinets at all? Carefully, not moving anything out of place, I searched all her drawers for other keys, to Bar's office or the front door. I didn't find any.

Before I risked breaking into Bar's office, I needed a consultation with a professional detective. So I retrieved my coat and bag, and pulled the gloves out of the pocket so the guard could see them. Mr. Mudder sat on the sofa again, head thrown back, sound asleep. In my experience, breaking and entering wasn't usually this easy.

CHAPTER 15

The next morning, I felt better than I expected to, given the lack of sleep, but when I reached the office, Sophie took one look at me and croaked, "Coffee's fresh, honey. What are you doing here so early on a Friday? It's okay to sleep in, the other *Drake* people don't show up till ten."

"I heard the detective was coming. I wanted to be here. Anything to report?"

"There will be any minute." She raised her brows and cocked her head toward the front door. Peter came in.

"Good morning," he said to both of us. "I'm Peter Winslow. I'm here to see Mr. Keane."

"I'll tell him you're here," Sophie said. She turned to the PBX and slipped on the headset. "This is Mrs. Tanner, one of our writers." Peter nodded, and Sophie squawked into the mouthpiece, "Mrs. Embert, Mr. Winslow is here to see Mr. Keane." She pulled out the plug. "She'll make you wait. Want some coffee?"

"No, thanks," Peter said.

"So why haven't you called me?" she asked. "I thought you were making dates with all the girls, checking our alibis."

"I already know where you were. Did you think you could keep something like that a secret forever?"

"All right, who was it? Who ratted me out?"

"Father Michael."

"The fink." She turned to me. "Every Wednesday night, I

play bingo at my church and help them clean up after." She looked back at Peter. "So this means you're through with me?"

"Not at all. Tomorrow's Saturday. Could I take you to lunch?"

"Pick me up at my apartment?"

"Of course. One o'clock?"

"I'll bet you know the address."

Mrs. Embert came out. I hadn't thought it possible for her lips to get any tighter. "This way, please."

As soon as they left the room, Sophie said, "I want every detail. Go. Go."

The door to Henry's office was just closing behind them. I couldn't hear anything, so I went to my office and waited. After about a half hour, I heard Peter's voice. "Why don't we start with the alarm?" After he and Mrs. Embert passed, I strolled into the hall.

The alarm was set just above the rear door, a red metal dome six inches across. "I'm going to need a better look," he said to Mrs. Embert. She said nothing.

"There's a stepladder in the storage room," I volunteered.

"Thanks," he said. "But I think this trash can will work fine." He grabbed Josh's trash can, which was empty, flipped it over and climbed on. He took a small flashlight out of his jacket pocket and shone it onto the alarm's hammer mechanism through the space between the edge of the dome covering and the wall. He put the flash back in his pocket and climbed down. "Is this door always locked?"

"We can't lock it," Mrs. Embert said. "It's a fire escape. But the alarm works very well."

"Who has keys to the other doors, the ones that lead out?"

"There are no keys for these side doors," she said, indicating the one that, with its twin across the way on the *Love* side, led into the elevator lobby. "They can only be opened from the inside. As far as I know, there are only four keys to the front door: Miss Keane's, Mr. Benjamin's, Mr. Keane's and one set for the watchmen, which is kept at the desk in reception."

"When you say Mr. Keane, you mean Henry?"

"Yes. Mr. George Keane might have a key. I don't know."

"I'd like to test this now. I think we should warn everyone first. Maybe Mrs. Tanner would do that."

Mrs. Embert turned and jabbed me with her stare. "Of course," I said. I alerted everyone, then went back, told Peter and covered my ears. The alarm wouldn't knock your teeth out, but it was loud enough to be heard all over the office. Peter closed the door, then did it again.

"That's enough, Mr. Winslow," Mrs. Embert said.

"I agree." He examined the fit of the door all around. "Nice and tight." That settled it: the killer hadn't deadened the alarm by shoving a rag or something else into it, with a string attached, then pulled it out under the door to conceal his escape route. "Let's move on. Thank you, Mrs. Tanner."

I thought he was telling me to stop making myself conspicuous, so I went back into my office. I gave him another hour, long enough to finish, then took myself out to visit Sophie and apologize for not having much to tell her. "He still sounds like fun," she said. "I hope he doesn't change his mind about lunch."

"I'm sure he'll want to talk to you. He's probably heard that you know everything."

She grinned, layering the folds in her face.

The PBX hummed and she turned to answer the call, plugging the cord in with a snap. When the caller told her what he needed, she said, "One moment, please," pulled the partner cord from the base and plunged the tip into the destination hole. Then she removed the headphone and turned back to me.

I said, "Have you been here long?"

"Four years. I retired after thirty years working the switchboard at the Board of Education. Try living on that pension. I'd known Hazel a long time. We met up at Saint Kay's. Saint Katherine's. It's an orphanage up in Yorkville, way up on the east side, where I live. She and her mother did volunteer work there, like me. We read to the kids, take them out to the movies now and then, help the sisters in the office."

"Were you at the party, the going-away party they had the night she was killed?"

"Yes. Why?"

"I keep trying to figure out where that guy—what is his name, Cupp?—where he hid that nobody saw him."

"I saw him at the party, but I wasn't paying much attention. He was talking to Karen for a while, but that's about all I remember."

"Karen Dunn was at the party?" I asked.

"They showed up at five for the meeting, her and Sky. Sky said no one told him it was starting late, and you can bet Mrs. Embert didn't care for that, implying that she hadn't called him. Karen said that she'd forgotten. Sky pouted for a while. I think he'd choke before admitting he was wrong."

"Not your favorite guy."

"You talk to him, the whole time he's figuring out what you can do for him. And the way he treats Karen. Right in front of her at the party, he's giving Jeannie the treatment."

"I understand there was a witness, someone who actually saw Cupp outside Miss Keane's office."

"A friend of Hazel's came to pick her up for dinner that night. He saw the guy come right out of her office. That late at night, and he doesn't think it's a little strange."

"Was she dating this friend?"

"Don't get the wrong idea. It was only after she and Bar split up, and she never invited him here during business hours. When they went out to lunch, she'd meet him somewhere. I'd talked to him on the phone, taken messages for her, but that day at the party was the first time I'd ever seen him."

"The doctor was here that afternoon?"

"He showed up just as the party was starting and asked to see Hazel. You should have seen Bar's face. I called her, and she came out and they went back to her office. I had the feeling she wasn't too happy to see him."

"Did you see him leave?"

"If I did, I don't remember. You know, now I think about it, when the police asked me who was at the party, I'm not sure I told them about him."

"Maybe you should mention it to Mr. Winslow."

"I'd like to make him happy, sweetie, but not if it's going to help him try to stiff somebody on the insurance money. Cute as he is, he's not working for Hazel."

"I see your point. Well, good luck with him. I better get back to work." I took myself off, before my curiosity became too obvious.

Doctor Clayton was dating Hazel, so she might have told him about her fight with Cupp. But could he possibly have known enough about the routine of the office to avoid Willa and find a safe hiding place? Could he have known about the coveralls in the basement or that Cupp would be at the party, conveniently toting a bag of deadly tools? It seemed unlikely.

Sky and Karen both conveniently forgot the meeting time had been changed. They had the opportunity to steal the weapons, and knew something about the after-hours routine from being at the writers meetings. But did Sky have any reason to want Hazel dead? Karen's theater company stood to inherit, but was that enough to kill for?

I moved on. Time to get better acquainted with another suspect.

I found Ruth Linden in her office, tapping a pencil on the desk and staring out the window. I didn't think I made any sound, but she turned around. "What can I do for you?"

"I'll come back if it's a bad time."

"That depends on what you want."

I laughed. I hoped she meant it as a joke. She didn't smile. I said, "I just wanted to say that I hope I'm not stepping on anyone's toes coming here."

"I was trying something new, the other day, working on *Drake*. Do you want me to take a look at something?"

"Pardon?"

"Look over what you've got? Before you show it to Bar?"

"Would you?"

"I don't think he'd like it. He's not the picnic type."

"What?"

"Sharing things around."

"Which means you'll take a look at it."

"Of course."

"How about now?"

"All right."

I retrieved my draft. "I appreciate this."

"You might not when I'm finished."

I laughed again and left it with her.

Bar's office door was open, but he wasn't there. I nipped inside and took a look at the labels on the file cabinet drawers, checking to see if they could contain what Josh had been after last night. In my peripheral vision, I saw Bar come out of the men's room. I turned casually and gazed out the window at Madison Avenue.

He said, "Good morning."

"Oh, hello. I'll have the draft this afternoon, but you know the script has a storm at the opening, and as we used one last night. . . ."

"We can take care of that." He went around his desk and sat down. "How's Karen? I saw you go after her last night."

"She calmed down quickly. She's very talented, isn't she?"

"She has range."

"Yes. Well, thanks." I left.

I found Eileen setting a cup of coffee and two donuts on her desk. "Where did you disappear to last night?" she asked.

"I spent some time with Karen."

"Sky's not worth it, but you can't tell a girl anything when she's in love. You couldn't tell me anyway."

I stepped into the room and dropped my voice. "Bar seems upset with her. He may know more than we thought."

"If he knew she was drunk, he'd have fired her. Now that Hazel's gone, I hope Henry isn't letting his id get in the way and thinking about moving Karen out for some chorus girl. You heard what Josh said at rehearsal, about Henry looking for a new Maisie."

"Doesn't Karen have a contract?"

"It's up in a few months. Bar would probably keep her, just to spite Henry, but, to him, actors are just hired voices. He never liked it that Hazel let Sky and Karen come to meetings. I'm sorry, but I have to close the door now. I don't want Bar to see that I don't have the first idea for my next script. Got anything I can steal?"

"Jewel heists are always nice."

"Oh, guess who called this morning? That detective. He asked if we could get together tonight after work. I suddenly found myself saying okay."

"George said we should talk to him. One more thing, quickly. Should I be on the lookout for Karen drinking? Does she get tight very often?"

"She drinks more than she should, but I'd never seen her drunk at a show."

"I'll let you get to work." I went into my office, leaving my door open, although I wanted very much to close it, given the thoughts that were bumping around in my head.

Was Karen drinking more now, tempting fate, because something was eating at her, something like the fact that she killed Hazel?

I didn't get much work done.

In about an hour, Ruth appeared in the door. She stood there for a moment and just looked at me.

"Come on," I said, "it can't be that bad."

"Not at all. You have a nice touch with dialogue, especially the sidekick, but you've got too much going on. The wrap-up confused me and I read it a couple of times."

"Gulp."

She didn't smile. "I warned you."

"I'm not a kid. I can take it."

"I can see that. You're good, but don't settle for that. Of course, that's coming from a soap opera writer."

"I don't think that's your life's ambition."

"I came down from Boston, certain that Broadway was just waiting for me. That was eight years ago."

"I hear you have a theater company now."

"Down in the Village."

"How do you compress stories into fifteen minutes for *Love* when your instinct is two and a half hours?"

"I write the Ring Cycle, then chop it up into fifteen-minute segments." She set the script on the desk. "May I ask you something? If you're going to color your hair, why don't you go for something a bit lighter?"

"I have a lot of gray already. It's hard to cover."

"It's not a bad job, but it's too dark for your coloring. I know a good man. I'll give you his name."

"Thanks. Could I buy you a drink sometime?"

"Sure. Oh, and don't tell Bar I gave you any tips."

"That doesn't seem fair."

"What is?" She went out and shut the door. Whew.

I opened the script and went to work, humbled. She was right. I was coasting. I pulled a pencil out of the cup and started to work, scratching through whole sections, filling the margins and then my pad with notes. The blood started pumping. I rolled fresh paper into the typewriter and began all over again. The ideas started running into each other, jostling, bumping, shoving, like horses out of the starting gate. They took off and I went along for the ride.

There is no feeling in the world like it.

CHAPTER 16

I didn't realize how late it was until my eyes had trouble focusing. The room was getting dark. I looked at my watch. Almost five.

I stood up, stretched, and went down to the typists room. Mrs. Embert was gone, but Jeannie and Marty were still hard at work.

"Excuse me," I said. "Will you be here long enough to type my script? I'd like to turn it in Monday."

"We leave at five-thirty," Jeannie said, apologetically.

Marty spoke up. "We're almost finished with this. We'll split it up, do as much as we can." She had a tough little voice, even when offering to help.

I retrieved my script, then stood between their desks while I explained the arrows and notes, and what went where.

Jeannie said, "Oh, we've seen worse than this, haven't we?" She glanced at Marty, who said nothing. "You should have seen what Hazel used to give us." She smiled, sadly.

"Was she a good boss?"

"She was to us." She lowered her voice, even though no one was around. "When she found out what Henry was paying us, she said she'd take care of it. Next paycheck we found a nice raise, didn't we?" she asked, seeking affirmation, or maybe participation, from Marty.

"Bet we won't see another," was Marty's comment.

I said, "I heard Henry's a little tight with a dollar."

"He's tight with a nickel," Marty scoffed. "There used to be three of us, then Kathy left to get married, and he hasn't hired anyone else."

"We can't even go to lunch together anymore," Jeannie said, "because one of us has to fill in for Sophie. They think that you'll work harder and take less money because radio's glamorous."

"Glamorous?" Marty said. "Typing scripts and letters all day."

"I meant that it wouldn't be that hard to replace us, because girls think it's glamorous when they read the ads in the paper. It used to be fun, when Hazel was alive. She'd invite us to watch the shows, take us out to dinner sometimes after. Now Mrs. Embert says it's too many people in the control room and the engineer has to concentrate."

"As if we don't know how to behave," Marty said.

"When I came here to apply for the job," Jeannie went on, "Hazel talked to me herself, asked all about my family and things. Then I did terrible on the test."

"Terribly," Marty corrected.

Jeannie flushed. "She asked me what had happened, and I told her that I was reading the words, which you're not supposed to do when you're typing. I think she liked it that I was reading it, so she gave me another script, told me to go read it, then type it. Of course, Marty didn't need to do it twice. She hardly ever makes a mistake."

It was Marty's turn to blush.

"Last month," Jeannie went on, "Hazel took us to see a play Ruth wrote, then she took us out for supper and sent us home in a cab."

Marty's dark eyes suddenly glowed. "It was a wonderful play."

I said, "She sounds like a nice lady."

Jeannie said, "George is like that, too. He asked if we were coming to his party and said he'd see we got home safe—safely—in cabs. Imagine Mrs. Embert saying that."

"Imagine Henry paying for it," Marty said.

I said, "If you don't have plans for tonight, I was wondering if I could give you each five dollars to stay and finish the script."

"Okay," Jeannie said immediately for both of them. Marty stared at me.

"I appreciate it. I was supposed to hand it in today."

"Bar's been gone all afternoon. He and Henry went over to the ad agency to meet with George about the new show. They're trying to start a new soap opera."

I asked, "Have you two been here long?"

"I came here in June. This is my first job. Marty was already working here. Hazel tracked her down out of school, didn't she?"

"You knew her before you came here?" I asked Marty.

"Hazel started a secretarial class at Saint Katherine's. It's an orphanage. That's where I grew up."

Jeannie jumped in. "When a place opened up here, Hazel called the school and asked where Marty was, because she remembered how good she was."

"Jeannie," Marty admonished, embarrassed. Then she turned to me. "I was working at Bloomingdale's at the time, typing invoices."

"So you shouldn't complain about this," Jeannie pointed out.

"I'm not complaining."

"You were."

"I just said that it wasn't glamorous."

"You got to be the *Love* assistant all summer."

"Pardon?" I said.

Jeannie giggled and covered her mouth with her fingers. "That sounded terrible, didn't it? During the summer, *Adam Drake* isn't on live. It's all transcription recordings from earlier in the year. There wasn't a secretary then. Mrs. Embert hadn't come yet because Henry and Hazel couldn't agree on anyone. So Bar asked Marty if she'd be the assistant on the *Love* broadcasts."

"Did you enjoy that?" I asked Marty.

"Yes," she replied, her entire face glowing.

"Is that what you'd like to do?"

Jeannie answered for her. "Bar said she was good at it, too. He said if she had more experience as a secretary, she could have had the job."

"He was just being nice," Marty said, her face still flushed.

She's got a crush on him, I thought. I said, "So you two took care of the secretary's job all summer. Did you find out what everybody makes?"

Marty actually smiled, then said, "They wouldn't let us see the contracts. They keep those locked up in Bar's office."

"But," Jeannie said, "we got to see the references, didn't we, when Hazel was checking up on everyone?"

I expected both girls to stare at my ears. I was sure they shot forward. "Checking up?"

Jeannie said, "The network told all the shows to make sure there was no one on their staffs who might get them in trouble. You know how worried everybody is these days, with communists everywhere. We typed all the letters that Hazel sent out, to the places where people used to work, saying that she had to check their references, then she sent letters to the network and the advertising agency, saying she did it."

"Then she was able to verify all of them?"

Jeannie said, "It wouldn't be like her to say she did something and not do it. She was funny that way. Oh, I don't mean a person shouldn't keep her word. I just mean she took it very seriously."

Marty brushed that aside. "She thought it was hooey, but she was worried that it could hurt the shows."

I took a pause while Jeannie divided the pages and handed Marty her half. Then I said, "Did you know the man the police arrested?"

"I can't believe he did it," Jeannie said. "I know that there was a witness, that doctor says he saw him, but I still can't believe it. And his wife says he was home with her when it happened."

Marty explained, "Jeannie's mom is friends with his wife. He lives near Jeannie."

"That's quite a coincidence," I said, mildly, "in a city this big."

"My father's a plumber," Jeannie said. "He works for the company that manages this building and a lot of others. Mr. Cupp came up here a few years ago from West Virginia, to work for the company, too. He was looking for an apartment, and my father told him to come look in our neighborhood. Well, maybe it is. I mean, a coincidence that we both ended up working here."

"I've heard he was sort of surly," I said.

"Not to us," Jeannie said. "He wasn't a smiler, but he spoke whenever he came in."

"Some people I could mention," Marty said, and jerked her head toward Mrs. Embert's desk, "you work with them every day and they don't do that."

"We knew there was trouble," Jeannie said. "Hazel caught him drinking while he was fixing something in the ladies' room. You probably heard about that."

"Yes."

"You never know what's going on inside some people, do you?"

"I'd say inside most people. I appreciate your doing this for me. Let me throw in a couple of extra dollars. You can get some dinner, then come back and finish up." I laid the money on the desk and went back to my office.

Hazel was verifying backgrounds. She told the network that everybody was on the up-and-up, but she might do that even if it weren't true. To admit to having a communist on the staff could result in terrible publicity. What would she do if she discovered that one of her staff might be tainted? She wouldn't waste time on more letters. She'd get right on the phone. And there might be a trail of long-distance phone bills from August or early September in Alton's office. I had my lock picks in my handbag.

By five-thirty, Josh and Eileen were gone. I crept to the corner and listened. The typewriters stopped and I heard the girls happily planning some Saturday shopping while they retrieved their coats. I got to hear them say nice things about me.

When they left, I grabbed my picks, a pad and a pencil and scurried to the *Love* side. Ruth's office was empty. Alton had locked his door, probably because he kept the petty cash there, but it was no match for me. I closed his door and snapped on the light. The background checks had been done only a couple of months ago. Surely anything that recent would be in the top drawer of his filing cabinet. I unlocked it.

At the back was a folder marked "PBX/phones." In it, I found the monthly charges for the system and rental of the phone equipment, a bill for a repair service visit, and bills for this year's long-distance phone calls. I glanced through those. As there weren't that many, I decided to make a copy of everything from the beginning of the year, in case Peter could make something out of them. Throughout, several numbers were repeated, in Detroit, Chicago, Pittsburgh and Cleveland. Probably the stations Keane Radio owned.

Early in the summer, there were calls to Newport, Rhode Island. I remembered that Hazel's lawyer said Henry had inherited a home there. There were a few calls to Maryland, where Hazel had a farm. Then there were several to Los Angeles. I recognized Sam Ross's office number at Marathon among them. There were practically none from mid-July until mid-August. Then, about the time the reference work began, there were calls to Hartford (where Alton had worked), Boston (where Ruth came from), Baltimore (where Karen had a husband), Philadelphia and Charleston, South Carolina.

My hand cramped. I shook it out while I flipped through the last set of calls, which had been to Los Angeles, the week Hazel was there, all to the Beverly Hills Hotel. That was it.

I was tempted by the other files, which contained financial records, but I couldn't risk it. I'd been in there long enough. I needed to get one of those little cameras all the spies had in the movies.

When I reached the Marquette Hotel, I found a message from Peter's alias, Mr. Stone, waiting for me. I called him back, and he was at my front door within a half hour. "I came in the back way," he said. "I wasn't followed."

"Shouldn't I have met you somewhere?"

"Change your mind since Wednesday, gumshoe?"

"What happened here?" Peter asked.

We were lying naked in my bed, and he was employing his considerable investigative talents on the lower part of my body. He brushed his fingers lightly over the scratches on my thigh. "How'd this happen?"

"My lock picks. I had them in my girdle. Do we have to talk about this now?"

He apparently thought so. "What were you doing with those?"

"I opened a file cabinet."

Now he sat up. "You what?"

"Calm down. I was careful." I told him about finding Josh searching files in the storage room.

"Why didn't you leave me a message?"

"I don't think he found what he was looking for. It's probably in Bar's office, and Josh doesn't have the key. If he did, he would have broken in before the files were moved."

"What else haven't you mentioned?"

"There were a couple of things that happened today, which I would have told you about but you had other things on your mind when you got here." I told him about Clayton's having been in the office during the going-away party, and that Sophie couldn't remember if he'd left. And that Karen and Sky had both been at the party, too. Then I related what the girls had told me about Hazel's background checks. "I made a list of all the long-distance calls since the beginning of the year, if you'd like to see them."

"I think that can wait," he said and went back to what he had been doing, so it was a half hour before we started talking about the case again.

"Do you want me to search Bar's files?" I asked.

"No, the weekend watchmen don't know you. They might keep an eye on you. I've got Vanguard doing checks on the staff. Let's see what they turn up, and my interviews. I have to leave soon. I'm meeting Eileen Walters."

"Yes, she mentioned that."

"She seem worried?"

"No more than you'd expect. How was the artists party, by the way? Meet any friendly little actresses after I left?"

He grinned and pulled me closer. "I talked to some of Hazel's friends. They all said she seemed distracted the last few months, but they thought it was because of her marriage and her father's death. A couple of them thought she seemed less taken with Clayton recently."

"Really?" I told him about the flowers Willa had seen on Hazel's desk and what Hazel had said: " 'They think if they send a few flowers, we lose our memories.' She was going to break it off, maybe cut him out of the will."

"A theory and evidence are two different things, but he's an interesting prospect."

"Okay, what is it? What else have you got? Spill it."

"Our good doctor has a thriving little side practice in abortion."

I stared at him, astonished. "Somebody at the party told you that?"

He laughed. "I gave his receptionist two hundred of New York Mutual's money and she let me go through the files. It's all aboveboard. Hospital admission, routine uterine scrape to treat bleeding. Your typical cover for a rich woman's abortion. But he does far more than the average doctor."

"Hazel wouldn't stand for that. She was devout."

"We can't prove she knew. Let's see how the next few days play out."

I slipped out of bed and retrieved the list of long-distance calls. "Treat that with respect. My hand was cramped for an hour after I finished it." I eased down next to him. "I've been thinking. If the killer knew enough about the routine of the office to avoid Willa and Alletter, he would certainly have known that between eight-thirty—when Willa went into the *Love* side—and nine—when Alletter went to dinner—he was relatively safe. It was the best time to commit the crime. He could have slipped out of his hiding place, killed Hazel and then hidden in Josh's office until Alletter was in the kitchen, then gone right out that side door, across the elevator lobby, and down the service stairs."

"Yes."

"So why would the killer wait until nine-thirty? Anybody who was at that meeting heard Hazel tell Alletter that she might not work as long as ten. She might have been finished by nine-thirty. If Clayton's not lying, the two best suspects are Bar and Henry. Bar left the offices after the meeting. We know he left because there's no place to hide in reception. He would have had trouble getting back in until nine, when Alletter went to dinner. Henry didn't leave George's till after nine."

"The fallen rod works against it being either one of them. Why create a diversion so you can hide and not hide? Henry doesn't have much of a motive, and it would have been a tight squeeze to get back to the office from his brother's house and do everything he had to do before nine-thirty. We'll see what his story sounds like when I talk to him. He and George have agreed to talk to me, together, after work Monday, over at George's office. Everyone's agreed to talk to me, except Connally and Donovan."

"I can work on Sky tomorrow night at George's party."

"What's he like?"

"Tall, dark, nicely built."

"Hmm."

"Green eyes. Roguish smile."

"Hmm."

"Wears a long white scarf and carries a walking stick."

"I like him."

My new apartment building was on East 11th, off Fifth, a few bocks north of Washington Square Park. The landlord had been inventive, avoiding regulations that limited rent by carving several apartments out of one. What had once been the living and dining rooms now constituted the entire apartment, the rooms divided by two pillars and low, built-in bookcases. The pair of windows in each room overlooked a patch of land and the rear of buildings on East 12th. There was no fire escape. One ran down from the apartment next door, where I assumed the original bedrooms to mine had been. The building inspector had apparently overlooked that. Peter had not. For me, it made the apartment safer.

My kitchen was no more than the bare essentials lined up against one wall of the living room, whose furniture sat around a rose-and-gardenia carpet. There was a bed (single) in what had been the dining room, along with a built-in china hutch where the tenant stored her linens and whose top drawer had been emptied for me. The bathroom had probably been created from a hallway. It was so narrow that you could tumble into the tub if you stepped back from the sink.

The tenant or her people must have come from Germany or Austria. The hutch shelves contained a collection of Hummel figurines and fancy beer steins. Between each pair of windows hung heavy brass platters of bucolic Tyrolean scenes: chubby children in lederhosen, among bushels of wheat and bunches of grapes. Above the bed, a mediocre print of a mediocre Romantic painting, dark gnarled trees and windswept heights. Something out of Eichendorff.

I stowed my unopened trunk at the foot of the bed, and after unpacking my suitcases, slid them under it. That's when I noticed the phone on the night table. I got off my knees and looked into the living room. There, on the end table by the sofa, was another one. Nobody had two phones this close together, not even in Hollywood. The cord to the one on the nightstand ran tightly along the baseboard, beneath the window curtains and into the bookcase. My benefactor worked for Vanguard. Somebody at the office had tapped the phone company's line to give her a free extension. A perquisite of working for private detectives: You don't have to get out of bed on a cold winter morning to answer the phone.

The doorbell rang.

Not Peter's prearranged coded knock. The doorbell. No one

was supposed to know where I lived. Maybe it was a neighbor, coming by to introduce herself. Did they do that in New York?

"Yes?"

"Mabel?" I didn't recognize the voice.

"Who is it?"

"Zack."

I opened the door. Zack Eisler stood in the hallway, wrapped in a double-breasted British military coat, a red knitted scarf thrown around his neck. Beside him was what could only be a painting, wrapped carefully in padding and covered in brown paper.

"I thought I'd deliver it myself."

"How did you know where I lived?"

"You gave my agent your phone number. I called Information. Usually the girl'll give you the address if you ask nicely. Not hiding out, are you?"

"No, not at all. Come in." He hoisted the painting, hauled it inside and leaned it against the wall. "You know I haven't paid for this yet."

"I know. If you don't pay, I know where you live." He looked around. "Not your place. Can't see you with middle-brow German art."

"I'm renting from a friend. You didn't have to do this."

"Sure I did. I wanted to see you again."

"Zack, you should know that I'm seeing someone."

"Not that lawyer Lewis?"

"No."

"Thank God for that. Hard to compete with that kind of money. Your daddy got money?"

"I'm sorry?"

"This guy you're seeing. He rich?"

"No."

He pulled me to him and gave me another kiss, longer, with a little more technique. Actually with a lot more, rather good, technique.

"Thanks for delivering the painting," I said when we came up for air.

He laughed. "This guy good-looking?"

"Yes."

"Good in bed?"

"None of your business."

"What you need is something to compare him to. It's only fair to both of you."

"I'll remember that." I slipped out of his arms. "Zack, please don't tell anyone where I'm staying. I've still got a husband, technically."

"And two lovers, you say the word. Anything you like, and if you don't know what that is yet, I'll help you find out."

"You're a great painter, Zack."

"You could tell your girlfriends more than that. My card's on the back of the painting." He gave me a roguish smile, then a chaste kiss on the cheek and was gone.

CHAPTER 17

George Keane lived on East 80th, a half block from Central Park. On a street of Palladian mansions, the Keane home was the largest. Next to its pillared porch, a wrought-iron gate led to a set of stone steps descending to the service entrance. I took the other ones, the wide and well-lit ones, and rung the bell beside the gleaming black door.

Willa Mitchell, wearing a formal maid's uniform—black with white cuffs and an apron—opened the door. "Mrs. Tanner," she said. I stepped inside and she took my coat.

The entry foyer rose two stories. To my left, a mahogany staircase swept up past a chandelier bigger than my bathroom; straight ahead, a set of carved doors opened into the dining room. In the old-fashioned tradition, in this home one went "down to dinner" from the drawing and sitting rooms above.

A butler appeared, a Central Casting butler—tall, stiff, with impeccably groomed gray hair, an unreadable face and tucked chin. Mr. Hawthorne, I presumed. "Good evening, madam. The elevator is here, if you would care to use it." He gestured smoothly to a narrow door with an egg-shaped brass knob, beneath the stairs.

"How far am I going?"

"One flight."

"I'll take the stairs, then."

The L-shaped drawing room took up the entire second floor. At least sixty guests were already there. I knew hardly any of them, and despite what George had said about the party's being informal, several wore evening clothes.

Jeannie waved to me from beside one of the long windows that looked out over the rear garden and proudly showed me her glass of champagne. Marty frowned at her intently, then looked at me with an expression that said "What a rube." Over near the corner of the L, Eileen sat on a fringed velvet ottoman, talking to Sophie and Hal—the engineer from *Adam Drake*—who were trying to get comfortable on a wood-framed settee. Eileen's black taffeta cocktail dress showed off very nice shoulders. Sophie wore lilac and ropes of pearls, knotted low, like a flapper. She had a cigarette stuck in the corner of her mouth, and she was squinting through the smoke, which allowed every wrinkle on her face to get some exercise.

I walked up and said hello. "Who are all these people?"

"Some from Traveler cigarettes," Eileen said. "They'd be the overdressed ones. Some from the advertising agency. A few of the actors we use regularly. Oh, and Henry's new friend." She cocked her eyebrows toward the far end of the room where Lola Staton posed in the hollow of a grand piano, sparkling in a silver dress. Sky was handing her a glass of champagne. He knocked back a bit of something stronger.

"Where's Karen?" I asked.

"Hasn't shown yet. I hope he behaves himself when she does. Did you bring anyone?"

"No. How about you?"

"I'm looking for new friends."

"Any prospects?"

"Zilch so far. Go get yourself a drink."

Halfway to the piano, across from the fireplace, the bar had been set up: a waist-high ebony counter and, behind it, a table, covered in white oilcloth, crisp linen and rows of liquor bottles beside a large cut-crystal bowl of ice cubes. On the floor, champagne cooled in a tub of crushed ice. Nathan Mitchell was tending the bar.

"Hello," I said.

He set a cocktail napkin in front of me, "What can I get you, ma'am?"

"A gin and tonic, heavy on the tonic."

With silver tongs, he deftly plucked cubes from the crystal bowl and dropped them into a glass. "Lemon in or out?"

"In." He dropped the thin slice into the glass rather than hanging it on the side.

Hal Lombardi, the studio engineer, moved up beside me. "A very big Scotch, please."

"Shall I ruin it with ice?" Nathan asked.

Hal chuckled. "Good memory. How you doing, Nate?"

"Just fine. How are you?"

"Can't complain." Hal turned to me. "Nate's a cop, so don't try to lift the silver. He's married to Willa, the maid at the office. She's around here somewhere. And his mother-in-law's probably down in the kitchen, cooking the food. At least I hope she is."

Nathan set the short, fat ice-less glass on the counter's ledge.

Hal said, "Thanks. Good seeing you."

"You too."

As Hal and I moved away from the bar, I said, "Do you know everyone here?"

"Most. I've been with both shows since the beginning."

"Then you know all the gossip," I observed, lightly.

He said, "I know Sky's pushing his luck."

Lola had moved to a chair near the piano where Sky tried to protect his territory, which had been invaded by a jaunty tuxedoed trio doing their best not to ogle. Lola leaned forward, listening with rapt attention to whatever they were saying. I was sure they had their eyes on her face.

"Henry wouldn't fire him for flirting," I said.

"He has a two-year contract, but he's got a chance to go out to Hollywood for a screen test, and Henry said he'd let him go. If I were Sky, I'd be talking to the ugliest woman here."

"How about a tour of the place? Could you show me around?"

"Sure."

On the third floor, at the rear of the house, we found a smaller, far-less-formal sitting room, full of comfortable slipcovered furniture, probably for gatherings of closer friends. Several card tables had been set up for those who preferred not to eat out of their laps, and possibly for card games later. Opening from that, a paneled smoking and billiard room stretched back to the front of the house. Mash Burton, the soundman, and Lon Randall, *Adam Drake*'s announcer, were selecting their cues from a rack of ivory-inlaid sticks. "You don't get to play in a place like this too often," Mash said. "Want to play?"

"Thanks," Hal said, "but we're just looking around."

At the other end, at the front of the house, was George's study, furnished in Chippendale and lined with bookcases in the Grecian style. Hal stopped at the door, but I went in.

Here was the room where George and Henry had their fight, the one that took away an airtight alibi for Henry. Had he picked that fight so he would have an excuse to leave, having figured out how to get to the Emory Building, up the fire escape and into the offices in less than a half hour? But why would he do it for rights to the shows and some insurance money when he had two million in a trust fund?

This was also the room in which a routine examination of Morris Keane's papers had begun that had ended in a frantic search of the entire house. Had the Keane children found some indication that their father had made a new will, leaving their fortune to his fiancée, the yet-to-be-located Rachel? If the fiancée knew about that will, and thought the children destroyed it, she'd have a motive to kill. But she would never have been able to do it inside the offices. Besides, Morris Keane's lawyer was positive there had been no new will.

Had Hazel once been secretly married to Lawrence Clayton and discovered that a long-ago annulment wasn't valid? It would explain her questioning Lewis about bigamy and why she wanted to make a new will. And it would give Bar a reason to kill her. But of course we had no hint that there had ever been another marriage.

Beside one of the bookcases stood an oval table covered with old family pictures in silver frames, one of them the anniversary portrait of the Keanes that Adora Watson had shown us at her apartment. In another, Morris Keane stood proudly beside a console Keane radio, very much like the one that had been in the reception room and loaned to Radio City by Bar. Beside that portrait was one of Ethel Keane in a high-backed chair, with her three children gathered around her. Hazel looked to be about twelve. She had a serious face, with rather thick straight brows. George stood very tall, the young master. Henry held his mother's hand.

Another showed Morris and Ethel together, sitting in front of a group of children in uniforms who filled the front steps of a large Victorian brick building. Next to them, several nuns. Given my detective skills, I surmised that it was one of the orphanages the Keanes supported.

At the back of the display stood a photograph of a man in uniform and two nurses in front of a Red Cross tent. The nurses wore ankle-length skirts, white caps and aprons. The man's calves were wound with cloth wrappings called puttees, part of a uniform during the first part of the century. Behind them, two patients, bandages on their heads, peered out of the tent's shadowed interior. I picked up the picture, examining the face of the man in the foreground.

"That's my father," George Keane said from the hall doorway. "In the uniform."

"I hope you don't mind my being in here," I said, replacing the picture. "I've been admiring your home."

"Not at all, though I can't take much credit for it, except the billiard room. I was just going to show it to Gordon." He introduced me to the hawk-nosed man beside him. "Gordon's with Camay. They'll be sponsoring our new show this spring. I found that picture in a drawer after my father died. It's the only one we have of him in the first war. He never talked about it. He volunteered with the American Field Service. I think he saw terrible things, worse even than this last one. Please feel free to look around."

He took Gordon off, and Hal and I strolled into the hallway. "What's up there?" I asked, pointing up the stairs to the fourth floor.

"When he said look around, I don't think he meant his bedroom."

"I need the ladies'."

"There's one right down there, beyond the elevator. I'll see you downstairs. Save you a place."

Given all the booze flowing, I knew it wouldn't be long before someone else appeared. In fact, she passed Hal on his way down the stairs, a good, stout matron wedged into a corset that had taken her breath away by the time she reached me. I let her have the bathroom, and continued to the fourth floor, pretending to be looking for another. If I was caught there, I had an excuse.

Overlooking the rear garden was what I assumed was George's bedroom suite, full of heavy, masculine furniture. Two other suites occupied the rest of the floor. There was no one around, so I went into each, investigating only enough to determine that, if either had been Hazel's, there was no outward sign remaining.

I kept going up. On the fifth floor, I found more bedrooms, their doors all closed, which didn't stop me from looking. The sixth floor was tucked beneath the roof, with a lower ceiling, more like an attic. There was a small apartment. Mr. Hawthorne's, I presumed. At the end of the short hallway, a set of steep, narrow stairs led to the bolted door to the roof.

On the opposite side of the hall were two doors. I tried the first: locked. I pulled my picks out of my girdle, took care of that impediment, and felt for the light switch. It was an older one, with push buttons for on and off. Pushing the top one revealed a sizeable storage room, lined on three sides with shelves containing hundreds of transcriptions, each record in its own pepper-colored cardboard sleeve, labeled at the top right corner. There appeared to be a set for each *Love Always* and *Adam Drake* show ever done. Along the fourth wall ran a row of filing cabinets labeled to indicate that they contained copies of all the scripts.

I turned off the light and relocked the door. The other door was not locked. It was even larger, the standard sort of attic, only dust-free: trunks and boxes of the stuff of Morris and Ethel Keane's lifetimes and the memorabilia of a radio pioneer. A box receiver set, probably one of the first Morris Keane made, nothing more than a couple of tubes, a battery and a headset. Who could have guessed that such a thing would turn into one of the biggest industries in the country? There were two old consoles, as well, the next step in Morris Keane's fortune, both only slightly less ornate than the one that had been in the office reception room. Beside them, a rolling turntable cabinet, an early version of what Mash used on the *Adam Drake* broadcasts. On a shelf nearby sat two compact radios, the attempts of radio makers to save their businesses during the Depression by manufacturing smaller, cheaper models. Depression radios, they were called.

I took the elevator down to the first floor, coming out underneath the stairs. In the dining room, the chafing dishes steamed, but no one was there. I needed to talk to Adora Watson, but I didn't see a door. How did one get to the kitchen?

"Well, hello, there," Henry Keane said. He was still in his coat and hat; he must have used his key, as I hadn't heard a bell. He gave my body a close shave with his eyes.

I said. "I was admiring your parents' house."

"My brother's house," he corrected me casually, but there was a thread of bitterness running through it. "Would you like a little tour? We could get to know each other a little better." He moved closer. "Why don't you take off the glasses, just for tonight? Let us see those eyes."

"Well, then I couldn't see you," I said, matter of factly, but it was a mistake. He took it for flirtation. I had the feeling, however, that whatever I said, Henry Keane would take it for flirtation.

He took another step, and slipped his hand onto my waist.

"Henry."

"Come on, you're a long way from Los Angeles. New York doesn't have to be a lonely town."

He slid the hand down onto my hip.

"Gosh, Henry, I'm not that kind of girl," I said lightly, as lightly as I could when I wanted to slap his face. I picked his hand off me by the cuff.

Peter had once roughed up a guy just for looking at me the wrong way. The image of what he would do to Henry Keane if he were here right now—and we weren't trying to solve a killing—cheered me up considerably.

The butler came out of a door neatly concealed in the far wall, carrying a tray of wine bottles, which he set on the sideboard. "We'll be starting dinner now, Mr. Keane. May I take your coat?"

"Thanks," Henry said, "I'll take care of it." He gave me a wink, and went off. The butler followed, to tell the guests that dinner was ready.

The second they were out of the room, I slipped through the door and found myself in a butler's pantry, with a sideboard set in front of a large dumbwaiter. You'd need a big one in a house like this, to take food up from the kitchen—not to mention guests' luggage and other heavy or awkward items—to every other floor. At the other end of the pantry, a door led to a dog-legged stairwell. I went down into the kitchen.

At the sink under the windows that looked up to the front pavement, a tall, thin Negro woman washed glasses. She appeared to be the only one in the room. She didn't hear me; a small radio played softly beside her. Across from the stairs was a door. As I put my hand out for the knob, it opened. Adora came out and jumped.

"Oh, law!" she exclaimed. "You scared me."

"I'm sorry."

"This isn't a good time for questions, Mrs. Atwill. I'm busy."

"Tanner. They think my name is Tanner. Just one. The papers that the children were going through, do you have any idea what became of them?"

"Why?"

"They might give us a lead."

"You want me to help you look through their private things, look for dirt on them."

"No."

"Yes, you do. I want to see the right man punished, but I know it wasn't Mr. George or Mr. Henry, and I won't help you sneak around Mr. George's house. Let me tell you the difference between the Keanes and other people. My friend, Olive." She nodded toward the woman at the sink. "When the man she worked for every day for twenty years died, his children asked her to serve at the wake. When Mr. Keane died, when Miss Hazel died, we were guests. Excuse me, I have work to do." She went off to the front of the kitchen.

I stood there for a moment, but nothing would change her mind. Not tonight, anyway. I had a houseful of suspects. Maybe I should go take a look at them.

Hal was waiting in the buffet line, holding a plate for me, which I loaded with lobster thermidor, then we rejoined Eileen and Sophie, who had settled down on the settee in the corner of the living room. Karen had arrived and was arranging herself on the chair next to the ottoman, showing off a sea-green dress and plenty of cleavage. She pointedly didn't look at Sky, who had been pinned to the mantle by a gushing woman covered in emeralds. I took the ottoman and Hal sat on the floor beside me.

Ruth and several of the supporting actors from *Adam Drake* had settled in the other corner, with their food on the rug, like a picnic. Josh and some eager-looking young men, probably fellow copywriters from his days at the ad agency, stood by the bar with fresh drinks and no food. Bar sat by the fireplace and had acquired a plate and a stern-looking couple, who talked continually, in tandem, one speaking while the other chewed.

Jeannie and Marty came in, carrying their plates, and I waved them over to join us. Until tonight, I had never seen them standing up, had never seen them walking. Marty had a pronounced limp, which tossed her to the right, that leg shorter than the other. Her long black evening skirt concealed her crippled leg.

Neither Eileen nor Sophie mentioned their meetings that day with Peter, which was just as well, as it might make the others cautious in what they said tonight. I took a breath and started the small talk. I complimented Karen on her dress, then said, "I didn't expect to see so many people here from the sponsor."

"The rich like to show up at these things, rub elbows with people who've actually had a creative thought once or twice. It makes them feel like they're more than—what do you call them?—the fish that hitch rides on other fish?"

"Pilot fish."

"That's a great name." Karen laughed. "Makes them sound like they're actually doing something."

"Do I detect a little socialist sentiment?" I asked.

"Honey," Sophie said, "you can't swing a cat in this town without hitting a lefty."

"The sponsors must find the political discussions stimulating."

Karen said, "They think we're quaint. Nobody takes artists seriously."

"Miss Dunn?" said a voice behind me.

I turned and nearly toppled off my seat. Doctor Lawrence Clayton stood there, smiling down at Karen.

CHAPTER 18

He said, "I saw your production of *Glass Spindle* last month. Your company's doing excellent work."

"Thank you. Meet my friend, Mabel Tanner. She's a new writer on the show. This is Doctor Clayton, one of our patrons."

A frown formed between his blue eyes. "Have we met?"

"I haven't been in New York long."

He stared at me for another moment. I kept looking at him, smiling. There was nothing else I could do.

"I understand that Ruth is a gifted playwright," I said. "She's just over there."

"Good. I'd like to say hello."

Karen said, "We'll be doing her new play in the spring."

"I'm looking forward to it." He turned to me. "Good to meet you, Miss. . . ."

"Call me Mabel," I said.

The second he was out of earshot, Eileen said, "What's Bar doing?"

He was listening to the same couple, but watching Clayton. His expression didn't look friendly.

"What's going on?" I asked.

Eileen said, "Hazel was seeing Lawrence Clayton, after she separated from Bar. Henry probably invited him. You know how he likes to needle Bar. George has more tact."

Jeannie added eagerly, "He's the man who saw Mr. Cupp outside Hazel's office."

"And damned lucky for Willa he did," Karen said.

I said, "Surely, no one would think she did it."

"She and her mother got a lot of money in the will, I heard," Eileen said.

"But it would be crazy for her to do it, where she'd be the only suspect."

Hal said, "I hope this insurance detective isn't going to cause her trouble."

"This isn't the South," I said.

Sophie scoffed, "Sweetie, everywhere in this country is the South."

George appeared at Clayton's elbow, greeted him warmly, and guided him from the room. Maybe Henry had invited Clayton to needle his brother as much as Bar.

Karen said, "Hazel was kidding herself. He's one of those guys who keeps a half dozen well-heeled women on the line, then marries some heiress half his age."

I thought about the young woman he had been with at Zack Eisler's party. "How did Hazel meet him?" I asked.

"He came to a benefit we had at the theater before Christmas," Karen said. "From the moment he saw her, he was giving her the full treatment. I think they knew each other before. A couple of months later, she and Bar had split up."

I chewed on that with the rest of my lobster.

After eating, most of the sponsors left—dinner, a couple of drinks and they were off to the nightclubs. George invited the remaining men up to the billiard room for cigars and brandy. Half the women took cigarettes from the silver boxes scattered around the room, and it didn't take long for me to need some air.

The rear garden was empty, still, and well-painted in moonlight. In the far corner stood a small arbor, covered in bare, twisted fingers of grapevines. I dipped inside it and sat down on one of the benches. I should just go home and not push my luck. How much information was I likely to get, with one eye out for Clayton all night?

A shadow fell across my feet. Jeannie appeared at the end of the arbor. "Hi," she said.

Marty was right behind her. "We don't want to bother you."

"You're not. Sit down."

"See, I told you," Jeannie said to Marty, taking a seat while Marty remained standing at the edge of the arbor. "I knew it would be okay."

I said, "I was getting out of the smoke."

"I made Marty come with me. Of course, she might have anyway. I've had a glass of champagne, and she's keeping an eye on me."

"Her parents don't let her go out on her own, so now she wants to try everything," Marty observed, with the certainty one can only have under the age of twenty-one. "She doesn't have much judgment yet."

"I do, too," Jeannie protested.

Before Marty could retort, I asked, "Have you known each other long?"

"Most of our lives," Jeannie offered. "We went to the same Catholic school, and Marty spent a lot of time at our house."

Marty said, "Jeannie's mother grew up at Saint Katherine's too, so she knew what it was like."

"Was it bad?" I asked.

"I meant what it's like to be an orphan. That's why Jeannie brags on me so much."

"I don't," Jeannie stated.

"You do. About my typing."

"Well, you're very good."

"That's not the point. You brag on me."

I said, "It does sound as if Hazel sought you out to come work for her."

Marty shrugged. "She was nice to all the girls at the orphanage."

I expected Jeannie to contradict her, but she was staring at the ground. There was silence.

"Is there something you wanted to talk to me about?" I asked.

"I'm not sure." Jeannie was silent again.

I glanced at Marty, who said, "She only just told me. She's had a glass of champagne."

"It's not the champagne," Jeannie asserted, and turned back to me. "I think maybe I should tell someone, and you're new here. You weren't here when it happened."

I was proud of the way my voice stayed level. "You mean the murder? Is it something you should tell the police?"

She stared at me, alarmed.

Marty said, "You won't catch Jeannie Devine talking to the police. Her father says when you're Irish, you either hate the cops or become one."

"I see." I waited.

Jeannie said, "Maybe I could tell you, and you could help me decide what to do, whether it matters."

"Of course."

Marty said, "I think she should tell her mother first before she talks to anyone else."

I hated having to agree, but saying anything else would make me sound like exactly what I was, far too interested. "Let me give you my phone number. Call me tomorrow after you've talked to her. If you know anything, anything at all, that might help prove who killed Miss Keane, you should tell someone."

"That's what I thought," she said softly. Her lips were chattering. Nerves or cold, she needed to go back inside.

"Let's go find some coffee," I said.

Desserts, a silver coffee urn, cups, crystal decanters and

brandy glasses had been set out on the dining table. When we had poured ourselves some coffee—and the girls had each taken a slice of cake—we went back upstairs. I didn't want to risk running into Clayton, so I suggested that we give the elevator a try, just for fun. I let them off on the second floor, telling them that I needed to go on up to find a powder room, which I didn't.

In case Clayton was with George and the other men in the billiard room, I went on to the fourth to think. Was there any way to get Jeannie to talk to Peter? Did she know anything worth talking about? As I opened the elevator door, I heard a man's voice on the stairs above me. "Oh, come on, honey." There was more petulance than pleading in it.

"Not here," a woman's voice protested, a bit blurrily.

"Then let's go on up, there's plenty of places. How about the roof? You'll like the view."

"It's cold."

"I'll keep you warm. Come on."

"I don't know. I think I need to sit down a second."

I followed the voices, and found Sky Donovan and Lola Staton sitting on the steps to the sixth floor. He had a drink in one hand. With the other, he was sliding her skirt above her knees.

"Hi," she said cheerily when she saw me, and waved even though I wasn't five feet away. Sky removed his hand.

"Hi, yourself," I said. "Nice party. I was headed up to the roof. Someone told me the view was great."

They looked at each other. She said, "I think I better go back down." She stood up and toddled off.

"No, don't go," Sky entreated, jumping up. "Lola!"

I laid my hand on his shoulder and whispered, "Don't do anything foolish. You don't want Henry to change his mind about Hollywood."

"Who told you I was going to Hollywood?"

"I heard you were getting a screen test. Sounds exciting." I took Lola's place.

He remained standing, eyeing me cautiously. "My agent's got things lined up."

"Where?"

"MGM."

"I know some people at Marathon."

"You do?" He was suddenly forgiving of my interference.

"I could give them a call, but don't tell anyone else, all right? Or everyone will want me to make calls."

"Oh, sure. Sure. Our secret." He dropped back onto the step. "Our secret."

"Are you coming to the next writers meeting?" I asked. "I understand that you and Karen usually come."

"Bar's not interested in what we have to say."

"I'm sorry to hear that. We had a short meeting the other day. Of course, what we mostly talked about was that detective, the one who's working for the insurance company."

"Yeah, he wants to talk to me."

"As long as you weren't a beneficiary," I said, lightly, "there's nothing to worry about."

He snorted. "Yeah, I can see her leaving me money."

I made an interested, yet ingenuous face.

He took a long pull on his drink. "I haven't been in the business that long. She tried to take advantage of me."

"I wouldn't think that happens much." I gave him an admiring little smile.

"They think they're holding all the cards. When I signed, Karen made—I made sure I wasn't locked in, in case I got a call from Hollywood."

I nodded, encouragingly.

"Last year, a casting agent at MGM called Hazel to get my agent's name. She told him not to bother, I was under a long-term contract. She lied to him. I could have been out there last summer. I didn't even know about it. Meanwhile, she gets me to sign a two-year contract."

"You must have been furious when you found out."

"She said it didn't make any difference. They give hundreds of screen tests every week. I was better off in radio. She tricked me, then tells me I'm better off. I told her I'd sue her, and she said go ahead. I had a contract, so Hollywood wouldn't touch me. A lawsuit would take years, and the casting guy wouldn't testify. She said I was better off in radio. She kept saying that. I could have killed—" He snapped his mouth shut.

I patted him on the arm. "It's okay. People say that kind of thing all the time. It doesn't mean anything. Of course," I said with a laugh, "I wouldn't say it to the detective."

He waved the glass dismissively. Fortunately, it was empty. "I don't have to talk to him. My lawyer said so."

"You don't want anyone saying you were the only one who wouldn't talk, especially since you're going out for the test. My friends—my friends out in Hollywood—say this killing's getting a lot of publicity out there. All you have to do is tell him where you were."

"Karen was in one of her moods. I wanted to go over to her place that night, but she said no."

"So you went home?"

"She called about eleven, to see how I was. But I guess that's not an alibi." He stood up. "You want a drink?"

"I'm fine. I think I'll just sit here for a while, finish my coffee, and enjoy the quiet."

"Don't forget your promise."

"I won't."

Sky had no alibi, and he had a motive. With Hazel out of the way, he had a much better chance of talking Henry or Bar into letting him out of his contract. According to Alletter, the night watchman, Sky witnessed Hazel's fight with Cupp. And he was at the going-away party, so he had the opportunity to steal the weapons. And maybe the reason the killer was still in Hazel's office at nine-thirty was that he didn't know the office routine quite as well as the people who worked there every day.

How much did Karen know? Maybe I should find her and see how she was reacting to his flagrant pursuit of Lola. Maybe something would slip out.

As I reached the third-floor landing, I heard Karen's voice at the end of the hallway. "Three spades."

"Double," Josh said.

In the small sitting room, I found a team of Josh and Sophie playing Karen and Eileen. The other bridge tables were empty, cluttered with cards and empty glasses and cups. Josh led and Eileen started laying down her dummy hand.

In the window seat, Jeannie sat with Hal, staring into a crème de menthe. "I think I liked the chocolate better."

"Crème de cacao," he said.

"Cuh-cow?"

"That's right."

"Cuh. Cow. I liked that better."

Marty appeared in the doorway to the billiard room, a cue in her hand, a stern look on her face. "Jeannie, we have to leave soon. Do you want to play?"

"Oh, yes," she replied eagerly, then said to me, "My mother would never let me near a pool hall. Mash is going to teach us how to play." With her crème de menthe, she scurried, mostly in a straight line, to the billiard room.

"She's cute," Hal said.

"She's seventeen."

"Eighteen, and damned proud of it."

I deposited my cup on a nearby table and sat down beside him.

"What have you been up to?" he asked.

"Not as much as you." Then I dropped my voice, so Karen wouldn't hear. "I've been talking to Sky and Lola."

"In the same place."

"Not anymore."

"Karen could see Hazel was kidding herself about that doctor, but she hangs onto Sky. Why do women like men who treat them bad?"

"Men, of course, always go for the good girl."

He chuckled, then his gaze slid over my shoulder, down into the garden. "Well, well, what have we here?"

I turned to see Bar come out of the arbor. Immediately, Hal took my arm and lifted me off the window seat and against the wall. He fingered the drapes away from the outer edge of the window, so we could see into the garden without being seen ourselves.

Bar stood at the arbor entrance, lighting a cigarette. He tossed a glance at all the windows, then put his lighter back into his trousers and went into the house.

"What are you looking at?"

"A little cold for an outdoor smoke, wouldn't you say?"

"I was out there earlier this evening. By myself. You have an evil mind."

"You bet. I saw two shadows before he came out."

"So he's having a smoke with someone who—"

"Look. There it is again." Quickly, he closed the drapes, leaving a narrow gap in them. We moved in front of them, pretending to talk, but watching the garden.

Finally someone appeared. The woman smoothed her hair and took a step into the moonlight. She looked down at her dress, then stepped back into the arbor. When she came back out, the bodice was straight again.

Ruth Linden.

Hal said, "What the hell?"

"I thought they didn't even like each other."

"I'd say parts of them get along fine. I'd like to be a fly on the wall when they sober up."

In the billiard room, Jeannie squealed in delight. Hal took himself off to watch. I sought refuge up on the fourth floor, in a bedroom at the front of the house, full of peach-colored silk. I stared out the window down into 80th Street.

Bar and Ruth. I didn't think this was any alcohol-induced onetime encounter, as Hal believed. The two of them accidentally turned up in the arbor at the same time and were so overcome by champagne and moonlight that they immediately had to unfasten her dress? The question was whether one of them—or both—decided to get Bar out of his marriage while keeping Hazel's money. Could he be secretly married to Ruth, and that was why Hazel was asking questions about bigamy?

Someone came into the room. I felt another body behind me before I heard the door close. Then there were brisk steps, coming fast. A hand gripped my arm and slung me around.

"Who are you?" Lawrence Clayton demanded.

I jerked my arm free and backed away from him, further into the room. He kept coming at me. Stunned, I kept backing up.

"I know where I saw you," he snarled. "You were at Zack Eisler's. You were there with that detective. Who are you?"

I bumped into something solid, the tall poster at the foot of the bed. Suddenly, I had an image of one of those heroines in movie melodramas, trapped by the maniac killer, raising her fists to her temples and screaming. Hollywood thought that was what women did when they were frightened.

Me, I shove the maniac in the chest.

"Get the hell away from me."

"You were with that detective."

"He has a gun, and he knows how to use it, so don't get any ideas."

"What are you doing here?"

"I was invited."

"Don't fuck with me."

"Nice language, doc. You'd look a lot tougher if you weren't sweating."

He yanked his handkerchief from his trouser pocket and blotted his tan. "Do George and Henry know what you're up to?"

"They're big boys. They can take care of themselves. Besides, they have alibis."

"What does that mean?"

"We only have your word that you saw anyone in that hallway."

"I picked him out of a lineup!"

"You'd seen him working in the building. You saw him at the going-away party. You picked out the first man who looked familiar."

"If you ever repeat that, I'll sue you for—"

"Yeah, yeah, for everything I have, everything I'll ever have. I'm not scared of you, doc."

"Stop calling me that!"

"All right. Doctor. What are you afraid I'm going to find out?"

"He did it. He threatened her. It was his wrench, his knife. They found his coveralls."

"Did the cops tell you that?"

"You stay away from me or I'll have you arrested."

"For what? You know, maybe it's time to go have a talk with George and Henry."

"What?"

"Let's go." I pushed past him and strode to the door.

He was rooted to the spot, staring at me.

"Come on," I said. "Let's go see what they think about your story. Maybe I can act it out for them. How does this sound?" I grabbed the doorknob. "I'm in the hallway outside Hazel's office. I'm the killer, closing the door. If I'm turned this way, toward you, I see you, doc, and I run. The killer didn't." I grabbed the knob with the other hand. "If I turn around, and close the door the other way, with my back to you, I can't see you, but the trouble is, you can't see me either. The best you get is a profile for maybe, maybe two seconds. Two seconds of a man in a cap you'd never seen before in your life." I turned the knob. "Let's go."

"Wait!"

"Was he facing you, or turned away?"

"He threatened her. They have his prints."

"On his own wrench and his own knife."

"They have his coveralls."

"They were old ones, discarded a month ago."

"You're lying."

"Why do you care, if you saw him?"

"I don't have to talk to you!"

"Why do you care? Answer me!" Then suddenly, it was crystal clear. "You didn't see him."

"I did!"

"You don't have any idea who you saw in that hallway. You saw him with the police, before the lineup. That's why you picked him out. They told you they had the killer, that he'd threatened her, that they had his prints, his coveralls. They told you they had a case. So you walked into that lineup room and picked him out for them. Good work. You probably nailed an innocent man."

"You're lying! He killed her! It couldn't be anyone else!"

"How about you? Hazel was having second thoughts about you. Did she find out about your little sideline? A devout Catholic, who discovers her boyfriend's an abortionist."

"How dare you!"

"Let's go see what her brothers think about you as a suspect!"

"No!"

"Then keep your mouth shut. We're looking for the killer, and you better let us do it. Otherwise, we'll hire Nestor Cupp the best lawyer money can buy, and he'll make you look like the killer on every front page of every paper in the country. You can kiss your career good-bye. Think it over."

I threw open the door with a nice flourish, I thought, and sailed out. But in the fifteen feet to the stairs, my legs started shaking so badly, I had to grip the railing. I kept going, flight after wobbly flight, then straight through the dining room and down to the kitchen. Nathan Mitchell was polishing glasses and putting them away into a cupboard near the stairs.

"Are you alone?" I asked.

"Yes. What's up?"

"Clayton's upstairs."

"I saw him."

"He knows I'm working with Peter. He threatened to tell George and Henry, so I threatened to tell them that he couldn't possibly have seen Cupp. It scared him." I took a breath. "I think I know why you keep pointing us at the detectives' reports. Clayton saw Cupp before the lineup."

He started drying his hands on the towel and watched himself do it.

I said, "Did you see it happen, or just suspect it did?"

He kept watching the towel. "That night, after I called the Keanes to tell them what had happened, I went down to the precinct. I was sitting on a bench at the top of the stairs. The doctor was there, pacing the hall. Then I saw the detectives bring a man up. I'd never seen him before. Later I found out it was Cupp. They went around the corner. I looked down at the other end of the hallway. The doctor was standing there. I don't know how much he saw."

I said, "The detectives told him they had a better case than they had, so he decided to help them out by picking out the man he'd seen with them. I have to tell Peter."

"I told them the doctor might have seen the suspect. That's all I could do. Any story they tell now won't match mine, and I'm not going against them. It wouldn't make any difference. But the preliminary report might still be around. Take a look at what he told the detectives when they first arrived on the scene, how much he saw of the man in the hallway."

The door opened from the butler's pantry and Adora called down the stairs, urgently, "Nathan?"

"What is it, mom?" he said, and took a few steps up toward her.

"I need to find Mrs. Atwill. Do you know where she is?"

"I'm here," I said and stepped to the foot of the stairs.

"I've seen her," she said. "She's here."

"Who?"

"The woman who was seeing Mr. Morris before he died, his fiancée. She's here. I saw her just now when I took some desserts up to the drawing room."

"Show me."

Back upstairs, she whispered, "She's standing by the windows, talking to Mr. Benjamin. I didn't recognize her at first. She's colored her hair and she's gained some weight, but that's her. In the black dress."

"Are you sure?" It sort of caught in my throat.

"Yes. Do you know her?"

"It's Eileen Walters."

Chapter 19

The Fulton Fish Market was the perfect meeting place: we weren't likely to run into anyone we knew. In fact, given that it was the weekend, we were unlikely to run into almost anyone. Further down South Street, some juke joints were jumping, but our block was deserted.

The narrow, flat-fronted buildings that housed the wholesalers were locked, their loading docks shuttered. No trucks would pull up beneath their tin awnings today. No boats would dock at the piers across South Street to unload their catches in huge metal scoops to be iced down in barrels and boxes. No "taximen" would then haul those away on carts into the wholesalers or on down to the refrigerated railcars waiting at Pier 21, to be floated down the coast on barges or shipped inland on the B&O.

Still, the night smelled of fish, and of creosote and the inky, oily water of the East River.

The Meyers Hotel sat on the corner of Fulton and South Street. In another twenty-four hours, its restaurant would be packed with dockworkers, fishermen and Teamsters. At midnight on a Saturday night, it was practically empty.

Peter sat in a booth at the rear, a plate of eggs in front of him, smacking a bottle of ketchup on the bottom. I slid into the booth.

"Clayton saw Cupp before the lineup," I announced triumphantly, then went on, a little breathless in my magnificence. "He saw Cupp at the precinct before the lineup. Nathan

Mitchell told me. He saw Cupp."

"Yeah," Peter said and went back to slapping the bottle around.

"What?" I said, loudly enough to draw a look from the guys in the booth across from us, and both of them looked like the kind of guys who usually minded their own business. "Did you hear me?" I demanded, lower.

"It had to be that. After I saw the office layout up close, I figured there was no way he'd made an ID in the hallway."

I snatched the bottle out of his hand, smacked the "57" at the base of the neck, and ketchup smothered his eggs.

"Thanks," he said.

"No trouble."

The waitress came over, a hennaed honey with a face as hard as the neighborhood. In my mood, I was a harsh judge.

She swung one hip to the right and locked a fist on it. "What you want?" she asked me.

"A new partner," I replied.

"Know what you mean," she said.

"Maybe a cup of tea."

"Got a billy club under the counter, you need it." She went off.

Peter grinned and shook ketchup off his toast. "After a few years in this job, you train yourself not to look too excited when you hear something. Ninety percent of the stuff you get turns out to be worthless. But it's nice to have Nathan Mitchell's word," he offered, my consolation prize.

"He won't go against the detective. He said we have to find the preliminary report, see what Clayton said about the guy in the hall."

"We're working on it. How'd you get Mitchell to talk?"

I told him about my confrontation with Clayton. He said, "Damn it, I never thought they'd invite him."

"Do you think he'll keep his mouth shut?" I said.

"We can't count on it."

"I can't leave *Adam Drake* now. People are starting to talk to me."

He sliced into his rosy eggs. "What are they saying?"

I waited till he brought a forkful to his mouth before I said, "I found Rachel." He stabbed himself in the lip. I pick my own consolation prizes. "Eileen Walters." I told him how Adora had identified her. "She didn't notice her at Hazel's funeral or Morris Keane's, but there would've been hundreds of people there, and Eileen's changed her appearance. I take it she didn't mention her engagement to Morris Keane when you talked to her this afternoon."

"It didn't come up. Go on, what else?"

The waitress brought the tea, and gave Peter the hard eye before she left. I dipped my tea bag and told him about Ruth and Bar's tryst in the arbor, Sky's grudge over his contract and the better chance he'd had of getting permission to go out for the screen test if it were up to Henry instead of Hazel, and that those might be Karen's motives as well, then about Jeannie's request for a consultation.

He considered it all for a moment before he said, "I think I'll turn in my license. Want some eggs?"

"No, thanks," I said smugly. "I've had lobster thermidor." I set my tea bag on the saucer.

"If you don't hear from Jeannie by noon, call her."

I winced. "I forgot to get her number."

He slid his notebook across to me. "It's in there. Page ten or eleven."

"Did you get anything from those long-distance phone lists I gave you?"

"A couple of possibilities."

"Such as?" I picked up my cup.

"Josh Connally's an imposter."

The tea sloshed onto the table.

"Maybe I'll keep the license." He took a bite and chewed with satisfaction.

"Okay, spill it."

"You know he used to work for D.W. Davis, the ad agency, before he went to *Adam Drake*. Well, they had a record of what he claimed to have done before they hired him."

"And how did you get them to give it to you?"

"These days, you pretend to be the War Department trying to help a veteran, you can find out anything you want. He told the ad agency that he taught literature at the Martin School in Charleston, South Carolina, before coming to New York."

"Is that very high-toned?"

"The highest." He picked up a book from the seat beside him and handed it to me, a dark-blue leather-bound volume. The Martin School 1938. "Turn to page twelve."

On it were the faculty pictures of the English Department. In the second row, at the end: Joshua Connally, English Literature. His curly hair was already receding.

But it was not our Josh.

"Try History," Peter said.

On page fifteen, I found a half dozen men in ill-fitting suits gathered behind a writing table in what I assumed was the school library: bookcases and a stone fireplace with a solemn portrait above it of someone important to the Martin School, but not important enough to be in the Great Hall. At the edge of the group, wearing a bow tie and sweater-vest beneath his suit jacket was our Josh. "Robert Worth Estes," I read. "Three names. Sounds like family money."

"He couldn't have much, if he's teaching prep school."

I said, "Someone at the office made long-distance calls to Charleston around the time Hazel was double-checking the references. She must have found out he was a phony. Where's the real Connally?"

"He joined the Canadian Air Force in thirty-nine."

"He's dead?"

"Try not to jump to conclusions. This part of it has a happy ending. He married an English girl and lives over there. About the same time that the real Connally signed up, Robert Worth Estes came to New York and started tutoring, using Connally's name. The real Connally was out of touch. Estes could bluff his way through any questions the parents had."

"What's the part with the *un*happy ending?"

Peter pulled an envelope from the inside pocket of his jacket and handed me the contents. First, a photocopy of an editorial in the *Charleston Evening Post* dated September 5, 1939, which contained the editor's sincere wishes for the school's continued success in training the finest young men of the state to leadership. Clipped to it was a story from the same paper, dated six months earlier, about the conclusion of an investigation by Martin School authorities and the Charleston district attorney into the misbehavior of three—and the article stressed only three—teachers, who had apparently been allowing some senior boys to drink and break curfew.

"A district attorney gets involved because some teenagers are drinking and staying up late? I take it the teachers were encouraging the boys to do other things as well."

"You Hollywood people don't shock easily, do you?"

"I've heard worse." I'd heard lots worse, about kindly, affable, eager-fingered producers who were fond of meeting late at night with the little boys and girls under contract to their studios, and about the parents who let them do it.

Peter went on. "I called up Betts out in LA."

"You got the assistant DA for the city of Los Angeles to work for you?"

"Could be he thinks he owes me something for keeping my mouth shut about part of what happened out there last summer. He got the DA in Charleston to send those articles to me over the wire, and the real story behind them."

"The parents must have been out for blood."

"So was the school, but you don't stay in business dragging that kind of thing into court. It was hushed up, as long as the teachers agreed to get the hell out of South Carolina."

"And one of them came to New York and took a new name."

"Which worked out fine until Hazel Keane was told to verify her employees' politics. The Martin School headmaster said when she wrote to him to check on Connally's credentials, he told her Connally was in England. Then, about a week later, he got a phone call from the parents of one of the boys who'd been involved, complaining that a private detective was asking questions about Estes. Hazel Keane hired somebody."

"But our fake Josh is still working at *Drake*."

"Then I think we've got a pretty good idea what he was after in that file cabinet."

"I don't."

"The resignation letter Hazel Keane made him sign. She didn't want a scandal."

"But if he's the killer, why didn't he search the files in her office the night he did it?"

"No key. Not everybody's as good with a lock pick as you are. He wouldn't want to linger in that room and make noise breaking into the cabinets."

"You think he did it?"

"I never make up my mind till you tell me who the killer is. The insurance company won't let me play this forever. We've got a week, two at the most."

"When they tell you it's over, I'll start writing checks."

"When they tell me it's over, it's over. Unless I go to work for

Cupp's lawyer, and, if I do, reporters will find out who I am, and you'll be out of *Adam Drake* in two minutes."

"So, what do we do?"

"We could try shaking things up. Roll the dice and see if we can scare the killer. Make him think I'm getting close."

"What would you do to shake things up?"

"It's what *you* would do."

Jeannie called at nine. I was lying with my head stuffed into the pillow of my lonely single bed. I groped for the receiver and tried to find my ear with it.

"Did I wake you?" she said.

"Old folks need a lot of sleep." She giggled. I said, "Have you told your mother about wanting to talk to me?"

"She said it was okay, but she wants to be there."

"Of course." I said a silent thank-you to Jeannie's mother, and fumbled into the top drawer of the nightstand for a pencil and pad of paper. "Give me the address." She did. "Would two o'clock be all right?"

She agreed. We said good-bye. I pulled open the lower, deeper drawer, shut the telephone inside it, and went back to sleep.

Eighty-Sixth and Lexington was the heart of Little Germany, the streets lined with German pastry shops, book stores, marzipan shops, restaurants and brauhauses, many decorated in mock-Bavarian, with facades made to look like snow-covered chalets. Every now and then, the Irish history of the neighborhood poked through: Flannery's Bar or Hanratty's Haberdashery.

Marty sat on the stoop of 257 East 88th and looked as if she might have been to church. Her hat and what I could see of her cranberry-colored dress appeared fancier than what she'd normally wear. We climbed five flights of stairs. Even with her limp, she had to hold her pace for me. Old people certainly need more breath. Along the way, she gave me a short history of the neighborhood.

"When Jeannie's grandparents, her father's people, the Devines, were growing up, it was mostly Irish. Now, it's mostly German. Have you ever heard of the *General Slocum*?"

"It was a boat that sank, wasn't it?"

"A ferry. A church from what used to be Little Germany, down on the Lower East Side, hired it to take some people to a picnic, but it caught fire. A thousand people died, most of them women and children. The people who were left down there couldn't bear it. There were too many reminders, so they started moving away, up here mostly."

She knocked on a door. The woman who opened it wore a blue-checked cotton housedress and a chocolate cardigan with the sleeves pushed up. She was short and strongly built, with a plain, square face and thick black hair, shot with gray. Jeannie, I thought, must look like her father.

Then another woman appeared in the doorway to her right, even darker, like a well-tanned Spanish woman, or perhaps Mexican, given that her nose was a bit wider than most native Spaniards I'd seen. Her lively eyes and generous lips were Jeannie's eyes and lips. Her heavy black curls were gathered into a pink scarf at the nape of her neck, and she wore the sweater set that I'd seen on Jeannie the day I met her. "I'm Liz Devine, Jeannie's mother," she said. "This is Mrs. Cupp. This is her apartment."

Nestor Cupp's wife nodded an apprehensive greeting and looked uncertainly at her friend, who said to me, "Come on in, please. Marty, take her in and let her sit down."

Mrs. Devine took our coats, and, while she hung them up, I went with Marty into the living room, which was papered in deep-lavender irises as big as my hand. The armchair and sofa were both upholstered in dark-green tweed. Three hard chairs had been arranged in a row across from the sofa. Jeannie sat in one of them. On a fourth one, in the corner, sat a phonograph.

At the edge of the carpet stood a boy and girl of about eight, with dark, straight hair and serious faces, wearing matching blue corduroy robes and red corduroy slippers, a game of jacks at their feet.

"These are the twins, Delbert and Tansy," Mrs. Cupp said softly, in a heavy mountain accent. "They got a bit of cold today, so I'm keeping them inside."

"Hello," I said to them. They smiled shyly, then looked at the ground and said nothing.

Liz Devine said, "Jeannie, why don't you make us some tea? Would that be all right, May?"

Mrs. Cupp said, "Oh, now, I can do that."

"Let the girls. It'll give them something to do."

Jeannie and Marty went off into the kitchen. I sat down in the armchair. The other women took the sofa.

"May and I are friends," Liz explained. "Nothing's changed that. Jeannie told me she wanted to talk to you, that there might be something—"

Someone knocked on the door. Jeannie scurried to answer it, plumping her hair. A man came in and she brought him into the living room.

She said, "This is Mr. Winslow."

CHAPTER 20

Jeannie introduced the rest of us.

"I'm the private detective working for the insurance company," he said to me.

"Yes. I remember. I met you at the office on Friday."

"Are you really a detective?" Tansy asked. "Like in the movies?"

"Not much like the movies," Peter said, but he took out his license and showed it to both of them.

"You got a gun?" Delbert asked.

Peter said, "I own one."

"You ever shoot anybody?"

"That's enough, you two," Mrs. Cupp said. "Now go on to the back and play."

"Oh, maw!" they complained in unison.

"Go on. We have to talk."

With sighs of martyrdom, they gathered up their game and went off. Peter took one of the hard chairs. Reluctantly, Jeannie went back to the kitchen, carrying his coat and hat.

Liz explained, "Mr. Winslow called me a few days ago, and said that he wanted to talk to all the people who worked for Miss Keane, and that if Jeannie decided to talk to him, I'd be welcome to come with her. Then after what she told me last night, I thought we should invite him over."

"Liz says you might can help Nestor," Mrs. Cupp said to Peter, fighting to keep hope out of her voice.

"I'm working for the insurance company," Peter explained, frankly but gently. "They're only interested in making sure that they don't pay off the killer. So far, I haven't found any evidence to implicate one of the beneficiaries."

"Nestor didn't do it. He was here that night. He came home about nine. He goes to Finnerty's most nights, but he never stays past nine. The children were in bed, so they didn't see him, but he was here. That doctor is lying."

"He could be mistaken. Your husband's best shot is to cast doubt on that identification. If I find anything that would help, I'll give it to your husband's lawyer."

"You look at that doctor. You look at him good."

"I will. May I ask how you ended up in New York?"

"Nestor used to work in the mines, down in Harlan County, that's in Kentucky. He was foreman of the tipple. That's where they sort out the different parts of the coal. We was doing good, but there was an accident one day, and he hurt his back real bad dragging some of the men out. After that, he couldn't work much. Then the war come, and our Jimmy went overseas. Jimmy's my oldest. Twenty-two now, come January. One of the boys in his unit was from New York. His father hired men to work in some of the office buildings, to fix things up. Nestor could always fix anything. This boy—Pauly they called him— told Jimmy that Nestor should come on up and talk to his father. He did, and Mr. Grazzio gave him a job. Poor Mr. Grazzio. His Pauly was killed in Italy. I don't think he's ever going to get over it. That was almost three years ago now, that we come up here. Nestor was so glad to be working again. New York scared me a little at first, but things is so much better." She gestured at the room. "And the children get school just down the street."

"Where's Jimmy now?"

"Oh, he liked the army. He's a staff sergeant out in Fort Sill.

That's in Oklahoma." She stared down at her hands, her face puckering. "Nestor was so proud of him."

Jeannie and Marty brought in the tea on a tin tray. We took our cups and helped ourselves to sugar. Jeannie sat down next to Peter, and Marty took the last chair.

Peter said to Jeannie, "I understand that you knew Miss Keane before you came to work at *Adam Drake*."

She looked at him, her face suddenly pink. "A little, through Saint Kay's, but I didn't really get to know her till I started working there."

Marty said, "Hazel started a secretarial course at Saint Katherine's, the orphanage, after school. The one we had at school was awful, it didn't even teach stenography, so the school started sending students over to Saint Kay's. That's where Jeannie met her."

Jeannie said, "I wasn't as good a student as Marty. She graduated early, and started working at Bloomingdale's, but then Hazel called her and told her they had an opening at *Adam Drake*. I started there later, after I graduated."

"Hazel took an interest in the students," Marty said.

"Especially you," Jeannie said.

"She let you take the test twice."

Peter raised a hand, and they both immediately fell silent. He asked them about working at *Adam Drake*, and they went on to tell him, in tandem, everything they had told me. He listened attentively, as if it were the first time he'd heard any of it, then said to Jeannie, "Your mother told me that you might know something that would help, but if you'd rather talk to Mrs. Tanner, I'll understand."

I pressed my lips against the rim of my cup to hold down the smile. The way she was looking at him, she would have run off to the Casbah with him if he'd brought it up.

Jeannie and I were both saved by the sudden appearance of a

tow-headed baby in a yellow-flowered nightshirt, toddling happily from the hallway. His arms held high for balance, he careened toward me, grunting enthusiastically, and bounced into my knees. I set my cup down and laid my hand on his back for support. He giggled and grinned up wetly at me.

"I'm sorry," said Mrs. Cupp. "That's Orin." She called out to the back of the apartment, "Del, Tansy, how'd Orin get out of his crib?"

"Tansy let him out!" Delbert called back.

"Did not!" Tansy protested. "He wanted down!"

"He's all right here," I said, "if you don't mind." I picked him up and sat him in my lap. Contentedly, he stayed there, chewing on his fist.

I said to Jeannie, "Would you rather tell me first?"

"No, it's all right. I can talk to Mr. Winslow." She turned to him. "I was working late one day at the office."

"Let me have all the details. When was this?"

"The first part of July, not long after I started. I was typing a *Love Always* script, and the office was empty. It's like that late on summer days, everybody leaves early. There wasn't much to do, so Marty and I were taking turns leaving early, so one of us could ride the bus when it wasn't crammed full of people at rush hour. I was there, working on the script and . . . well, actually, I was coming back from the ladies' room, and I saw Hazel and Bar standing in her office door. I went back to my desk and started typing again, and later—I think it must have been about fifteen minutes—I heard them yelling. I couldn't tell what they were saying, just a word here and there."

Peter said, "Me, I would have been curious about what was going on."

"Well," she said, and flushed, "I did go out into the hall a little way. The door was closed, but I heard her say—and I heard this clearly—she said, 'You leave her alone, I mean it. If

226

you lay a finger on her, you'll pay.' I could barely hear him, but I did hear him say, 'You're out of your mind.' And something about being ruined. I'm pretty sure he said ruined. It didn't seem right to listen, so I went back to my desk. I didn't hear them leave, but when I finished an hour or so later, they were gone. Last night, at the party, everybody was talking about how Hazel had been seeing that doctor and I remembered hearing the fight. I guess Bar was seeing someone, too. I don't know if it means anything. Do you think it does?"

I thought it meant Hazel had found out about Bar and Ruth, and he denied it to save his job.

Marty's brows had edged into a frown and she pressed her lips together. I had been right. She had a crush on Bar. And Jeannie didn't know about it. I thought that must have been a hard secret to keep from a best friend.

"Did you mention this to anyone else?" Peter asked.

"I didn't even think about it until last night."

"One other question, if you don't mind. It's just a formality. I know you weren't beneficiaries. But could you tell me where you were the night Miss Keane was killed?"

Jeannie stared, but Marty sat up straight and said, "I was at home. My apartment's on West Twenty-Third. I got there about seven, after I ate dinner, and stayed in all night."

He turned to Jeannie.

"I was at home, too, reading in my room, listening to my radio."

"Thank you for your help," Peter said. "Thank you, Mrs. Devine. Do you think it would be possible for me to talk to Mrs. Cupp alone for a while?"

"Would that be all right with you, May?" Liz asked.

"I think it'd be best," Mrs. Cupp said.

I said good-bye and started to hand Orin to her. He picked that moment to throw his arms around my neck and give me a long, moist hug.

"He likes you," said Mrs. Cupp. "How many children do you have?"

"I don't have any." Not for lack of trying. Not for lack of wanting. I kissed Orin on his soft curls and handed him to his mother, who was polite enough not to look surprised by my answer.

"He took to Miss Keane, too, did Orin."

"Hazel Keane came here?" I said.

"There was some trouble at work. That's why the police say Nestor did this, but it was all settled. I told the police, but they didn't believe me. I called her after it happened, the argument she and Nestor had. I didn't think she'd even talk to me, but she did. I told her how Nestor didn't drink till he hurt his back, and how bad it hurt him sometimes. She came here, right here to the apartment, and we talked and she met the children. I told her how sorry I was about what had happened, and how much better things were for us now. She said she'd give him another chance, and she did. He didn't do this. That doctor's lying."

When we reached the sidewalk, Jeannie and Marty went along ahead, their heads together, probably discussing whether a private detective could make a good husband. I knew how they felt.

Liz said, "From the moment they saw each other, they've been friends. I was visiting the sisters at Saint Katherine's one day and had Jeannie with me. She wasn't much past two then. She pulled her hand out of mine and went right over to Marty. It was the sweetest thing you've ever seen. They're just like sisters, except they don't fight as much."

"Where did Marty get her name, being an orphan?"

"Martha, the nuns gave to her. She took Lubrano from an

old man and his wife who used to own a candy store not far from here, near Saint Kay's. They were always nice to the children."

"Saint Kay's is nearby?"

"A few blocks. Would you like to see it?"

We caught up with the girls and told them where we were going. They preferred to walk on over to the park and enjoy the Sunday afternoon. And their discussion, I was sure.

Saint Katherine's was five stories of maroon brick, with three ponderous basket-handle arches at the top of the steps leading to a portico and three doors. The stone lintel on the door to the right had Boys carved in it. The one on the left, Girls. Except for a statue of the saint above the center arch, there was no ornamentation. No money wasted. A solid, serious building of the late nineteenth century meant to do solid, serious work.

"That's where Marty and I grew up," Liz said.

I didn't say any of the obvious things, such as, it looked nice. It looked stifling. It did, however, appear to be in excellent repair, and I could hear the happy shouts of children playing in the yard behind it.

Liz went on, "I wanted to adopt Marty. Jamie, that's my husband, knew I'd like to have another little girl with all my boys, but we just couldn't manage it. You know what things were like back then. Worried every day whether your man would have a job at the end of it, but we found a nice couple for her. Then I found out no one could adopt her."

"What?"

"She had parents, one parent. Sister Luke had to tell me the truth when I told her we'd found Marty a family."

"How can that be?"

"Not all the children in Saint Kay's are orphans. Sometimes parents leave a child until they can afford to have him back, sometimes a mother's too ill to care for the child. Sometimes it's an unwed mother, and if the family is forgiving, the girl's parents will leave the child there for a while, then bring him home, pretending to have adopted him. It happens more than you'd suppose. Sometimes, the nuns will keep a child because there's still a chance the girl's young man will marry her. That's what it was for Marty. Sister Luke said she'd speak to the mother, but it didn't do any good. Selfish, nothing but selfish. Marty was almost three. If the young man was going to do what's right, he would have done it by then, even if he was in jail. The couple took another little girl, and then six months later, Marty caught polio."

"Does she know about her real mother?"

"She knows some of it. When she was ten, she found out about the couple somehow. I didn't want her to think that they'd changed their minds because she got sick. So I told her the truth. She took it very hard, knowing that if the mother had let her go, she could have had a family. She got into quite a bit of trouble at school for a while. They even caught her breaking into the records, trying to find out who her mother was. She made everyone call her Marty, which she still does. Maybe I did the wrong thing, but I didn't want her to think badly of that couple, that they didn't like her because she got crippled. I know what that's like, thinking no one could want you. Of course, for me, it was being so dark. This skin, this nose. Even today, but forty years ago . . . the names some of the kids used to call me. I never let my boys use that word, no matter what the other parents let their children say. Jamie's family gave him plenty of trouble when he married me, but they don't say anything now. He's the only one of their sons who's stayed out of trouble and out of the bottle." Suddenly, she flushed heavily. "Listen to me, talking like this to a total stranger. I can see why Jeannie and Marty came to you."

"I'm glad they felt they could trust me."

We walked on quietly for a moment, then she said, "What do you think of this man, this detective?"

"He seems to know what he's doing."

"I'll have to have a word with Jeannie, a man like that."

"She seemed taken with him."

"I couldn't blame her."

"No."

CHAPTER 21

The night turned cold. I woke up huddled under the covers. I fished my robe from the foot of the bed and snuggled into it before crawling out. I turned up the radiators, and, by the time I'd made coffee, they were clanking loudly, something I hoped they weren't planning to do at night.

It was my first day going into the office from the apartment, the first day taking the subway. I did fine, stuck my nickel into the turnstile slot, and squeezed onto the F-train at 14th Street at exactly eight-thirty.

I did fine, until I realized I was going downtown.

I wiggled out at Canal, dashed to the uptown side and had to wait through two trains before one arrived that I could stuff myself into. I popped out at Fifth Avenue, and made it to the office by nine-thirty.

Sophie raised an eyebrow.

"I went downtown on the subway by mistake."

"Train, if you want to sound like a New Yorker. What were you doing on the train? You get an apartment?"

"I need to give Mrs. Embert the address."

"Give it to me. I'll pass it on."

"Thanks." I gave her the phony address that Peter and I had agreed to. He didn't want anyone knowing where I was really living. I hadn't told him about Zack Eisler finding me. "I didn't get a chance to ask you Saturday night, how was your lunch with the detective?"

She raised her penciled brows. "Twenty-One, sweetie."

"Really?" I said, impressed.

"That was on the expense account, you can bet, although he was wearing a nice suit. Maybe there's more money in being a detective than I thought. Could be why Jeannie's got her eye on him. She and Marty were talking about him in the ladies'. I guess they had their interviews this weekend."

"Bet they didn't rate Twenty-One."

She grinned. "Maybe he likes older women."

"What was Marty's advice?"

"You know Marty. She's a tough one."

"Really?"

"You can't blame her. She's had a hard life. Raised in an orphanage, the polio and all. She's lucky Hazel took her under her wing. When she first came here, she could do the job, but she would have made Winnie Embert look like Little Miss Sunshine. Henry wanted to fire her, but Hazel wouldn't hear of it. She had a little talk with her, then a few months later, she arranged for Jeannie to come here."

"Arranged?"

"The girl who used to do that job, Hazel found her a better one, then she asked the school to send Jeannie over. Marty's been fine since." The PBX buzzed, and I let Sophie get back to work. I was late enough already. As I hung up my coat, I said hello to Jeannie and Marty, who boldly smiled and returned the greeting, despite Mrs. Embert's scowls.

On my desk was the draft of my script that the girls had typed on Friday. I took it to Ruth Linden.

"Will you have time?" I asked her.

"Sure, later this morning."

I left it on her desk and went along to Alton's office and stuck my head in. He didn't see me, his attention concentrated on an old leather-covered album sitting on his blotter. He smoothed his long fingers gently over the worn tooled rose on the cover. The expression on his face pressed at my heart. I backed out of the room and came in again, making more noise as I approached.

"We missed you Saturday," I said.

His warm smile was back in place. "You're very kind, young lady. I had plans for that night. Ballet tickets I'd had for some time. Besides, I don't sit on the floor these days, and I don't play bridge." I wondered if the house held too many memories of friends now gone.

"I play a mean game of rummy."

"As do I."

"Maybe we could play next time, and we won't sit on the floor."

"I would enjoy that."

"What a lovely album."

"Yes, that detective called," he said, as if that explained it. When he saw my frown, he chuckled. "No, I have not lost my mind. You'll find that, as you get older, your mind moves quickly from a thought to its genesis, and you will be surprised that young people cannot make that leap without explanation. That detective called and asked to meet with me. I started thinking about Hazel, then about Morris and Ethel, those were her parents. I found this album and thought I'd show it to Henry and George, to see if there were any pictures in it they might want to have copied. Would you close the door? It's pulling a draft in from the window."

"Of course." I shut the door.

"It's a curious thing," he said then, "that detective. When I first met you, I thought you looked familiar, but that happens sometimes, you think you've seen someone before. Then Friday morning, when I saw him here at the office. . . ." He reached into a drawer, pulled out a magazine and handed it to me.

"Page five," he said.

I folded it open, and there in all its cheap-paper glory was the picture of me and Peter getting into the car outside Chasen's the night I met Hazel Keane.

"I wouldn't have taken you for a reader of *Movie Star*," I said. I sat down and told him the real reason I was at *Adam Drake*. "Have you told anyone else?"

"No, and no one else has seen that. I brought it from home today. I made the appointment to meet Mr. Winslow here tomorrow, but, perhaps, under the circumstances, I should meet him at my apartment."

"I think that's a good idea."

He slid the album toward me. "Would you like to see it?"

"I would, very much." I folded the magazine and tucked it into the waistband of my skirt, buttoning my suit jacket over it, then pulled the album into my lap.

It was held together with a wide, well-worn grosgrain ribbon of pearl gray, which was strung through holes in the cover, the back, and the sheets of aged black construction paper between. The pictures were each captioned in silver ink.

The first series of photographs was of two couples at the beach. The women wore bathing costumes of the early century, dark, knitted beach dresses that brushed the knees. I recognized Ethel Keane. The other woman had shy eyes and a lovely figure, what little I could see of it. I assumed that she was Alton's late wife. One of the men was trim, with nice shoulders: Alton a quarter century ago. Morris Keane had already begun to show signs of a successful engineering career around his middle. There were other pictures of summer vacations together: the friends sitting on canvas lounge chairs, squinting into the sun; standing by a badminton net, racquets in their hands; eating huge crabs at a long table with a dozen other friends, toasting some long-ago event. As I turned the pages, the settings moved on to the city.

Alton said, "We would go to the beach in the summers, then when Morris made his money, he bought a house in Rhode Island, and my wife and I would visit them there, then come down to New York every December for a week. New York is such a festive city at Christmas. When Mary got sick, he paid for the best doctors—and gave me a job here when she died. I'd lost my other job, you see, because I wanted to be with her. Morris and I were war buddies. That was it, I suppose. They say men make their closest friends there."

Further back, I found the military pictures; among them, one of Morris and Alton standing on one of the frozen-mud fields where an entire generation had been decimated in World War I. They wore long, dark coats with Red Cross bands slipped over one sleeve. Behind them, the ambulance appeared to be a converted touring car, the stretcher-bearing compartment built onto it behind the chauffeur's seat.

I said, "I think the family might like some of these as well. George said they had only one of their father in the war, that he never liked to talk about it."

"No, that one hit him hard. There's some glory in this last one, some nobility of purpose, but there was none then. Just a million dead young men, and maimed bodies and ruined nerves for a million others."

I lifted the page. The pictures were still old, but the construction paper was brand new, as were the shiny black holders at the corners of the photos. At the top, on the right-hand side, there was Morris again, this time in puttees, standing with two nurses in front of a hospital tent.

"I've seen this picture, in George's study. It's the only one he has." The silver caption said, "Near Santiago."

"Santiago?" I asked.

"Cuba."

"This isn't from the first war?"

"No, that's a soldier's uniform Morris is wearing, not an ambulance volunteer's. But I can understand the mistake. The girls' dresses didn't change much, not for nurses. But I'm certain where it was taken, because I'm one of the men in the tent, the one on the left." He pointed to the scar above his ear.

I looked closely at the man in the photograph. I would never have recognized him, couldn't tell it was Alton, even now that I knew. The interior was too dim, the bandage too heavy, the face too gaunt.

"Lovely nurses," he said. "The ones in that picture are Americans, of course, but the Cuban girls," he smiled wistfully, "so lovely and kind. Gentle as they could be, with their melodic accents, and skin the color of warm syrup. It was no wonder we fell in love." He blushed suddenly. "Every soldier in his right mind did."

"I'm sure," I said, seeing him through new eyes.

I turned through the last pages, all brand new, and all filled with other pictures of Morris and Alton in Cuba, but there was no picture of Alton's Cuban love. If there had ever been any, they were probably long destroyed. I closed the book and laid it on the desk. "I'm sure George and Henry will love to see these." I stood up. "Thank you for your confidence in us."

He nodded. I opened the door. "And don't forget the rummy. The next party, we'll play."

"It's a date."

"A date?" Henry Keane asked, appearing at my elbow.

Alton stood up. "This young lady has kindly offered to play gin with me some evening. Here is the album I mentioned." He handed it to Henry, who accepted it gently.

"I appreciate this. I'll get it back to you next week."

"There's no hurry. Take as long as you need."

Henry turned to me. "Do you have a minute?"

We went into his office and he closed the door. He set the album on his desk and patted it a few times with his fingertips, finding words. "I think I might have been a little out of line Saturday night."

I waited to see where he was taking this. I had enough experience in Hollywood to know that a wolf's apology was sometimes no more than a prelude to the next pass. It was also possible that he was having second thoughts about messing with what he thought was Sam Ross's property and hoping he hadn't queered the deal with Marathon. And then, of course, it was possible he was truly sorry. A few stranger things have happened than a playboy trying to grow up.

"I'd had a couple of drinks. It helps when I have to go to my brother's house. We've been having some disagreements about the new show. I won't tell you that I don't usually do things like that. I do things like that all the time."

"I'd heard there was a reason Mrs. Embert was hired."

"My sister threatened to give me Sophie."

I laughed, and he grinned, with a charming sort of abashed look that probably had saved him dozens of times.

"Does this mean that as long as I'm working for you, I only have to write?"

"Yes." He put out his hand, and I shook. "That *was* a damn nice dress you were wearing."

He kept his eyes where they belonged, and I left. I went down the *Love* side to the ladies', locked myself in the stall and quietly tore the picture of Peter and me out of the copy of *Movie Star*, ripped it to pieces and flushed them down the toilet. I hid the rest of the magazine in the bottom drawer of my desk, then took a moment to collect myself before I tackled my assignment for the day: stirring things up.

I found Eileen coming out of the kitchen, a cup of steaming coffee in her hand. "My legs are freezing," she said. "My blood must be thinning."

"Can I talk to you?"

"Sure, come on in."

I did and closed the door. She sat down at the desk. I remained standing. I said, "I saw that detective yesterday. I didn't know why he'd want to talk to me, but I met with him anyway. He asked me a lot of questions about how people were behaving now, then he asked about you, if I knew that you'd been engaged to Morris Keane. I didn't know what to say."

She set the coffee down. "Well, I guess he wouldn't be any good if he didn't find out about that sooner or later."

"You didn't tell him?"

"It's none of his business."

I pulled over a chair and sat down, the sister with the ready ear.

She said, "I met Morris a couple of years ago, at a broadcast. He was one of those guys who actually listens when a girl talks. It started with dinner, just dinner. Two people who got along. Neither one of us saw it coming." She was quiet, and I was too, letting the silence force her to talk. "The children tried to break it up. Mostly Hazel. That doesn't sound good, does it?" She laughed, without much under it. "Henry wasn't too happy either. I think he was always a little too fond of his mother and didn't want a replacement. George was worried about his sponsors and his social circle, if it got out that his stepmother was a Jew. I guess Mr. Winslow mentioned that."

"No, actually, he didn't."

"The real name's Rachel Wallenstein, nice to meet you."

"Why did you change your name, in New York?"

"God, everybody thinks this town's full of Jews. This town's full of people who think the Jews killed Christ. Do you ever listen to the radio? Read a magazine?"

"I'm sorry. Go on."

"No, I'm sorry, I shouldn't take it out on you. And I can't say the kids didn't have something to worry about. In show business, it's not so important, but in their circles. . . . Morris didn't care anymore about what clubs he'd have to resign from, who wouldn't be inviting us to dinner. Still, he didn't want to hurt his kids' lives. He told them he was going up to Rhode Island for a couple of weeks, to make a final decision, but he'd already asked me, gave me a ring. While he was up there, he had a stroke. I would have married him anyway, but, after a few weeks, I realized he was never going to remember me. So, they got their way in the end."

"How can you keep working for them?"

"Instead of doing what? Quitting wouldn't teach them anything. I like what I do and I like the money. There aren't many places a girl can earn this much. I think Hazel was sorry in the end. She never said anything, but she showed up there in the doorway one night. Stood right there and said that she'd heard I was trying to buy an apartment, said she'd like to pay for it, just like that. I said sure. She bought me a two-bedroom on East Sixty-Third. Paid off. What the hell."

She turned and stared out the window, her eyes suddenly very bright. I said, "Would you rather be alone?"

"Yeah. If you hear anything else from the detective, let me know."

"Sure." I went out and closed the door. I felt bad, but I reminded myself that murderers can lie to you. They had lied to me before. And tried to kill me when I dropped my guard.

Maybe Eileen hadn't stayed at *Adam Drake* only for the income. She blamed the children, especially Hazel. She was the one who invited Nestor Cupp to join the going-away party.

I went along to Josh's office, more stirring up to do.

He was crossing out a long passage in a script with a heavy, angry X. As I came up on the other side of the desk, I saw a note in the margin that said, "Boring!" If I had been him, I wouldn't have appreciated the exclamation point.

"Yeah?" he asked abruptly and flipped the script over.

"I'm sorry to bother you. I'll come back later, if you want." I dropped my voice. "But I thought you should know that I saw the detective this weekend, and he asked a lot of questions about you."

"What?"

"I don't know why, but he kept asking about your teaching school. I told him that you'd taught a little in New York before you started at the ad agency, but he kept asking if I'd ever heard you mention teaching anywhere else. I said no. What could I say? Anyway, I thought you should know."

He sat back casually, but it was a bit too studied. "What else did he ask?"

I pretended to think about it for a moment. "If I'd ever heard you talk about Hazel Keane, and I said no, not a word. Then he said, didn't that seem odd? I said I didn't think so. And he asked me if you'd ever mentioned where you'd gone the night of the killing. I said we'd never discussed that night, but that Mr. Alletter told me that you'd stayed here a while after the meeting."

"Why the hell did Alletter say that?"

"You did stay for a while, didn't you?"

"Five minutes. I was gone long before anything happened."

"It's too bad Mr. Alletter didn't see you leave."

"He was probably still fixing the rod that broke in the closet. I went out that side door, like I always do. Everybody on the *Drake* side uses that door. I can't believe he's running his mouth about my being here. It wasn't even five minutes."

"Did someone see you after you left? A girlfriend, maybe?"

There was just a moment before he said, "I went straight home. Look, I've got to get back to work."

"Of course. Sorry."

About noon, Ruth brought back my script. "Well," she said, as she handed it to me, "congratulations."

"Thanks."

"I'm serious. It's good work. Better than good."

"I owe you that drink."

"I'll take it."

"How about tonight after work? You know any places a couple of women can go without an escort?"

"The Plaza. If we don't stay past six or so."

"Good. See you about five then." She turned and went out. I was curiously pleased to get her approval.

CHAPTER 22

I took the script down to Bar's office. He said, "I won't be able to take a look till tomorrow."

"I'll start on the next one, then." I took a breath. "Do you have a second? I met with that detective this weekend. I only did it because George said it was all right. I thought I should tell you, since it's your show. He was asking questions about the people here, what they're like, what they said about Hazel, if I'd heard anything about grudges. Maybe he's just trying to wrap things up, but I thought you should know."

"What did he ask about me?"

"About you and your wife and, uh, that doctor."

"Some people around here can't keep their mouths shut about what doesn't concern them. What else?"

"Whether I'd heard about your fighting with her."

"What did you say?"

"I didn't say anything, because all married couples argue, but he said that he'd heard you had fights with her here."

"We never brought our problems into the office."

"That must have been hard."

"Well, we didn't do it. Never."

"I shouldn't have mentioned it."

"No, I want to know if people are saying things like that."

"Well, I'll get back to work."

I was able to work, because no one interrupted me, even though I kept the door open. Peter had told me not to expect visitors. Yet. If we had a killer at *Adam Drake,* he'd be working out his next move, if my information shook him up. Actually, I wasn't eager to see who the next person through that door would be.

It turned out to be Ruth, promptly at five. We pinned on our hats, grabbed our coats and headed out. As I laid my hand on the door to reception, I heard Alletter's voice, huffily aggrieved. "I know what I saw, Mr. Connally."

Josh shot back, "Haven't we got enough trouble without you flapping your lips?"

"I don't think there's any reason to be insulting."

I was ready to eavesdrop, but Ruth pushed the door open and sailed past me. "Evening, boys. What's up, besides tempers?"

"Nothing," Josh said, and started buttoning his coat.

Alletter said, "Mr. Connally has accused me of lying."

"I accused you of not knowing what you're talking about." He turned to Ruth. "He told Mabel here that I was in my office after the meeting ended, just like that, out of the blue. With that detective asking questions."

Alletter said, "I know you were here. I saw those paper things in your wastebasket."

"And *that's* how you decided I was here?" Josh said, his voice rising again.

"Gentlemen." It was Mrs. Embert, standing in the hall door. "Is everything all right?"

"Yeah, everything's fine," Josh snapped. "I always shout when things are just dandy." He stalked out, stiff-arming the glass door. He punched the elevator call button with the side of his fist, then strode over, slammed open the service door and disappeared through it.

"Well," said Mrs. Embert, "I will have to mention this to Mr. Keane."

"Why?" I asked, cajolingly. "It's over."

Ruth put her hand under my elbow and guided me firmly to the door. "We're all a little wound up these days," she said over her shoulder. "I'm sure Josh will apologize tomorrow. Good night, Al, Mrs. Embert." She took me out, just as the elevator door slid open. We got in. She said, "If you try to talk her out of it, she's sure to go to Henry."

In the Oak Room, we were given a table behind a pillar, so no one would see two ladies drinking at sundown, the province of the businessman. I spent a few minutes asking her advice on where to buy clothes, as California's version of a winter coat was not going to make it in New York. We sipped our drinks and discussed rumors that skirts might be longer next season, then I pounced. Of course, I had to pounce casually, appearing to be merely interested in a budding romance.

"How long have you been seeing Bar?" I asked brightly.

"I beg your pardon?"

I pretended to be confused by her shock. "I—Well, I saw you Saturday night. I was upstairs, looking out at the garden."

She turned cold in a hurry. "I don't like gossip."

"I didn't mean to pry. There's nothing wrong with it. He and his wife were separated."

She pulled a black enameled case from her handbag and took out a cigarette. She set it between her lips and tore a match from the book in the table's ashtray. When she struck it, it let out a long hiss. As she put the flame to the cigarette tip, she asked, not quite as offhandedly as she might have, "Did you tell anyone else?"

"Of course not. I wouldn't do that. But Hal saw you, too."

"Christ. Then it'll be all over town."

"I guess this isn't the best time, with that detective asking questions."

"It could be better. Have you talked to him?"

"Yesterday, but just for a few minutes. He didn't ask me

anything about you and Bar. If I see him again, I won't tell him. He can't possibly think either one of you was involved."

"Who knows what that kind of man thinks? I'm supposed to see him later tonight. Thanks for the warning."

"Sure." I took a long sip and watched her calculating the impact of this information, then said, "Karen told me the theater company's doing your new play this spring."

"Providing I finish it. I'm having a reading of the first act tomorrow night, six-thirty, at the theater. The company, a few guests. Why don't you come along, pay me back for what I said about your script? It could make for some fine melodrama as well. Sky and Karen will both be there."

I went back to the office, starving, and none the better for a gin and tonic on an empty stomach. But I couldn't go home yet. I needed to do some more breaking and entering.

I made a quick reconnaissance. No one was there except Al-letter and Willa, who was cleaning the men's room. I tossed my coat and handbag in my chair, pulled out my picks and slipped into Bar's office. I closed the door and had the file cabinet open in two seconds. I rifled through the Correspondence files. I found nothing, but then a resignation wasn't correspondence.

Where would it be? Not in any of the files Bar regularly looked at, or he would have found it.

Contracts. Josh had been searching files marked Contracts/Correspondence. I broke into the next drawer and pulled out Josh's contract. Paper-clipped to the back was a letter of resignation: he was asking to be released from his contract to pursue another opportunity, and offering to work another sixty days until a suitable replacement could be found. There were a few mistakes in the typing, the kind you might make when you're agitated and maybe even angry and don't give a damn about the impression you're making. Across the bottom, in longhand, was written simply, "Accepted. HK. September 5, 1946." Hazel had died about a month before Josh's sixty days would have been up.

I returned the letter to its place, then relocked the cabinet drawer. I eased the office door open far enough to be able to see the coast was clear, then slipped out and strolled casually to the *Love* side and the storage room. I closed its door and went into the *Drake* files, looking at every script that had been done since last April, when Hazel had questioned Ed Lewis, her lawyer, about bigamy. Although Hazel had said she wanted the information for a show, none of the scripts had anything to do with inheritances or bigamy.

Could Hazel have been asking about herself? Had she, a devout woman, accidentally committed bigamy? Or had she, in fact, been talking about Bar, had found out that he was married and had changed the sexes around so Lewis wouldn't suspect she was talking about her own life? Ruth said that she came to New York eight years ago, which was about the time Hazel met Bar. They could have married, then decided to get themselves a fortune. Bar would marry Hazel, stash money away for a few years, then get an annulment with a nice settlement and "marry" Ruth. Bar's refusal to have a child could well have been part of the plan. But if she found herself in that kind of trouble, why didn't she tell Lewis? Wasn't that exactly the sort of thing you confided to your lawyer?

Nevertheless, Peter was searching for a marriage license with Bar's name on it, as well as one for Hazel Keane and Lawrence Clayton.

I closed the files and went home. Before I took off my coat, I turned up the radiators, and they began to hiss and clank enthusiastically. I closed the drapes and changed into slacks and a heavy sweater, then made a sandwich and called Peter at the Vanguard number, but he wasn't there. His late afternoon and evening were filled with meetings. First, George and Henry at George's office, then Ruth. He called back about eight. I told him about finding the resignation and the other results of my day. I left for last the fact that Alton had recognized us.

Peter said, "I'll be there in a half hour."

In exactly thirty minutes, I heard his coded knock. By that time, I had heaved my Zack Eisler painting into the bathtub, concealed it behind the shower curtain and replaced it with the old print. I didn't want to have to construct a complicated lie about how the painting got there. I certainly didn't want to tell Peter that Zack Eisler had delivered it personally.

Now all I had to do was convince Peter that Alton Peake wasn't going to tell anyone. It didn't work. "He might trust the wrong person and let something slip."

"He's not a fool. He knows this is dangerous."

"We've got enough to worry about getting the doctor to keep his mouth shut. I want you to meet me at Clayton's office tomorrow. One o'clock."

"He's agreed to see you?"

"He's agreed to see you, under another name, and your concerned husband."

"Call Alton now. Go see him tonight."

"I have an appointment with Sky Donovan. I don't know when I'll be finished." He pulled his notebook out and found Alton's number. Alton was home. They arranged for Peter to come to his apartment the following evening at seven. "He doesn't live far from here," Peter said when he hung up. "I'll have time to talk to him, then meet Karen Dunn at ten."

"That's pretty late for a meeting."

"It must be after this play reading Ruth Linden invited you to."

"She couldn't meet you during the day?"

"She was busy, doing a couple of other shows, some auditions. I can't blame her for not wanting to see me before she has to perform."

"Are you going to upset her?"

"It's one of the things I do best."

The next morning, I got on the right train, so I arrived on time, with my frozen feet having only been trod on a dozen times. In my office, the radiator was blasting warm air, silently. I stood beside it until my legs warmed up and the feeling returned to my feet. My stockings had survived the trampling, but I decided that, for their protection and to keep my feet warm, I needed a pair of boots. Maybe a cute little pair with a nice fur lining.

My office door flew open.

Sky Donovan stood in it, still in his overcoat, fedora and scarf. "What the hell did you tell that detective?"

"What?"

"You heard me." He slammed the door dramatically and shook the head of his walking stick at me, the carved head of a snarling griffon. Suddenly, I wondered if he had killed Hazel with it, then used Cupp's wrench to disguise the shape of the wound. "What the hell did you tell him?"

"Nothing. What's the matter with you?"

There was a light tap on the door, and it opened immediately. "Sophie called," Henry said calmly. "She said you looked a little upset, Sky. What do you say we take this into my office?"

"Fine by me," I said.

Sky grumped his agreement, still glaring at me.

We went down to Henry's office. Josh and Eileen stood in their doorways, full of curiosity. Bar was waiting at the corner and fell in behind our little parade. We passed Jeannie and Marty, who gaped wide-eyed. Even Mrs. Embert stared. Bar shut the door.

"Let me take your coat and hat, Sky," Henry offered.

Sky handed them over. Henry also took the cane and put it away in his closet, then he sat down at his desk, gesturing for us to sit opposite. Bar chose to lean on the wall beside the window, much as I had seen him do on my first day.

Henry turned to Sky. "What's going on?"

"I talked to that detective last night, and he started making accusations."

"What sort?"

"About how you're letting me go to Hollywood for the screen test. He said he'd heard Hazel wouldn't let me go."

"May I ask what Mabel has to do with that?"

"She told him," he stated, petulantly. "He knew everything I told her on Saturday night."

I explained to Henry. "At the party, Sky told me that your sister wouldn't let him go out to Hollywood, but that you were, that's all."

"That's not all!" Sky insisted. "He knew about the argument we had!"

"We didn't argue," I said to him.

"Hazel, with Hazel," he snapped.

Bar said, "Your fights with Hazel were no big secret."

"Fights?" I said. "More than one? You only mentioned one to me. You didn't call it a fight."

"It wasn't. We never fought," Sky affirmed, affronted.

Bar said, "There was that day at rehearsal last month, you two were going at it up in the control room. Most of us were there, but not Mabel."

Henry's expression hardened. "I don't believe I heard about this one. Did the detective know about this *argument*?"

"Yes," Sky admitted mumpishly. Without thinking, he had stormed theatrically into the office. Karen wasn't here to rescue him, and he didn't know how to get what he wanted except through petulance and temper.

"This is exactly why we wanted you to meet the detective here," Henry said in exasperation. "We need to know what he's implying, and we want to avoid bad feeling among the staff. Mabel, I think you can go on back to work. Thank you for your time."

Sky had the temper and lack of control necessary to commit murder, but did he have the foresight to plan and carry out this particular killing? It could explain why the escape plan seemed so haphazard: Sky hadn't thought the entire thing out.

"Okay, what was that about?"

I had barely sat my rear down in my chair when Eileen appeared in my doorway, Josh right after her.

"Spill it," he said, and closed the door.

I told them what had happened, then said, "Sky and Hazel had a fight at the studio?"

Josh said, "Maybe a couple of weeks before she died. We were doing one of my scripts, so I was there. He had a bad rehearsal, and Hazel marched right down to the floor and told him it wasn't going to do him any good to screw up. He wasn't getting out of his contract. She invited him to step up to the control room. She sent Hal out, and they went at it hammer and tongs."

"And she still let him come to the writers meeting?" I asked.

Eileen shrugged. "She was like that, blow up and get over it."

"I'm surprised he showed up."

She and Josh stared at me, as if a not-very-pleasant thought had occurred to both of them, the same one that had occurred to me, but none of us said it out loud.

Instead, Eileen said, "Henry will settle him down. What are you doing for lunch? Want to help me look for a new hat?"

Josh groaned and stood up. "Oh, God, hats. I'm leaving. Good-bye. Tell me if you hear anything about what Henry says to him." He went out.

Eileen said, "A moment ago, were you thinking what I was thinking?"

"Yes."

"This is awful. I was sure the police got the right man. Now I'm starting to suspect people I work with."

"Well, I think we can eliminate Alton."

She laughed. "Thank God for that."

"I can't shop at lunch. I have a doctor's appointment, and I'm going to Ruth's reading tonight."

"Me, too. Let's duck out early, shop, grab some dinner and go on down to the theater."

"Sounds good."

CHAPTER 23

Peter gave Clayton's receptionist our names. Mr. and Mrs. Stone to see the doctor.

The women in the waiting room eyed Peter with a mixture of suspicion and envy, the husband who comes with his wife. At one-thirty, the nurse showed us into the doctor's consulting office and left us there to examine the impressive credentials hanging on the walls. Clayton arrived, reading from a file folder. By the time he looked up, Peter was on his feet and had closed the door.

"You've got a roomful of patients out there," Peter said. "Give us five minutes, and we leave quietly."

"I have nothing to say to you. Either of you."

"It might not be in your best interest to force us to hire a new lawyer for Nestor Cupp. Have you told anyone that she's working with me?"

"No," he said, after a moment.

"Why don't you sit down, doctor? Five minutes, that's all we want."

Clayton glared at him for a moment, then sat down. "The police have a very good case, without me."

"I'm sure they told you that before they let you pick Cupp out of the lineup, but the truth is, without your identification, they probably couldn't have held him overnight."

Clayton looked shaken. He said, "I have only your word for that."

"It's what the evidence says. The coveralls weren't his, his tools could have been stolen that day while he was at the going-away party. If you have any doubts, doctor, if there are circumstances that might have led you to pick out the wrong man, there's still time to make it right with the cops. Take a lawyer with you, and explain it to them. It might be uncomfortable, but it won't be anything to what it'll be like if all this gets into the papers."

"Are you threatening me? If I don't take back my identification, you'll vilify me in the press?"

"Let's lay our cards out here, doctor. I don't think you killed Hazel Keane. I think you were trying to help find her killer, and you were misled by the cops into identifying a man who might be innocent. I'll make you a deal. You don't tell anyone that Mrs. Tanner and I are working together, and I won't tell Cupp's lawyer anything I find out until I've given you another chance to clear things up with the cops. How does that sound?"

"I don't think you're working for any insurance company."

"That's who's paying me, but there's another party involved. Someone who'll find out who killed Hazel Keane. No matter what it costs or how long it takes."

"Does that person think it's me?"

"That person relies on us to do our jobs. I hope you're going to let us."

His eyes shifted back and forth between us a few times. Then he said, "I think I can make that agreement."

At four, Eileen came by my office, her handbag over her arm. We pinned on our hats and walked down to Franklin Simon. Within fifteen minutes, I had a pair of toasty, fleece-lined, ankle-high boots with beaver cuffs. Then we went searching for Eileen's hat in what the store called The Mirror Room, raised above the ordinary millinery collection, reached by shallow semicircular steps and decorated in white pickled wood and frosted glass.

Two salesladies bumped hips hurrying to greet us. Eileen told one of them what she was after. I told the other I was only looking, but she could tell from the hat I wore that I could afford what she had, and obligingly helped me while I amused myself. I tried on an elegant aquamarine pillbox with detachable netting that could be dropped across the face, a snappy scarlet beret with trailing grosgrain ribbons, a midnight-blue velvet cap with a long, arching feather, and finally, a marvelous concoction shaped like a crusader's chain-mail helmet, but made of parrot-blue velvet that caressed the cheeks and would keep the neck and ears warm in winter. I bought it. We wanted to wear our new hats, but didn't want to tote hatboxes around with our other hats in them, so we arranged to have those delivered to the office.

We ate with our knees touching at a New York–size table in a coffee shop on 34th, then took the train at Sixth Avenue down to West Fourth, where I followed Eileen through the crowded, labyrinthine corridors, until we came out onto another platform just as a train slid into the station and we jumped on. We got off at the next stop and came up at Spring Street and Sixth. She charged off. I had no idea in which direction we were headed.

The neighborhood consisted mostly of turn-of-the-century buildings with long, arched windows on every floor—stores, showrooms and factory lofts where everything from shoes and pots and pans to machine tools and office equipment were made and sold.

Squeezed between two of them was a chipped gray-brick building, whose ground floor was the home of the Off–West Broadway Players—appropriately just off West Broadway. Later I discovered that West Broadway had nothing to do with Broadway, except that, for its mile-and-a-half length, it ran roughly parallel to the more famous street.

The lobby was tiny, its floors covered in linoleum tiles. Squeezed into the far right corner was the box office, which would have been large enough for one stool, one cash box and one starving artist. Open double doors on the right led into the theater, although my first view of it was a black triangular wall that marked the side of the raked audience seating. We went in and down the side aisle to the front of the house, the only way to reach the seats. In total, the theater might seat a hundred, on unforgiving wooden folding chairs, which I thought would encourage Ruth to keep the action moving.

A long table sat on stage with more wooden chairs gathered around it. Behind it was the ghost light, which was basically a floor lamp with no shade, only a solitary bulb—theater tradition dictated that it be kept lit after performances, in the center of the stage, company for theater ghosts when no one was there. At the table, two women and a man—actors, I assumed—were deep in discussion with Ruth over the script, all still wearing their coats and scarves, as there didn't seem to be any heat.

A dozen people, likewise still in their mufflers and mittens, were already in the audience. One of them was Lawrence Clayton. He looked right through me.

We climbed the steps of the narrow center aisle. On the opposite side from Clayton, two rows further back sat Mash Burton, the soundman from *Adam Drake*. He had a knitted woolen cap pulled down over his wild hair, which gave the cap a sort of electric fringe. Josh sat beside him, his scarf wrapped up to his ears and his fedora low on his brow.

They moved over to make room for us.

"I do some of the sound work for them," Mash explained.

"You must be dedicated, to come to a reading. I can see my breath in here."

"But a great excuse for alcohol afterward."

"Or before," Josh said as he pulled a flask out of his pocket and unscrewed the lid. He took a sip and offered it to the rest of us. "Kentucky bourbon, aged ten years."

"That's a sound I love to hear," Mash said. He took the flask. "Ladies?"

Eileen and I declined. Mash gave it a try, then another, and returned the flask.

George and Henry Keane came in from the lobby. From where we were sitting, the audience rake was steep enough that I could only see the tops of their bare heads, the identical shade of auburn hair, in the same tight waves: thick on one head, surrounding a bald pate on the other. When they reached the center aisle, and saw the rest of us bundled up, they put their hats back on.

The doors opened again, and Sky and Karen came in. As they reached the front of the house, Sky surveyed the audience with a hint of a man expecting adulation for deigning to do this reading. Then he saw me, and immediately the expression turned to a scowl.

"What's up with Sky?" Mash asked me.

"It's me," I said. "He thinks I told the detective some things, even though I'm the least likely one." I did it, but I was still the least likely.

Josh took another sip from the flask. "I wouldn't worry. He doesn't have many friends at the show. It's all ambition with him. Most radio people aren't like that."

I thought it was an odd remark from someone who liked to detach himself from his coworkers, but then Josh was showing signs of attaching himself, at least tonight. I told myself that there was no chance he was being friendly because he suspected I was investigating.

Ruth stood up and greeted us. "Our landlord seems to have forgotten that I asked for heat this evening. Why don't you grab some chairs and come up on stage?"

We did, and formed a rough circle around the table.

As we settled in, the lobby door opened again, and there was Bar. Jeannie and Marty came in behind him. "Mind if we join you?" Bar asked.

"Not at all," Ruth said.

They grabbed chairs, too. Bar set his down as far from Clayton as possible. Marty positioned hers beside Bar. Ruth took no more notice of him. They were both damn good actors.

She introduced the play only by its title, *The Lip Reader,* and let the work speak for itself, the story of a middle-aged woman, who had sacrificed the chance for happiness to take care of a fragile, demanding mother and a ne'er-do-well brother. Everyone's old grudges resurface with the return of the pretty, petted younger sister, now successfully married.

Afterward, Ruth accepted comments from the actors. A few of the guests offered their two cents as well, unsolicited, to which she listened attentively, with more patience than I would have had to what was basically amateur opinion. But then, they were patrons.

She offered to buy a round of warm drinks. The patrons all declined and went back to their heated apartments. Clayton lingered. Maybe he was taking George and Henry's temperature, making sure they hadn't heard anything he'd rather they didn't.

Karen tossed her script on the pile in the center of the table. "I'll have to take a rain check," she said to Ruth. "I'm meeting that detective tonight."

George said, "Are you sure you want to do that at your apartment?"

"I'm not. We're meeting at Dunleavy's, not far from here, up on West Third."

"I'm going, too," Sky said. "He won't pull anything."

"No, you aren't. That's why I didn't tell you until now," Karen said. "You'll only pick a fight." She turned to us. "I've invited some girlfriends for dinner, first. They'll stick around. They want to meet a real private detective, and he won't get out of hand with them there."

"Oh, Ruth," Henry said, "I forgot to tell you. Alton asked me to convey his apologies. He would have been here, but he's meeting with that guy tonight, too, at his place. I couldn't talk him out of it. He said he didn't want the guy coming around the office again and he wanted to get it over with."

"I don't blame him," Ruth said.

"How was it?" Karen asked, as she fitted her scarf up around her neck.

"Not bad, but he wants the dirt on all of us. Knock yourself out."

Karen laughed and went off.

Clayton said good night, then, graciously to Ruth and the Keane brothers. The rest of us got a nod. I wasn't sure I even got that.

Everyone else decamped to a neighborhood watering hole around the corner and squeezed around three small tables. We ordered hot cider for the girls and buttered rums for the adults. Most of the gathering pulled out cigarettes. Soon the air was gray-blue with smoke. The drinks came and we took turns guessing where the play was going. Ruth smiled mysteriously, but with the obvious pleasure of an author whose work inspires discussion, the highest compliment.

She might be the killer, but she could sure as hell write.

She offered to buy another round, but Mash and the actors had to go. Paying jobs began early. One of the actors locked eyes briefly with Josh. If I hadn't known about what went on in South Carolina, I wouldn't have made anything out of it. Josh said, "Well, I guess I'll take off, too. Great work, Ruth. See you tomorrow." He buttoned up his coat, fitted his fedora on firmly, and went out.

"I think I'll call it a night too," Bar said, and pulled on his coat. "Plenty to do before *Love* tomorrow. Want to share a cab?" he said to the girls.

Marty's eyes lit up. "Yes, please."

George stood up as well. "And me. Meetings in the morning. Good night, all."

The rest of us were content to stay in the warmth of the room. Another drink, and the conversation moved on to the theater group's next season and Ruth's plans to eventually move to a larger space, something I knew was now possible, since her company had inherited fifty thousand from Hazel.

I glanced at my watch. Nearly ten. It was time for me to go home, before I was tempted by too much alcohol to forget I was surrounded by suspects. I stood up, remarkably balanced, and said good night. The others decided to break up the evening, as well. Henry offered to get me a cab, and I accepted before it occurred to me that he might want to share it. I could remember the fake address I had given them at the office, but what if he insisted on waiting until I was actually inside the building? What if its front door was locked or the doorman refused to let me in?

He hailed a cab and put me in it. And said good night.

When the door closed with me alone in the backseat, I was so relieved that it took a while to realize that the cabbie was waiting for me to tell him where to go. I gave him the phony address. We eased down Spring Street carefully, as the pavement looked as if no one had worked on it since before the war. Maybe the Civil War. I checked through the back window for any hint that I might be followed. It wasn't likely, but Peter insisted I always do it when headed home. We turned north on Sixth Avenue, and I saw nothing but a sea of headlights behind me. If anyone was tailing me, I wasn't sure I would spot it.

Within a few blocks, just above Bleecker, we ran into a traffic snarl that seemed to extend far ahead. Something had happened—a wreck, a broken traffic light, a girl in a short skirt—and cars had come to a standstill, all honking madly, as if enough nerve-grinding noise would induce the Fates to act. "I think I'll get out here. You can make the turn up ahead there and get out of this."

"Thanks," he said dryly. "I never would have thought of that."

I paid him and got out. He jigsawed his way across Sixth, his left arm waving out his window at the cars to let him over, and shot away west.

I headed off uptown on the east side of the street, faster than the traffic, glancing over my shoulder. No one got out of a car to follow me. At West Third, I turned the corner and stopped immediately at a newsstand, flipping the pages of a *McCall's*, but watching the corner. No one came around it, saw me, and suddenly loitered. I pulled a small neighborhood map from my handbag and unfolded it beneath the street lamp, pleased with myself for having thought to carry it. I could continue up to 11th Street, then go east to my apartment, or go east from here one block, follow the edge of Washington Square Park to Fifth Avenue and on north. That might be a more pleasant walk. I could avoid some of the Village crowd. Then I realized that Dunleavy's, where Peter was meeting Karen, must be close by. She'd said it was on West Third.

I bought the *McCall's*. "Do you know where a restaurant called Dunleavy's is?" I asked the news seller.

"Sure. Three blocks east. You got McDougal, Sullivan, then Thompson. Just past Thompson. Right side."

"Thanks."

"Try the chops."

I was not going to Dunleavy's. I waited for the light to change so I could cross West Third, heading home.

And there was Peter. He was up on Fourth, crossing Sixth Avenue, still a block away, coming from his meeting with Alton. Funny how I could tell it was him, at that distance, in that light, in the crowd, by some unconscious signal his body had for me that made my face snap into a smile. God, I was head over heels.

When the light changed, I didn't cross Third. I stepped out of the way of the other pedestrians, dropped my head over the map again and waited. He turned and headed down Third on the opposite side of the street. He must have seen me, because he pulled a handkerchief from his left coat pocket, folded it and placed it in the right, the signal that it was safe for me to follow, discreetly.

I dropped the map back in the handbag and the *McCall's* into a trash bin, and wrapped my scarf over my head and the lower part of my face. I followed, a half-block back on my own side of the cracked, cobbled street, down the canyon of fire escapes.

On the far side of Thompson, Peter turned and crossed Third, heading south, away from Dunleavy's walking faster now. I turned as well, still keeping to my side of the street, hanging back, although not as far behind as before. If it was all right to make contact, he would cross to my side. A long Chrysler with New Jersey plates came toward us. As it passed, Peter stepped out into the street between the parked cars, watching the Chrysler move away and not the cracked cobbles. He missed his step on the uneven paving and tripped. He stumbled forward onto his knee, catching himself with his hand on the pavement.

I couldn't resist. I stepped out into the street. "Jeez, Winslow," I said, as I approached. "I thought I was the one who'd had too much to drink."

He reached up and yanked me to the ground. I hit the pavement hard, sliding on my rear end in the oily grime. He pulled me beneath him, rolled on top of me, held me to the ground. His gun was already out and pointing straight above my head toward Third.

"What is it?" I whispered, urgently.

"Somebody's shooting at us," he said.

"Hey, buddy!" called a man from the curb. "What do you think you're doing? Get off her." Then he saw Peter's gun. He stepped back and showed his palms.

"Someone's shooting at us!" I shouted at the man. "Call the police!"

He dashed off in the opposite direction.

Peter rolled onto one hip and I scuttled from under him and tucked myself against the fender of the nearest car.

Peter shifted into a crouch, his gaze still on the top of the street. Slowly, he rose and edged past me over to the sidewalk on the east side of the street, scanning for anyone coming at us that way. He shook his head. "Nobody here."

"Are you sure they were shooting?" I asked. "I didn't hear anything."

"Neither did I."

"Then how did you know? Oh, God!" I jumped up and jerked the front of his coat open, then his jacket. "Peter, you're hit!"

CHAPTER 24

"You're lucky," the doctor said. "It missed your ribs."

"Not much of a shot," Peter commented.

The emergency-room doctor finished sewing up the wound, a nasty deep gash about three inches long, just below Peter's rib cage. "Get that looked at again in a couple of days. Don't get it wet. The nurse will give you some antiseptic and some bandages. Change them every twelve hours."

"Can I sit up now?" Peter asked.

"Suit yourself, but it won't hurt to lie there." He tossed a glance at the police officer standing not far away. "You're not going anywhere." He left.

I put my handbag on the floor and poured Peter a glass of water from the carafe on the cabinet by the bed. "Drink it all." He did as he was told.

His bloodied shirt lay in the trash can; his jacket and coat were folded on a chair. His hat and empty shoulder holster sat on top of them. The officer had Peter's gun in the pocket of his tunic. He hadn't asked us any questions. It wasn't his job. His job was to watch men with gunshot wounds, especially when they carried guns themselves.

I had already called Alton Peake to make sure he was all right, then Vanguard, so they could send someone over to Dunleavy's to escort Karen Dunn home. Until we could figure out why the killer had picked that time and that place, we had to make sure they were safe.

We waited.

The detective arrived ten minutes later, thin and hangdog, the skin sagging from his jaws. He was so bony that I could see the shape of his suit's shoulder padding and the outline of his shoulder blades beneath it.

"Detective Barnes," he said.

"Peter Winslow."

"Can I see some proof of that?"

I handed Peter his wallet and he showed Barnes the photocopy of his detective's license. "I suppose you got someone out in LA can vouch for you."

"You might try the assistant DA, name's Betts."

Barnes's eyebrows went up an entire quarter of an inch.

Peter told him the truth about who we were and the reason we had left LA.

Barnes said, "Don't bring your trouble here. We got plenty of our own."

"This has nothing to do with the LA case. He was shooting at me, not Mrs. Atwill. She was on the other side of the street, and he didn't wait for me to cross to her." He told Barnes what he was doing for the insurance company.

"Think we need some help with the Keane case?"

"It was just routine, until tonight."

"So what happened?"

Peter explained where he had been, then said, "The shooter was at the top of the street. I'm sure he didn't follow me there, so he was waiting. When I turned in another direction, he must have panicked, maybe thought I'd seen him, and started shooting."

"Let's go take a look. That is, if you think our boys can handle it."

Peter put on his jacket over his bare skin, then buttoned his overcoat to the throat. We went out to the admitting desk, where

Peter paid the bill: five-fifty for stitches and a few bandages. I wondered if they raised the price when you had a police escort.

Barnes took us back to Thompson, where six officers with powerful flashlights were waiting. Barnes set three of them to work searching for spent bullets where Peter had fallen; the others went back toward the intersection, looking for casings.

"Do you mind if I go get a cup of coffee?" I asked Barnes.

"Okay."

Peter eyed me, but said nothing. I headed toward Third.

The shooter had been waiting for Peter, probably somewhere close to Dunleavy's.

On the northeast corner of the intersection, there was a drug store, closed, then a narrow house with a low wrought-iron railing enclosing a postage-stamp garden beside its stoop. Crammed against the rail was a waist-high, battered boxwood. Dunleavy's was almost directly across the street. The boxwood was the perfect place for an ambush. But then Peter turned away before reaching the restaurant. The shooter must have panicked. His target was getting away. He rushed out and emptied his gun.

Where had he fired from?

I went back to the intersection and examined the first car parked on the east side of Thompson, its hood well lit by the streetlamp in front of the drugstore. Maybe there was too much light for a killer.

I went on down to the second car, which was parked in gloom, took off my gloves and pulled the cigarette lighter out of my handbag. The hood was clean, but there was something on its windshield, like shreds of burned paper, and more of it caught in the wiper blades. And something mixed with the paper. Something dark and woven. I could see the interlocking threads.

I stepped out into Thompson and called to Peter and Barnes.

"Homemade silencer," Peter commented after they had stared

at the windshield for a minute, now better lit by the officers' flashlights.

"Heavy blanket, maybe," Barnes grunted. "Fold it inside some paper wrapping, look like a package. Stick your hand in, pull the trigger."

"Good for close-up work. Not too accurate at sixty feet." Peter started to pluck off one of the fibers.

Barnes said, "Leave it. I get to keep the evidence. How'd he know you were headed for Dunleavy's?"

"Good question."

I kept my mouth shut. I would wait to tell Peter that everyone who had remained at the theater at the end of the play reading knew he had been at Alton's and was going to the restaurant to meet Karen.

Barnes said, "Well, I'm glad nobody got killed tonight, even if that nobody was you." He handed Peter a card. "I'll be there tomorrow, you can make a statement. You check out all right, I might let you have your gun back."

An officer escorted us to Sixth, where we caught a cab and headed uptown. "You're staying at the Marquette tonight, and I'm putting a guard in the room," Peter said, low enough that the cabbie couldn't hear over his radio.

"He wasn't after me. And the way I was wrapped up, walking behind the parked cars, that far behind you, he probably didn't even notice me."

"I don't care. I didn't come to New York to get you killed, even by accident."

"Here, this will make you feel better." I opened my handbag and took out a handkerchief. I showed him what I had wrapped inside it before calling him and Barnes over to the car: a few shreds of the paper and several of the fibers.

"Good girl," he said and took the handkerchief from me. Then I told him what had happened at the reading, that everyone knew where he was.

"Karen probably has witnesses that she was in the restaurant," I said. "Eileen, Ruth and Henry were with me. I don't see how they could have had time to get what they needed and make it up to Dunleavy's."

"It's not that far, five, six blocks."

"If any of them wanted to shoot you, they would have left earlier. Clayton and Sky had two and a half hours. Josh maybe an hour and a half, a little less for Bar. He was sharing a cab with Marty and Jeannie, so he had to at least pretend to go home. Where does he live, I wonder?"

"In the East Forties."

"Not that far."

"Anybody who left early had time to lay hands on a blanket and some wrapping paper, check a phone book to find out where Dunleavy's was. And get their gun."

"But why tonight?"

Something had scared the killer badly. Badly enough to make him take a gun he didn't know how to use well and, rather than wait for a better shot, empty it as soon as Peter made the first move that he might get away.

We'd set out to shake up the killer, and we had. But we still didn't know who.

"I'm going back to work tomorrow," I said.

"Lauren—"

"I'm going. I'll take cabs door to door, but I'm in this. We can't stop now."

He didn't argue anymore. It wouldn't do any good, and he knew it.

No one at the office looked as if he'd been shooting at people the night before. I said hello to all of them. If the killer was there, and knew who I really was, I wanted him to see my eyes.

To see that I wasn't afraid.

I could lie, too.

I reached Ruth's office just as she hung up her phone. "You'll never guess what happened last night," she said. "That was Karen. That detective didn't show, but another one did and insisted on taking her home. He seemed to think she was in danger. Scared her to death. She's coming over after I get back from *Love*. I'm calling George. He has to hear this." She picked up the phone again. "That's all I know so far."

"Oh. Okay." I went into Alton's office and closed the door. We kept our voices down.

"There was nothing in the newspapers about the shooting," he said.

"Detective Barnes said he'd try to keep it quiet."

"Your young man is close to something."

"I hope we figure out what it is before this guy's aim improves."

Bar and Ruth went to the *Love* broadcast. Within minutes of their return, Karen arrived, then George. Henry guided them into his office, and the rest of us floated in behind them as if we'd been invited. Karen told her story. She had been waiting at Dunleavy's. The detective was late. The only reason she hadn't left was that her girlfriends wanted to see him. Then a man appeared, very serious, showed her his license, said Winslow had been detained, and he'd make sure she got home all right. She insisted she was fine. He insisted that she let him take her home in a cab, but it wasn't chivalry. He looked up and down the sidewalk before he let her leave the restaurant. He walked her inside her apartment building and made her promise not to let anyone in.

She had not slept all night.

George took a card from his wallet and reached for Henry's phone. "I can take care of it, George," Henry said. He asked

Sophie to get Mr. Winslow on the phone, then turned to Alton.

"Did you see him last night? What did you talk about?"

"Baseball, mostly. I had nothing to tell him."

"He didn't say anything about you being in danger?"

"No. No, he didn't."

"Bar, if you'd stay." The rest of us, except George, melted back into the hall. Ruth took Karen to an early lunch. Eileen went into her office and closed the door. Josh loaded his doorway with paper footballs. I tried to figure out if it was significant that his aim seemed to be off. Then I went in, rolled some paper into my typewriter, and pretended to be filling it up with a story.

Bar appeared in my doorway, handed me my script and said, "We'll do this next week. I made some comments. Take care of those, then get it typed." He ran his fingers through his lank hair and it settled back into pieces. "Ruth tells me you saw us together."

"Hal and I saw you in the garden."

"You know my wife and I were separated."

"I'm not a gossip, Bar."

"Yeah. Thanks. Well, I'll let you get to work."

I flipped through my script. His comments were mild, the sort someone makes when he feels he has to say something. When I finished making the changes, I took it along to the typists room. As long as I was there, I asked Mrs. Embert for a copy of Josh's script, the one we were doing this week. Glumly, she handed me one from the stack on her desk.

I said to the girls, "Want to come to the broadcast?"

Mrs. Embert said, "We don't like to crowd the control room."

"I'm sure the girls won't disturb Hal."

"We'd love to," Marty said, her gaze slanted at Mrs. Embert.

I hoped Bar wasn't the killer. It would break Marty's heart.

I went back to my office and read "A Race to Death." Adam

Drake is called in by the owner of a champion racehorse when his stable's head groom is found dead the day before the big race, trampled in the horse's stall. Drake discovers what the police, of course, don't see: the blunt-instrument wounds that actually killed him.

Mash, the soundman, would be happy. The script began with the killing. The groom sees someone in the stables who shouldn't be there, accosts him with the always useful, "What are *you* doing here?" and then is struck down.

At lunch, I called Vanguard from a phone booth and got a message from Peter. Barnes's men had found casings and spent bullets for a Colt M-1911, the same kind of gun Peter carried. Pawnshops were full of them, sold by veterans. The paper shreds I'd found on the car turned out to be ordinary brown wrapping paper, impossible to trace. The fabric was wool, densely woven, probably a blanket. Again, impossible to trace. Our only hope was the gun.

It would take a lot of footwork to canvass gun stores and pawnshops with pictures of our suspects. If the insurance company wasn't willing to pay for the men it would take, I was ready to pull out my checkbook.

Rather than stare at a typewriter all afternoon, I decided to go over to rehearsal.

I found Peter in the studio, talking to Karen.

I sidled over to watch Mash work while I eavesdropped. He had just finished scattering sand and a layer of straw into a wooden box on the floor, about two feet square and four inches deep. Now, he rolled the lower half of the stable door into place near the end of his turntable console—it was less than half the size of a normal stable door and built to tilt ever so slightly toward the front. A length of wood extended vertically on the latch side with a large eye screw near the top of it. Mash tied a length of cord to a hole in the latch handle, threaded it through the eye screw, then tied the end to another eye screw at the end of his console. I noticed, among his props, a good-sized squash to represent the victim's head.

Peter said, "I'm sorry he gave you the impression that you were in danger. He takes his work a little too seriously. I hope it didn't scare you."

"Not so much that I fainted."

"Will you forgive me, and let me take you to dinner tonight?"

"I'd like that."

"Eight o'clock? I'll pick you up at your apartment."

Bar came in, carrying a script. When he saw Peter, he said, "Could I have a word?" He led Peter to the control booth. I watched them through the window. After what appeared to be a gentlemanly discussion, Peter left. I hoped he managed to smooth things over. If George complained to the insurance company, they might assign someone else.

When I returned from rehearsal, I told Sophie about Peter's studio visit. As I was wrapping up my tale, a cabinetmaker arrived to refinish the battered console radio. He had big, sad eyes and a nose that took several detours before its end. "You were supposed to be here at one o'clock," Sophie said. "Traffic must be murder."

"Hey, I got held up," he said.

"A mile from a phone?"

"I'm here now." He dropped his canvas bag of tools beside the radio.

"We're not paying you to lay out your stuff, then decide you can't finish before five. So why don't you just pack it back up and tell me what time you won't be here tomorrow."

"You're a tough act, sister."

"My boss doesn't waste money. He said if you have to go into overtime, you don't work on it."

"I might not get back here for a week."

"We'll see you then, if we don't find someone with a watch first."

"You tell your boss he isn't going to find better work. I'm an artist. Make this look like new. You tell him that."

"You bet. What time next week?"

"Okay, okay, tell you what, as long as I'm here, I'll finish it up today, and no overtime."

"All right. Get started. The night guard will be here at five-thirty. I'm leaving then."

"A blessing for us both."

CHAPTER 25

Apparently, Detective Barnes decided to let us stay in New York. There was nothing about the shooting in Thursday's papers, either.

Before I left the apartment that morning, Peter called.

"How was dinner?" I asked. "Did Karen flirt?"

"I prefer my blondes taller. She didn't have much new, said Sky left her at Dunleavy's when her girlfriends arrived, about eight-thirty. He had enough time to set up the ambush."

Barnes gave him his gun back, then took him over to see the detectives assigned to Hazel's murder and told them about the attack. They had at least listened.

The insurance company had agreed to pay for three other men to tackle a long list of gun stores and pawnshops. The killer could have had the gun for years. He could have bought it out of town. But maybe we'd get lucky.

I took Marty and Jeannie to dinner at the Crossroads Café in Times Square, figuring that Jeannie's family probably didn't let her visit that part of town after dark, with its huge movie and burlesque houses, dance palaces and arcades, which drew swarms of young men, in and out of uniform, trying to meet girls and not shy about expressing their interest.

We lingered, played a few games, and I acted as chaperone, deflecting the sailors who flocked around Jeannie. "Why don't you come out with us? Bring your sister. And your mother.

Come on. We're meeting up with some guys and their girls, go dancing maybe. Our chief'll be there. Your mother'd like him."

Hal was happy to see Jeannie again, and set a chair next to his, so she could watch him work the show. Marty and I pulled chairs to the far end of the console, where we'd be out of the way but still have a good view.

The supporting actors arrived, then Sky and Karen, together. The clock ticked down. Josh appeared with five minutes to spare.

The "On Air" light went on.

Bar cued Mash, and the *Adam Drake* theme began. He cued Sky.

"In the city, trouble never sleeps. It tosses and turns, gives up the fight and heads out into the street. Trouble doesn't care where it's going, who it runs into. Sometimes it finds me. Sometimes I return the favor." The sax rose and fell.

Bar signaled Lon. "Traveler cigarettes, with the smooth taste that comes from only the finest tobacco, proudly presents *Adam Drake, For Hire*. And now, Act One of 'A Race to Death.' "

Out of the music came footsteps, hard soles on a stable floor, as Mash, in shirtsleeves, walked in the box of straw and sand.

Lon said, "It's midnight at the Seneca Springs Racetrack. But the air is full of expectation. In only two days, Sea Admiral, the favorite, will race for a purse of one hundred thousand dollars."

Mash stopped walking, and leaned toward a standing mike. From his mouth came the sound of a champion thoroughbred, tall, proud, demanding to know who was trespassing in his stable.

One of the supporting actors spoke, with a mild Irish accent. "There, boy, and how are you? Are you glad to see me?" Mash, his right hand precisely cupped, slapped himself on the left shoulder blade: the slapping of a horse's neck. "Would you like a bit of sugar? Our secret."

Mash made nuzzling sounds, the horse nibbling up the sugar. As he did, he picked up two short boards, nailed together. He twisted one, and, in the distance, a floorboard creaked.

"Is someone there?"

In the box, Mash produced new footsteps, slower, sinister. "Who's there? What—what are you doing here?" A gasp, a cry of alarm. The sound of a heavy weapon against human flesh.

Then Adam Drake was on the scene, called in by the owner, and is thrown out of the crime scene by the police even though he points out to them that the death was no accident. The next day, he returns, with Maisie along to take notes and ask pert questions. The guard tells Drake that he just can't understand how anyone could have got past the dogs. They always bark when anyone comes around at night.

And Mash made it sound as if they were all three in the stables. In the straw box on the floor, he walked as Drake. In a smaller box, on the table, he walked as the guard and Maisie, wearing a woman's high heel on one hand and a man's work boot on the other. Then Mash's feet worked briskly in the floor box and the police lieutenant arrived, in high dudgeon.

"Who let you in here?" the lieutenant demanded of Drake.

"Lieutenant Jaffe," Drake said. "Good to see you, too. I heard your boys were finished with the crime scene. Let's take a look."

As Drake spoke, Mash set down the high heel, grabbed the cord stretching from his console to the stall door, and pulled it. The latch lifted. He released the cord slowly, and the stall door swung open, with a whisper of a creak. Drake walked into the scene of the crime.

Karen flipped softly to the next page of her script. As she did, she casually discarded the old one, and it floated away. She took no notice of it. Neither did anyone else. It would make no sound. It would be in no one's way. No one paid any attention. Except me.

At precisely the same moment, Mash reached out, gave the door a gentle push, and it swung closed again with a soft clack.

And the gleaming white paper drifted to the floor, lazily sweeping from side to side, as if in slow motion, caught on some small current from the air vents perhaps. Or maybe it was all in my imagination. It sailed as gently as an autumn leaf and finally touched lightly to the studio floor among a dozen others.

"What's the matter?" Marty said.

"What?" I asked in confusion. I realized that I was standing up.

"Are you all right?"

"Fine. I'm fine."

She kept looking at me.

I turned back to the window. I stared down into the studio, at the stable door now quietly closed, at the pieces of paper lying on the floor, and the answer to how Hazel Keane's killer had escaped.

"I don't understand it," Maisie Lane was saying to Adam Drake. "Why didn't the dogs bark?"

The moment the show ended, I gave Marty and Jeannie cab money and dashed out. In the lobby, I shut myself in a phone booth and called Peter's number at Vanguard. I had to talk to Peter, I told the woman. She had to find him. I wasn't in danger, but I had to talk to him. I was on my way back to the office. He should call me there, after ten, when Alletter would be the only person around.

I told Alletter I was going to work a bit, was expecting a call. He said he'd ring it through and went back to the desk, his portable radio and his Katzenjammer Kids comic. The room smelled of wood stripper and paste wax, the refinisher having finished his work. He'd been right: he was an artist. The console radio looked brand new.

I dumped my coat and handbag on my desk and slipped into Josh's office. By the time I reached his desk, my palms were sweating. I rifled through his bottom drawer. "Let it still be here," I whispered, although there was hardly any sound coming from my dry throat. How long had it been since I had last seen it? A week. A week ago today. I stopped rifling, took a deep breath, and began a systematic search, removing handfuls of the paper triangles and sorting through them on the blotter.

A handful. Another. Another. How many of these things did he have?

Another handful. And there it was. Splayed at the bottom, like a little paper party hat, with both sides mauled by nickel-sized blisters, much as I remembered it from the day Josh had tried to teach me how to hit the trash can. He had said the marks were made by a woman's high heel. At the time, I hadn't thought anything about it, even though the marks were too rounded for high heels.

I had also noticed, fleetingly, the tear in one of the corners. Now I looked at it closely. It was, in fact, the result of a tiny hole having been made through all the thicknesses and the paper being ripped from there to the edge. That tear was every bit as important to my theory as the impressions made in the paper.

I searched through the dozens of remaining triangles. There were no others like it. Should I take it or leave it here? I'd decide later. For now, I picked it up with my fingernails, folded it into my handkerchief, and slipped it into the pocket of my jacket. Into my other pocket, I slipped two brand-new ones.

I went over and stood in Josh's doorway, next to his trash can, calculating height, angle and the distance between it and the alarm door. Then I stepped back into his office, reached up and searched along the top of the lintel with my fingertips.

There were imperfections, but I couldn't tell what they were. I grabbed one of the hard chairs, kicked off my shoes and climbed on.

I found it immediately. All the way at the end, just above the trash can, a tiny screw hole. My heart slammed around in my rib cage and perspiration stung my entire body. Could I possibly be right?

I climbed down and moved the chair underneath the alarm, then climbed back on and felt around beneath the red dome covering. It appeared to be a fairly simply mechanism. With the door closed, a shunt held the ball-tipped hammer stationary. When the door opened, the shunt would drop, releasing the hammer, which would then strike back and forth sharply till the door closed again.

I took out one of the new paper triangles and fitted it over the hammer like a tent. It was a nice, snug fit. But was it tight enough not to be shaken off?

I got down and laid my hand on the door handle. I figured it would have taken at most five seconds for the killer to open the door, squeeze out fast and close it again. I took a long breath and opened the door. The alarm purred loudly, but not loudly enough to have been heard above Willa's vacuum and, tonight, above Alletter's radio. Five seconds. I closed the door.

I retrieved my paper tent and examined it. The marks on either side were identical to those on the mauled triangle in my pocket. I stared at it, my hand shaking.

Of course, I said to myself firmly, all this meant nothing if I couldn't replicate the experiment. I took the other new triangle, slipped it over the hammer, then opened the door again. There was another round of drumming purring. I closed the door, retrieved the triangle and examined it. It was just like the others.

"What are you doing?" a voice said.

I leapt straight up. As the chair toppled beneath me, I managed to jump free, landing without any grace at all, but at least on my feet.

Alletter stood at the corner of the hall, his comic in one hand.

I said, "You scared me, I didn't see you there." Slowly, I put my shoes back on to give me time to gather my thoughts. The paper tent lay on the floor where it had flown out of my hand. I hoped he placed the same significance on it that he had the night Hazel died. "I was thinking about using an alarm in a script and I needed to see if it was too complicated to explain on the air."

He gave me a look, but it was one of those pitying looks the sane working man gives the crazy artist. "There's a call for you. A Mr. Stone."

"Be there in a second. I'll just put the chair back." He disappeared around the corner. I snatched the triangle off the floor, returned the chair, grabbed my things and took the call in reception where I could make sure he wasn't listening in on what Peter said.

"Thanks for calling back, Mr. Stone. I forgot where we were meeting."

There was just a beat, then Peter said, "The bar at the Marquette. Ten minutes."

"Okay, see you there." I handed the receiver back to Alletter with a sweet, innocent smile.

I hopped into a cab and told the driver to just drive up the street for a while. I scanned traffic out the back window. There wasn't much of it on Madison that late, so I could tell no one was following. At 60th, I told him to take me back down to the Marquette instead. He shrugged and did it. I wasn't the oddest customer he'd ever had, not even that night.

I waited in the Marquette's lobby. By the time Peter appeared—having satisfied himself from some vantage point that no one was watching—I was shaking. He took me into the bar and ordered me an Irish coffee, which turned out to be heavy on the Irish, and, gradually, I stopped shivering. Then I took the triangle that I'd found in Josh's drawer and laid it on the table on top of the handkerchief. Beside it, I placed the two I'd experimented with.

"I think the killer escaped through the alarm door, and used this thing to deaden the ringing." I told him briefly how I had seen it a week ago in Josh's office and what I had done tonight. "It works. And see that little hole there in the corner? The killer wouldn't want the police to know he disabled the alarm, because that would point back to the staff. No outsider would have had the opportunity to experiment. He had to get that thing off the alarm hammer. So, he punches that little hole in one corner and ties a line to it, maybe fishing line because it's transparent and would fit easily up under the covering of the alarm."

Peter nodded. "But he can't just take the line out the door with him, and pull the thing off and under the door. The door's frame's too tight."

"Exactly. So, at some point, he fit an eye screw into the top of Josh's doorframe, where no one would notice it. And then, on the way out that night, he uncoiled the line from inside the alarm, draped it across the hall, threaded it through the eye screw, and took the end out with him. The alarm is activated, but no one hears it. The door closes. The alarm goes silent. He then tugs on the line till the tent pops off the hammer. It swings across the hallway and reaches the eye screw. A good yank on the line, and the tent breaks free and drops right into Josh's wastebasket, with a couple of others the killer planted because Alletter found more than one that night after Willa had finished cleaning. It's what made him think that Josh had stayed late that night. Alletter put them back in Josh's drawer, not the least suspicious. I probably should have left it there, but Alletter

281

caught me up on the chair, looking at the alarm when he came to tell me about your call. I told him I was thinking about using an alarm in a script. I think he believed me. But after that, I just wanted to get out. I forgot to put it back."

Peter stared at the triangles. "It doesn't matter. It's not really evidence, and there might be prints that could give us a lead. If you're right, Connally's out. He never would have left this laying around."

"No." I took another sip, my shivering being slowly replaced by a nice, warm glow. "What are you thinking?"

I thought he was going to ask me how I'd come to my brilliant deduction and I was prepared to impress him. Instead, he said, "I'm wondering whether maybe the killer didn't hide after all. Whether he not only left through the alarm door but came in that way too."

"What?"

"We know there weren't that many places to hide, and none of them really safe. And we've never been able to explain why—if he hid out—he didn't kill Miss Keane before nine, hide briefly in Connally's office, then slip out the *Drake* side door while Alletter was at dinner. Maybe this could explain it, I don't know."

He frowned and continued, working it out as he went. "Maybe instead, he left that night, just like everybody else, then came back. The fire escape would take him as far as the fifth floor. He could climb in a window, if he'd unlocked it earlier. During the party, anybody could have slipped down the service stairs long enough to unlock that window. He'd have to relock it after he got back in—because Nathan Mitchell found all the windows locked after the killing—then he comes up the service stairs to the eighth floor. He could peek out the service door and make sure Alletter was at the desk. Alletter's so nearsighted he'd never notice the door moving. And the killer could hear

Willa's vacuum, know she was on the *Love* side."

"And he wouldn't need a key," I said. "The alarm door can't be locked. But he'd have to know there wouldn't be anybody working late on the *Drake* side."

"Willa told us at the club that Hazel was the only one of the *Drake* people who ever stayed late after the meetings."

"Right. So he puts this thing over the alarm hammer, maybe during the party when everybody—"

"No, remember the delivery boy. He set off the alarm."

"So it must have been after the meeting ended."

"Possibly, or during the meeting. Someone excuses himself to go to the restroom, but instead grabs a chair from Connally's office, fixes everything, and is back in two minutes. Of course, he'd have to avoid Willa."

"So then after the meeting ended, he leaves with the others, with the weapons he stole from Cupp's tool bag during the party, and then waits in the alley until he knows the *Drake* side is clear."

Peter was silent for a moment, then shook his head, "But we still have the same hole."

"What?"

"Whether the killer came back in through the alarm door or hid in the offices, we still have the same problem. The killer knew the routine. He had to know everyone's schedules or he never would have been able to experiment with these things. He knew Willa Mitchell went into the *Love* side at eight-thirty. Alletter went into the kitchen at nine. Between eight-thirty and nine, the killer could have easily killed Miss Keane and escaped her office unseen. But he's still there at nine-thirty, when Clayton sees him. Okay, we have one question we can't answer right now. What are the others? Let's go over them, see where they lead."

"All right. The killer must have removed the eye screw. Why

didn't he retrieve this thing?" I asked, giving the triangle a little flick with my fingertip.

"This could be the one part of the routine the killer *didn't* know. Willa—and Alletter following her example—put these things back into Connally's drawer. He figured Willa would throw them out."

"What about the broken rod in the closet? If the killer didn't need a diversion to hide—I mean, if you're right and he came *in* the alarm door as well as going out—why did he break the rod in the hall closet?"

"Confusion. If the Cupp frame didn't work, for whatever reason, the cops could be led to think some other outsider had hidden in the closet. It gave him a little extra diversion from the staff. I know you wanted it to be Clayton."

"It's more my not wanting it to be anyone else."

"I'm sorry."

"Maybe that's why he shot you."

"What?"

"The killer. You said the killer had to practice. What if someone saw him in the office late, fooling around with the alarm? Maybe that's why he shot you. He was afraid that person would let something slip while you were talking to him. Or her."

"But I've already talked to everyone who was ever there late at night. He'd have shot me before I talked to them. Are you drunk?"

"Of course not." But of course I was.

He motioned to the waiter and ordered me another coffee, this time with no Irish, and a sandwich, which came in record time: The Marquette bar was used to sobering up customers.

After I'd had a few bites, Peter said, "So what gave you the idea that the killer used that thing on the alarm?"

"Mash," I said, chewing.

"What?" He scooted the coffee toward me.

"Mash. The soundman on *Adam Drake*. Mash and Karen, what they were doing." I told him what had happened at the studio, then said, "There was that piece of paper, dropping to the floor and nobody paying any attention, because they're used to seeing that. And there was Mash with a high heel on his hand, and I guess it reminded me of what Josh said, that those marks had been made by a high heel. And Mash had to work the stable door from a distance using some eye screws and a piece of string because he doesn't have an assistant anymore, and he was busy walking in the straw box."

"The what?"

"The straw box. A box, with sand and straw in it. He walks in it and it sounds like somebody walking through a stable. He's very good at it. He can walk like different people: the groom, the killer, then Drake, Maisie, the guard and the police detective, some of them at the same time." I gestured with my sandwich and slung a bit of mayonnaise onto the table. "You should have seen him doing Maisie and the guard. He had a box on the table and that high heel on one hand and a man's boot on the other, and you'd swear it was two people walking. It was amazing. Just like two people. You'd swear . . . you'd swear. . . ." I sat there, the sandwich in midair.

"What? What is it?"

"You'd swear it was two people."

CHAPTER 26

I sobered up fast.

We spent the next half hour trying to figure out if it were possible. Then, when we decided that it was, another hour trying to figure out why.

But it was just an idea. We didn't have anything like proof.

It was after midnight. It didn't matter. We needed answers.

We hailed a cab downtown. The elevator operator was reluctant to take us up so late. Peter told him we were expected and slipped him a dollar to prove it. Nevertheless, he remained with his head poked out while I rang the apartment's bell.

Alton Peake opened the door, wearing a rust-colored smoking jacket over a starched white shirt.

"We have to talk," I blurted out as I rushed in. "We think we know who killed Hazel."

He raised a hand in warning, but it was too late.

In the arch to the kitchen stood Mrs. Embert, wearing an apron over a silk dress, a mixing bowl in the crook of her arm. Then I remembered that she and Alton were the only two people from the office who had not attended George's party. Alton told me he had ballet tickets.

He said, "Mrs. Embert and I have been to the theater. She's making waffles. She makes excellent waffles. Please come in. Let me take your coats. May I offer you some tea?"

The room was filled with inviting furniture, too much of it for the size of the room. On the coffee table was a silver tray, a rose-covered porcelain pot and two cups. "Sit down," Alton said. I took a seat on the sofa. Peter remained standing near the door. "Do you take milk or sugar?"

"Sugar," I said. "Some sugar."

He sprinkled it in, then handed me the cup with a teaspoon on the saucer. I stirred, then took a sip. The near-scalding liquid spread through my chest.

"Mr. Winslow?"

"No, thank you."

I glanced at the arch. Mrs. Embert was still standing there, although she had gotten rid of the mixing bowl.

"Who are you?" she asked me.

"My name is Lauren Atwill. I knew Hazel Keane. I came to *Adam Drake* to find her killer."

Alton said, "I saw Mrs. Atwill's picture in a magazine a few days ago. She and Mr. Winslow solved that murder case out in Hollywood last summer." He turned to me. "What may I do for you?"

I set my cup down and squeezed my hands into fists a few times. "Perhaps we should talk privately."

Mrs. Embert said, "You can't think that Alton had anything to do with this."

"No," Peter said, "but we need his help."

"I'm sure he's told you everything," she insisted.

"I have," Alton said. "I have no idea who killed Hazel."

"I think it would be best if we spoke alone," I said.

"I've told you everything."

"Very well," I said. "I need to talk to you about a baby girl who was left at Saint Katherine's."

He drew a breath, and it wasn't easy for him to do it.

"Alton." Mrs. Embert hurried to his side. "What is it?"

I said, "I think there is something you haven't told us."

"I can't see that it's important," he said finally.

"May we talk privately?"

Mrs. Embert said, "I'm not leaving him with you."

She glared at Peter, who said, "Then won't you sit down?" He gestured her to the other armchair. "Go on," he said to me.

"We believe that several years ago, a baby girl was brought to Saint Katherine's orphanage, a baby connected to the Keanes. Am I wrong?"

He dropped his head then and looked at the carpet.

I continued, feeling my way through it. "She was given to the nuns to rear, but she wasn't entirely deserted. She was looked after from afar, as much as was possible without causing comment. And the nuns who knew the truth kept a special eye on her. She grew up. She left and set out on her own, but not far away. If anyone wanted to know what was happening to her, it would be easy to find out."

Alton said nothing to stop me.

"Earlier this year, Hazel made a special effort to bring a girl over from the secretarial school she started, made a place for her, made allowances for her. People thought she was just being nice, but I think she felt guilty. She felt responsible for what had been denied that girl. She might even have hoped that everything could be made right, and forgiven. But she didn't realize how dangerous it would be to bring this girl into her life."

"This is scurrilous!" Mrs. Embert exclaimed, deep red patches of fury blazing on her cheeks. "Stop this right now! How dare you say things like that about Hazel Keane! How dare you! Marty Lubrano is not Hazel Keane's child!"

Alton said, "Winifred. Please."

"Marty was devoted to Hazel! She would never have done anything to harm her! Never!"

Peter stepped forward. "We know that," he said quietly.

"Then what are you talking about?" Mrs. Embert said, her voice catching in her attempts to control her anger.

I turned to Alton. "Are we wrong?"

"I didn't know until last year," he said. "How on earth did you find out?"

"It's mostly conjecture. That's why I wanted to talk privately. After Morris Keane's stroke, he hid things, mostly items of little value, but, just after he died, his housekeeper found the children tearing the place apart. Whatever they were looking for, it had to be paper because they were looking between the pages of books. And it had to be very important. I think that, in the process of a routine examination of his papers, they discovered something that scared them enough to make them ransack their father's home and make Hazel ask her lawyer questions about bigamy and inheritance. A marriage license. A birth certificate. Maybe both."

Slowly, Alton got to his feet and walked over to the window. He stared out it.

I said, "You told me that the nurses were lovely in Cuba. You said, 'It's no wonder we fell in love.' I thought you meant soldiers in general, but you meant that both you and Morris Keane fell in love down there."

I could barely hear him, he spoke so softly. "Mine was a passing fancy, an injured young man and a beautiful nurse, but Morris fell deeply. Her name was Miranda, like the island child in *The Tempest*. She was quadroon, perhaps, not dark, but dark enough that her heritage could not be hidden. Nevertheless, they married. I was living in Connecticut, and he was trying to get his start in New York. She didn't stay with him long, perhaps a year. I received a letter from him, saying that she had returned to Cuba. It was too hard for her in this country. He never said anything about a child. Morris didn't have any immediate family left, and I doubt any of his other relatives would have been eager to rear the child while he made his way. I wasn't married at the time, so I couldn't have taken her either. Still, I wish he had confided in me."

I said, "But he did later."

"Last year. Last spring, before his stroke. He was thinking of marrying again, and because the woman was young, there was the chance of another baby. He was thinking about the little one he had hardly seen. He told me then that her name was Elizabeth, that she had grown up a beautiful woman, was married, with children of her own . . . happy, he thought."

"She is," I said. I tried to make it easier for him, lead him to tell me all he knew. "I've met her."

"When he told me, he said that for a while, he thought that Miranda would send for the baby. He tried to find her, but he didn't have the money then, to search in Cuba. Perhaps she died. Perhaps she married again, and didn't want to tell her husband about her other marriage. Morris couldn't rear the child on his own. He took her to Saint Katherine's. She was fair-skinned enough that they could take her there, but not fair enough that it would be easy to find her a family. The nuns cared for her, and he looked after her from afar, as you said."

"His children ransacked that house trying to find a death certificate for Miranda," I said, "or a record of an annulment or divorce, because, not long after, Hazel asked her lawyer what would happen if someone discovered a spouse was already married. The lawyer told her that, if the bigamist died, he would be declared intestate. The second spouse, and any children, would get nothing. Everything would go to the first wife. If there was no proof that Miranda died before Morris married Ethel, Ethel's children were illegitimate.

"Given what Miranda's age would be, she might well be dead. But what about the child? Where was she? What if she reappeared, claimed the Keane fortune? They knew that, given Morris' interest in orphanages, there was a chance that the baby had been given up for adoption. If she were, they'd be all right.

She wouldn't be an heir. Hazel was already a volunteer in the offices at Saint Katherine's. She started her search there and discovered that Elizabeth Devine was Morris' child. Hazel's own sister had grown up an orphan because Morris had not been able to care for her alone and, later, because he feared to tell his wife the truth—especially if his second marriage was not valid. It is certain that, had he claimed the little girl, he would not have been able to move in some of the social circles he was later welcomed into.

"Hazel adored her father. However hard this news was for her, she wanted to help her own niece. She loved children. She longed for a child of her own. She brought Elizabeth's daughter, Jeannie, into the business, created a place for her, even allowed her to take the typing test twice. Nevertheless, she had to have known that telling the truth could ruin her fortune. If Elizabeth Devine was never formally given up for adoption, then she could be the legal heir. And if it got out that the founder of Keane Radio had married a woman with Negro blood, there would be parts of this country where Keane radios would never be purchased again, where *Adam Drake* and *Love Always* would be boycotted."

Alton turned back into the room. "You don't think Jeannie Devine killed Hazel."

"No."

"Then who?" Mrs. Embert asked.

Peter said, "We think her brothers killed her."

"That's ridiculous," Mrs. Embert declared. "They were at George's house."

Peter shook his head. "George was at George's house."

"Henry was there," she insisted.

"There's no evidence that he was there after eight-thirty."

"He was seen," Alton insisted.

"He was heard. Anything else might well have been illusion."

I said, "Henry arrived at George's sometime around eight-fifteen, after the writers meeting, and went down to the kitchen, still in his coat and hat, so the housekeeper could get a good look at them. When Henry and George left the kitchen, Henry left the house, leaving the coat and hat behind. Mrs. Watson, the housekeeper, came up from the kitchen a bit later, to ice a cake, something she always does when she makes a cake.

"When she took slices up to the study—something else she always did—George was watching for her. He started a transcription recording on an old set of turntables that he brought down from the attic. I saw them there Saturday night. The recording was of a man playing billiards, even Henry's voice, angry. It continued the illusion of a fight brewing. Mrs. Watson was now concentrating on the trouble between the brothers and not on what she was actually seeing. And, of course, it would never occur to her that they would deceive her.

"She returned to the dining room and continued setting up for a party, a routine the brothers knew as well as the routine of the office. Just after nine, George starts a second record and opens the study door, turning the sound up so that Mrs. Watson can hear it. The brothers' fight begins. Henry's voice declares that he is leaving.

"This is where their years in radio really paid off. They have to make it seem that Henry is coming downstairs and that he leaves the house. George looks enough like him from the back to carry it off, if he's wearing Henry's coat and his hat to cover his bald head, but he could never sound like him. They need one final touch to prove to Mrs. Watson that it's Henry she's seeing: He says good night to her. He doesn't have to look at her. If he says good night and calls her by name, he must have seen her. It must be Henry. How do you do that? The same way that sound is carried from the studio into the control room, through wires to speakers. George turns on a speaker he's set up in the elevator with a long length of cord attached to it. He sends the elevator down, then heads downstairs in Henry's coat, hat and scarf, making enough racket to cover any sound of the elevator descending. Mrs. Watson hears Henry's voice seeming to come downstairs. George's voice has been recorded off-mike, so that he sounds as if he is still upstairs. The recording delivers Henry's good-bye to her. Henry appears to have left the house and George seems to still be upstairs. The study door slams. George has his radio on in the study to cover any sound the speakers might make when the recording ends.

"But he doesn't have much time. He reaches the sidewalk and immediately darts back into the house through the kitchen. He climbs into the dumbwaiter, takes himself to the third floor, turns off the speaker. He sends the dumbwaiter back down, throws off Henry's coat and recalls the elevator, covering any sounds it makes as he descends the stairs. He talks to Adora for a while, they listen to the radio. When she goes back to the kitchen, he returns upstairs and removes all traces of his deception."

There was silence in Alton's living room, a lot of it.

I picked up my cup and sipped some tea. I had begun shivering again.

"I don't believe it," Alton said.

"I'd be surprised if you did," Peter said. "Even if we're right, the records were destroyed, but we might be able to get some proof they were made. The Keanes own radio stations in other cities. We might get lucky and find a witness."

"I won't believe it," Alton stated. "Why would you even consider such a thing?"

"Because it adds up that way." Peter told them about the paper triangles and how the killer had defeated the alarm. "It has to be an inside job, and someone who could work late without causing comment. That leaves out Sky Donovan, Karen

Dunn. Jeannie and Marty, you and Mrs. Embert. And it's not Connally. He never would have left evidence in his desk. Who does that leave? Eileen Walters, Ruth Linden, Bar Benjamin and Henry Keane. But anyone who knew the office routine knew that the best time to commit the crime was between eight-thirty and nine. Yet the killer was still there at nine-thirty. Who's the only one who couldn't have made it to the offices in time to do everything he had to do before nine? Henry Keane. And who had the best opportunity to disable the alarm and pull down the rod in the closet? George Keane. He left the writers meeting early. And he had the best reason to have shot me."

"You were shot?" Mrs. Embert exclaimed.

"Tuesday night, as I walked from here to my meeting with Karen Dunn. We can eliminate Eileen Walters, Ruth Linden and Henry Keane from our list of shooting suspects. They were with Mrs. Atwill. That leaves Bar Benjamin and George Keane. Whoever it was emptied the gun at me. He wasn't very good with a gun, but he sure wanted me out of the way. He was panicked. And that had to be because of something that had happened recently, if he picked that time and place to do it. Tonight, Mrs. Atwill and I went back over everything that had happened Monday and Tuesday, looking for anything that could have scared the killer bad enough to risk pulling out a gun in the middle of the street. Then Mrs. Atwill told me about an album you gave to Henry on Monday. Some of the pictures were of you and Morris Keane in Cuba. The brothers realized how much you might know, and they couldn't risk what you might have told me Tuesday night."

Alton said, "Then why wouldn't they kill me?"

Peter said, "I'm an investigator. In my line of work, my killing could have plenty of motives. Yours would be different. However, if they'd discovered that you had any suspicions about them, they probably would have. They killed their own sister for money."

I said, "Last summer, not long after Jeannie came to work at *Adam Drake,* she overheard Hazel arguing with a man she thought was Bar because, earlier, she'd seen him standing in the door to Hazel's office. She overheard Hazel warning someone to keep his hands off a woman. 'If you lay a finger on her, you'll be sorry,' she said. Yet she and Bar had been separated for months, and she was seeing another man. And it didn't sound like the sort of thing a woman says when she wants a man to cut off a romance. It sounded more like she was protecting someone. And the man said something about being ruined.

"When the fight started, Jeannie had been at her desk for at least fifteen minutes. She couldn't see Hazel's door. And she hadn't been at work there long enough to recognize voices. I think Bar left and Henry came in. Hazel had brought Morris Keane's granddaughter to work for her. He and George must have been terrified that she would do something to ruin them, lose them their inheritance."

Alton shook his head. "It's not enough."

Peter said, "Not to prove they did it, but if we can prove they made recordings, it might be enough to get the police to reopen the case."

"And subject her brothers to the most vicious gossip, all because their father once fell in love?"

"I can't let an innocent man die for this."

"It's a terrible thing you're about to do."

Peter stayed at my apartment. I had to explain the Eisler painting, although I told him I'd gone to the agent's to pick it up. I didn't need him distracted.

At nine the next morning, while we were having cups of strong coffee, Alton called. In the end, his—and Mrs. Embert's—desire to find Hazel's killer had tilted the balance in our favor. They had agreed not to say anything to anyone about us, and Alton had agreed to do us one last favor.

Alton was at the office. He said his records showed that Henry had submitted travel expenses for a trip to Detroit in August. He gave us the dates and the name of the hotel. He had called the billing clerk at D.W. Davis, George's ad agency, pretending to be checking on the possibility that *Adam Drake* had been billed for some of George's expenses by mistake. The clerk confirmed that George had traveled to Detroit on the same dates and stayed in the same hotel.

August was an odd time for a business trip, but the perfect time to find a station far from home with studios free and engineers on summer vacation. We'd start in Detroit. I'd have to pull out my checkbook. There wasn't time to get the insurance company to agree to pay. Peter needed to hire detectives out there immediately. In addition to finding out if George and Henry had done any recording at the station, they would have to question pawnshop and gun store owners, accompanied by wire photos of the two men. Meanwhile, Vanguard detectives would continue questioning owners in the New York area, adding shops near Henry's Rhode Island house.

"Do you think there's any chance they haven't tossed the gun in the river right next to the recordings?" I said.

Peter got up and poured himself another cup, then leaned his hips on the kitchen counter. "I've been thinking about those recordings and the timing of the argument. It started too early. To give Henry a rock-solid alibi, the recording needed to start closer to nine-thirty, when it would look like Henry had no chance whatsoever to get to the offices and kill her before her body was discovered. Remember, Alletter was supposed to call her at ten. So they could be pretty sure the body would be found close to that time. Henry got a fair alibi, but only because the doctor saw a man in the hall."

"Maybe Adora broke her routine and George was about to lose his witness."

"He couldn't have seen what she was doing in the dining room from his study."

"If Henry got caught that night, George could claim he had nothing to do with it."

"Exactly."

"Henry must have been furious. I'd want to kill George."

"Maybe you'd settle for scaring him, having something to hold over him. George had a lot of work to do that night, removing all traces of the deception. His guests would be arriving soon, and the police wouldn't be too far behind. He wouldn't have had a chance to safely dispose of the records. Maybe if you're Henry, you grab one of them, or the pieces if George had broken them up. Maybe you'd keep it for a while. But it would have to be someplace safe."

"I'll say."

"Someplace he could lay his hands on it fast. Not in a safe-deposit box. Banks are closed most of the time. Lockers are too public. Not his apartment. George could search that too easily. Same for his office."

"But once the insurance company started asking questions, it would have been insane to hold onto it."

"Yeah," he said after a moment, "you're right." He shook his head. "Thanks for the dose of logic." He tossed the last of his coffee into the sink and left. I went to work, too.

The second I hit the front door, Sophie squawked, "The sun's shining. Sourpuss is home sick today."

"Thanks," I said, although I had already known Mrs. Embert wouldn't be coming in. She had been far too upset. She had promised not to tell anyone, but I didn't trust her to keep her mouth shut for long.

"Anything else to report?" I asked Sophie.

"All's quiet. Ruth and Bar are over at *Love*. Eileen and Josh aren't in yet."

"Henry?"

"Not yet. You could have slept till noon."

I shut my office door. I wasn't up to facing Henry unless I had to. I set to work on my script.

Eileen dropped by and invited me to lunch. I declined. Nose to the grindstone, I said. About two, I tucked lunch money into my jacket, so I wouldn't have to carry my handbag, and called Vanguard from a booth around the corner. Peter was there. He would be staying in all day, overseeing the other detectives, not wanting to miss any scrap of information that came in.

He said, "Henry and George were both in the Detroit radio station and worked on a recording. No engineer, of course, and they did it after hours. Told the manager they were working on an idea for a new show."

"That's good, but not proof."

"How does a pawnshop sound, one that sold Henry a Colt M-1911? Last week, in Providence."

"My God."

"Positive ID. We got a statement. The owner doesn't see all that many guys who look like they could afford new guns. Looks like our boys were already worried I might get too close. How's the script coming?"

"What?"

He laughed. "It's killing you to be there and not out looking for clues, isn't it?"

"It's killing me to do nothing."

"I'll call you tonight, at the apartment." He said good-bye and hung up.

I wasn't hungry. I strolled over to Fifth and looked in a few store windows, then on to Sixth, thinking I'd walk up to the park, then back to the office. The traffic was thicker than usual, bosses leaving early on a Friday afternoon and trucks delivering to restaurants for the weekend. As I approached 50th, the foot traffic increased as well, with the Rockefeller Center tourists and Radio City matinee-goers.

During the six months that I had lived in New York after graduating from Vassar, working for a magazine—which meant I answered phones and lived on oatmeal—I treated myself once a month to a movie at Radio City and, in my sophisticated city-girl way, tried not to look too impressed by the sweep of the Grand Staircase, the gold leaf in the Grand Foyer, the extravagant auditorium with a sea of red velvet seats, and the huge Wurlitzer consoles, which could reproduce an entire orchestra.

I waited for the light, looking up at Radio City's block-high marquee of blue-and-red neon.

Then it occurred to me that Peter just might be right.

CHAPTER 27

Edward Lewis, Hazel's lawyer, sat behind his desk, looking devastated. As the executor of her estate, he was the one we needed now. "I don't believe it."

"I know. It's a long shot, but it's all we've got," Peter said. "It's something Henry could keep an eye on, something the staff wasn't allowed to touch. A place he had easy access to. Nobody would question him. Something he never cared two cents about, until Bar Benjamin loaned it out, then he was yelling to get it back. Yeah, it's a long shot. Will you do it?"

"Yes," Lewis replied finally. "Well, then, let's go. Let's get it over with."

The Radio City manager escorted us to the Grand Foyer, where, behind red velvet ropes, stretched a display of famous radios from the medium's earliest days. He lifted one of the ropes and we followed him slowly along the exhibition, as if taking a tour. First, an RCA box receiver kit from 1924, light enough to carry, little assembly required. Two tubes, batteries and headphones, which had cost eighty-five dollars back then, according to the small printed sign next to it.

The receivers got larger, until, with the invention of the AC tube in 1927, the console radio was born, meant to be a piece of furniture suitable to the finest homes (at over five hundred dollars). Some were made to look like sideboards, others like fancy highboys, or even a grandfather clock. Finally we came to the Keane Eagle, the one that Bar had loaned the exhibition. Lewis handed the manager the signed letter he had prepared, absolving Radio City from any responsibility for damages. Carefully, Peter and Lewis slid the radio away from the wall, revealing the panels that covered its back, like cabinet doors, with a tiny gold keyhole in one of them. There was no key. I handed Peter my lock pick. He inserted it and turned. That was all it took.

And there, in its own pepper-gray paper sleeve, leaning against the glass tubes of the chassis, was the one piece of evidence we had never expected to find.

"You're not going back to the office," Peter said.

Around us, in front of the precinct house, officers and detectives, including the one who had thrown me out of the *Adam Drake* offices the day after Hazel died, climbed into their cars. Armed with warrants, they would pick up George and Henry for questioning and start searching their offices and homes for other evidence.

I didn't protest. If I went back, I'd be standing there among the staff during the search, either pretending I was still Mabel Tanner, which seemed a grotesque charade, or admitting my involvement and facing the people I had deceived. The police didn't need any eruption of bad feeling and recrimination to distract them.

"Go pack," Peter said. "We'll get you on a train tonight. By tomorrow, every reporter in town will be looking for you. I'll call, let you know what we find."

I nodded. "Bring my handbag. It's in my desk."

When I had left the apartment that morning, I'd forgot to turn down the radiators. Under normal circumstances, the apartment would feel stifling. But my body was chilled, deeply chilled. I poured a brandy, and sipped half of it before I took off my coat. Then I pulled one of my suitcases from under the bed and plopped it onto the spread. But instead of packing, I took my brandy to the bedroom window and stared out across the courtyard, lit only by the sliver of moon and the scattered glow from windows in the surrounding buildings.

The radiator was too hot. I took a step back and made plans to leave another town. If the police didn't need me to stick around, I'd probably take the overnighter—sixteen hours—into Chicago. Then on to San Francisco and Sally Wallace's loaned cottage, where no one had yet discovered Juanita.

On the roof of the brownstone across the way, someone had left laundry on the line, one narrow sheet, perhaps for a child's bed. They'd have to wash it again, I thought, if they left it out through a damp, dirty winter's night. Maybe it had been children playing, trying to make a tent, and they'd left it up there when they went in to dinner. Did mothers let children play on the roofs? I squinted at it. No, it wasn't a sheet. The fabric seemed thinner than that, almost diaphanous, with an odd sort of shimmer. Too much shimmer, I thought, for the struggling moonlight.

Then I realized that what I saw was not on the opposite roof but was, in fact, a reflection in the window pane, the illusion of movement being created by the waves of heat from the radiator. It was something white, something solid, something behind me.

I whirled around. I dropped the brandy.

Henry Keane stood at the end of the china cabinet, a gun in his hand. Absurdly, I examined it, to see if it was the Colt, as if the fact that George couldn't kill Peter with it at sixty feet made any difference here, at twenty. His overcoat and jacket were open, revealing a shifting rectangle of white shirt front.

"Henry," I said stupidly. I didn't ask how he had found me. If Zack Eisler could give Information my phone number and get my address, so could Henry Keane. Still, I wanted to keep him talking. "You can pick locks."

"I can get a key copied," he said. "What were you doing looking at the alarm?"

"You copied my key?"

"You shouldn't leave it in your purse when you go to lunch."

"Where's George? Does he know you're here?"

George came out of the bathroom, bare-headed, his wool trench coat tied tightly around him. He looked chastened and more than a little afraid.

"Yes," Henry said derisively, "time to come out now." But his gaze never left me. "What were you doing with the alarm last night?"

I looked at George. He was as close to an ally as I was going to find. "Alletter told you he saw me."

"It's his job," Henry snapped. "What were you doing?"

"Finding out how you got in and out of the offices."

"Who are you working with?"

"Peter Winslow. We met Hazel in Los Angeles." I wasn't sure how to tell them Peter knew everything, that the police were looking for them. They'd committed one murder. I'd rather they didn't decide one more wouldn't make any difference. I tried to think of a way to tell them that wouldn't get me killed. Last time a gun had been pointed at me, Peter had arrived at the last minute to save me. It wasn't going to happen this time. I was on my own.

I had to get George into the conversation. He didn't look like he wanted to be here. I said to him, "It couldn't have just been my playing around with the alarm. Was it too many questions?"

George said, "Henry told me Sky came to the office, saying that everything he had said to you, Mr. Winslow knew."

"Not everything," I mildly corrected.

"You were looking at pictures in my house."

Henry said, "And pictures in that album. You screwed up. Where is he?"

"I'm not sure. He's supposed to meet me here later."

"Maybe we'll wait for him." He punched the gun briefly toward the suitcase. "Where were you going?"

"I'm expected back in Los Angeles for a trial that's starting soon. You might have read about it." I told them who I really was. "That's why it was easy for me to get Sam Ross to call you."

George's frown deepened. He was quicker to figure it out than Henry, but Henry wasn't much slower. "Why are you leaving now? Don't give me that trial shit."

"Peter knows about the alarm, and more. You don't have much time, if you want to get out of New York, out of the country. Don't go home."

"Why?" Henry demanded.

"Because the police will be there. Do you have any place, anybody you could get money from? Anyone who would give you a lot of money and not ask too many questions? Call them now. Get the money, head for Canada."

"Henry," George whispered.

"Pull yourself together. She's lying."

"Think it over," I urged George. "Think about who you could get money from. I'm not lying."

"Shut up," Henry snarled.

I pressed my shaking lips together.

George said, "If she knows something, make her tell us." He turned to me. "What do you know?"

"Look, I don't want to get shot. I know some things, and you're not going to like it, but I'm not the only one who knows, so let's all try to stay calm."

"What have you got?" Henry shouted. "Tell us or shut up!"

"We know about the alarm. I found the paper triangle you used, still in Josh's drawer. Alletter put it back there along with the ones you planted the night Hazel died. We know about the trip to Detroit and the recording session. We know about the recording and how you made Adora Watson believe Henry was still in the house. That was very clever, by the way. And we know that you bought a gun at a pawnshop in Providence, the gun George used to shoot Peter. And. . . ." I paused so they could see what I was about to say was going to be trouble, and maybe Henry wouldn't pull the trigger. "The police have the recording."

George staggered. Henry's face flushed with fury. "You're lying!" he screamed.

"How could I make that up?"

"Henry," George said.

"She's lying. She's guessing."

I said, "The police have the record. They found it in the radio."

Henry fell back against the cabinet.

George's mouth opened, pulling in long, desperate breaths. I could hear them across the room. Then he turned on his brother. "You bastard! You bastard!"

"You tried to set me up!"

"It was a mistake! Mrs. Watson was—!"

"Bullshit! You tried to keep yourself clean if it didn't work!" Then he wheeled on me. "Where are they?"

"The police? I don't know. Your house. Your office. They have warrants to arrest both of you."

"Let's go, Henry. Now," George begged. "We can get some money. We know people. Let's go."

"She's lying. They wouldn't have had time to get warrants."

"They're looking for you. It won't do any good to hurt me. Don't go home."

"Then they've closed the bridges and tunnels."

"Henry, let's go," George urged. "We'll switch plates on the car. For Christ's sake, let's go. Tie her up. Let's go!"

"No!" He pointed the gun at my heart.

George jumped forward. "For the love of God! Let's go!"

"No!"

George laid his hand on the gun. Henry yanked it away.

Then there was a crack, a simple crack. I remembered gunshots being so much louder.

I staggered from the sound of it nonetheless.

We froze. They stared at me. I stared at the gun.

Then one of the brass plates between the windows behind me crashed to the floor and skidded across the wide strip of wood between the radiator and the rug. Then it settled, circling on its base, whirring on the floorboards.

"Jesus," I said.

George found his voice as well. "Henry. We have to go. We have to go now. Here, I'll do it." He marched into the living room and ripped the cord out of the phone. "See? She can't call anyone. We'll tie her up. Break the key off in the lock. There's no fire escape. No one's going to find her till we're long gone."

"Tie her up."

"That's right." He disappeared briefly into the bathroom and came out with a stocking. "See, we'll use this to tie her up. We'll gag her, too."

He came over to me. I wrapped my arms around me.

"Give me your hands!"

"No."

"Don't be an idiot! Give me your hands!"

I took a step back, tottered and sat down on the rug.

Funny thing about ricochet. Funny that of everything the bullet could have hit—the window, the wall, the bookcase—it hit one of the brass plates. It hit the plate, ricocheted off it and went straight into my back.

I'm not sure what Henry did, or George. I was staring at my

blouse and how the side was now covered in blood just above the waistband. Already covered in blood. I knew I had one chance left to stay alive. Convince them I was dying. Which I was, I was sure. But I had to convince them that I would be dead in minutes, fewer minutes than I actually had left. If they tied me up, I'd never make it.

I slid down onto the floor, onto my side, so that I was looking at George's shoes and started making little gasping sounds. I'd heard them once before, when a man died in my arms. They were awful. When you heard them, you wanted to run.

I think they said something to each other. My ears started to buzz. But George's shoes moved away from me. The floor vibrated with their running. Then I felt the door slam.

With tremendous effort, I pushed myself up and crawled to the bed, to the night table and opened the deep drawer. Out of it, I took the extension phone, which had been there since I dropped it in after Jeannie woke me up Sunday morning. I used my left hand, because my right hand was busy holding the blood in. I didn't know the number for the police precinct. I could call the operator, but how long would it take for an ambulance to get here?

I called the office.

And there was Sophie. Sophie, with her sweet, familiar gravelly croak.

"Sophie. It's Lauren. Mabel. It's Mabel."

"Sweetie, get yourself back over here and see what's—"

"I need help. Please. I've been shot."

"What?"

"I need the police."

"They're right here, a bunch of them. Did you say 'shot'?"

"Is Peter there? The detective? Peter Winslow?"

"Yeah. I'll get him. You hang on."

I heard her calling down the hallway in that magnificent voice:

"Hey, you, detective man. Get out here. Mabel Tanner's on the phone. I think she said she's been shot."

I heard footsteps moving very fast and the sound of Peter's snatching up Sophie's headset. He didn't ask me what had happened.

"Where are you hit?"

"In the side. Henry. But they left. I'm in the apartment."

"Do you have a belt? Can you get a belt?"

"Yes. I am."

"What?"

"I'm wearing a belt."

"Get a towel. Can you?"

"Yes. In the china cabinet."

"Lauren, stay awake. Can you get a towel?"

"Sure thing. I'll be right back." I crawled to the cabinet and pulled out the bottom drawer, which seemed to take a very long time. It was so heavy. There were the towels. I took out a nice white one. I was sorry it was white. It was going to be ruined. I hoped the tenant wasn't too angry about that. I crawled back to the bed. I heard Peter shouting at the police. Shouting my address, telling them to get an ambulance there and more cops and break down the door if they had to.

"Lauren?"

"Yes, I'm here. I found a towel," I said proudly.

"Fold it. Press it against the wound, and strap the belt over it. Can you do that?"

"Yes."

"Tightly. Do it."

I made my fingers pull the belt from the buckle and out of the prong and slid the towel in. I was glad that I remembered not to take off the belt so that I just had to tighten it again. And make the prong go through the hole.

"I did it," I said. "I'm kind of tired."

"I'm on my way. Stay awake. Keep talking. Just keep her talking," he said to Sophie. "Can you do that?"

"No problem," she said.

Then there was only Sophie. "So, let's start at the beginning, sweetie. Who the hell are you, and what the hell is going on?"

I told her everything. Everything about the case, every single piece of evidence, and how we had put it all together, about Jeannie and her mother, and how they might end up with the Keane fortune, and I hoped they did. I was sure that even if Elizabeth wasn't the legal heir, Peter would figure out how to convince Bar that she and her husband deserved a nice little retirement nest egg. He was good at convincing people. He was good at his job. He would find George and Henry because he made sure the police were watching all the bridges and tunnels, all the marinas and patrolling the rivers. They were watching the train and bus stations, too, just in case. I was sure they would be caught.

And I was glad for the Cupps. They had a sweet little baby named Orin, who had taken to me. I wondered what it would be like when I finally met Nestor Cupp. He didn't seem like the friendliest guy, and gratitude can be awkward.

And then I was telling her my life story, about my upbringing at the hands of two intelligent, distant, neglectful parents; about my childless uncle, who had preferred to love men and was my salvation; about the soaring happiness and ultimate misery of my marriage; about how badly I had wanted a baby and my inability to have one; and about Peter. Plenty of things I shouldn't have told her. She kept me talking for the eternal minutes it took until the apartment door exploded and Peter rushed in, very tall and blurry around the edges. He looked scared. I'd never seen him look scared. I wondered why. There were police with him who started fussing with me and moving me when I was so comfortable there on the floor, lying back against the side of the bed, talking to Sophie. Peter took the receiver gently out of my hand.

"Thank you," he whispered into it.

"No trouble," I heard her say.

Whatever secrets I told Sophie Millsinberger that night, she kept to herself.

ABOUT THE AUTHOR

Sheila York grew up traveling, the daughter of an army officer. She spent much of her childhood in Munich, Germany, and later studied abroad as an exchange student in both France and England. After post-graduate studies in psychology, she took a sharp turn and enjoyed a long career as a radio disc jockey and occasional news anchor and sports reporter, with assignments on all three coasts, including stints in Los Angeles and New York, where her books are set.

She lives in Bloomfield, New Jersey, with her husband, novelist David F. Nighbert.